FALLEN

FALLEN

A KATE BURKHOLDER NOVEL

Linda Castillo

MINOTAUR
BOOKS
NEW YORK

First published in the United States by Minotaur Books, an imprint of St. Martin's Publishing Group

FALLEN. Copyright © 2021 by Linda Castillo. All rights reserved. Printed in the United States of America. For information, address St. Martin's Publishing Group, 120 Broadway, New York, NY 10271.

www.minotaurbooks.com

Designed by Omar Chapa

The Library of Congress Cataloging-in-Publication Data is available upon request.

ISBN 978-1-250-14292-4 (hardcover)
ISBN 978-1-250-82803-3 (international, sold outside the U.S., subject to rights availability)
ISBN 978-1-250-14294-8 (ebook)

Our books may be purchased in bulk for promotional, educational, or business use. Please contact your local bookseller or the Macmillan Corporate and Premium Sales Department at 1-800-221-7945, extension 5442, or by email at MacmillanSpecialMarkets@macmillan.com.

First Edition: 2021

10 9 8 7 6 5 4 3 2 1

This book is dedicated to all of my wonderful friends at the Dover Public Library in Dover, Ohio. Thank you for hosting such lovely (and fun!) events for the last eleven years. You always go above and beyond and it means a lot. Seeing you and your patrons has become a tradition I cherish more than you know. Your library is my home away from home when I'm on the road, and I very much appreciate each and every one of you.

FALLEN

CHAPTER 1

She knew coming back after so many years would be difficult, especially when she'd left so much hurt behind when she departed. She'd hurt the people she loved, never wasting a moment on the notion of regret. She'd sullied relationships that should have meant the world to her. She'd blamed others when misfortune reared its head, never admitting she might've been wrong. Mistakes had always been the one thing she was good at, and she'd made them in spades.

Once upon a time she'd called Painters Mill home. She'd belonged here, been part of the community, and she'd never looked too far beyond the cornfields, the quaint farmhouses and winding back roads. Once, this little town had been the center of her universe. It was the place where her family still lived—a family she hadn't been part of for twelve years. Like it or not, her connection to this place and its people ran deep—too deep, in her opinion—and it was a link she could no longer deny no matter how hard she tried.

This saccharine little town with its all-American main street and pastoral countryside hadn't always been kind. In the eyes of the seventeen-year-old girl she'd been, Painters Mill was a place of brutal lessons, rules she couldn't abide by, and crushing recriminations by people who, like her, possessed the power to hurt.

It took years for her to realize all the suffering and never-lived-up-to expectations were crap. Like her *mamm* always said: Time is a relevant thing and life is a cruel teacher. It was one of few things her mother had been right about.

Painters Mill hadn't changed a lick. Main Street, with its charming storefronts and Amish tourist shops, still dominated the historic downtown. The bucolic farms and back roads were still dotted with the occasional buggy or hay wagon. Coming back was like entering a time warp. It was as if she'd never been gone, and everything that had happened since was nothing more than a dream. The utter sameness of this place unsettled her in ways she hadn't expected.

The Willowdell Motel sure hadn't changed. Same trashy façade and dusty gravel parking lot. Inside, the room was still dressed in the same god-awful orange carpet. Same bad wall art. Same shoddily concealed cigarette smoke and the vague smell of moldy towels. It was a place she shouldn't have known at the age of seventeen.

If life had taught her one lesson that stood out above the rest, it was to look forward, not back. To focus on goals instead of regrets. It took a lot of years and even more sacrifice, but she'd clawed her way out of the cesspit she'd made of her life. She'd done well—better than she ever imagined possible—and she'd forged a good life for herself. Did any of that matter now? Was it enough?

Tossing her overnight bag onto the bed, Rachael Schwartz figured she'd waited long enough to make things right. The time had come for her to rectify the one wrong that still kept her up nights. The one bad decision she hadn't been able to live down. The one that, for years now, pounded at the back of her brain with increasing intensity. She didn't know how things would turn out or if she'd get what she wanted. The one thing she *did* know was that she had to try. However this turned out, good or bad or somewhere in between, she figured she would simply have to live with it.

The knock on the door came at two A.M. Even as she threw the covers aside and rolled from the bed, she knew who it was. A smile touched her mouth as she crossed to the door. Recognition kicked when she checked the peephole. The quiver of pleasure that followed didn't quite cover the ping of trepidation. She swung open the door.

"Well, it's about damn time," she said.

A faltering smile followed by a flash of remembrance. "I didn't think I'd ever see you again."

She grinned. "No such luck."

"Sorry about the time. Can I come in?"

"I think you'd better. We've a lot to discuss." Stepping back, she motioned her visitor inside. "I'll get the light."

Her heart strummed as she started for the night table next to the bed. All the words she'd practiced saying for months now tumbled in her brain like dice. Something not quite right, but then what had she expected?

"I hope you brought the wine," she said as she bent to turn on the lamp.

The blow came out of nowhere. A sunburst of white light and sound, like a stick of dynamite igniting in her head. A splintering of pain. Her knees hit the floor. Shock and confusion rattled through her.

She reached out, grabbed the night table. A sound escaped her as she struggled to her feet, teetered left. She turned, spotted the bat, saw the other things she'd missed before. Dark intent. Buried rage. Dear God, how could she have been so naive?

3

The bat came down again. Air whooshed. She staggered right, tried to escape it. Not fast enough. The blow landed hard on her shoulder. Her clavicle snapped. The lightning bolt of pain took her breath. Mewling, she turned, tried to run, fell to her knees.

Footsteps behind her. More to come. She swiveled, raised her hands to protect herself. The bat struck her forearm. An explosion of pain. The shock pulsing like a strobe.

"Don't!" she cried.

Her attacker drew back. Teeth clenched. The dead eyes of a taxidermist's glass. The bat struck her cheekbone, the force snapping her head back. She bit her tongue, tasted blood. Darkness crowded her vision. The sensation of falling into space. The floor rushed up, struck her shoulder. The scrape of carpet against her face. The knowledge that she was injured badly. That it wasn't going to stop. That she'd made a serious miscalculation.

The shuffle of feet on carpet. The hiss of a labored breath. Fighting dizziness, she reached for the bed, fisted the bedsheet, tried to pull herself up. The bat struck the mattress inches from her hand. Still a chance to get away. Terrible sounds tore from her throat as she threw herself onto the bed, scrabbled across. On the other side, she grabbed the lamp, yanked the cord from the wall.

The bat slammed against her back. A sickening wet-meat punch that rent the air from her lungs. An electric shock ran the length of her spine. Unconsciousness beckoned. She swiveled, tried to swing the lamp, but she was too injured and it clattered to the floor.

"Get away!" she cried.

She rolled off the bed, tried to land on her feet. Her legs buckled and she went down. She looked around. A few feet away, the door stood open. Pale light spilling in. If she could reach it . . . Freedom, she thought. Life. She crawled toward it, pain running like a freight train through her body.

A sound to her left. Shoes against carpet. Legs coming around the bed. Blocking her way. "No!" she screamed, a primal cry of outrage and terror. No time to brace.

The bat struck her ribs with such force she was thrown onto her side. An animalistic sound ripped from her throat. Pain piled atop pain. She opened her mouth, tried to suck in air, swallowed blood.

A wheeze escaped her as she rolled onto her back. The face that stared down at her was a mindless machine. Flat eyes filled with unspeakable purpose. No intellect. No emotion. And in that instant, she knew she was going to die. She knew her life was going to end here in this dirty motel and there wasn't a goddamn thing she could do to help herself.

See you in hell, she thought.

She didn't see the next blow coming.

CHAPTER 2

The winters are endless in northeastern Ohio. People are stuck indoors for the most part. The sun doesn't show itself for weeks on end. When the relentless cold and snow finally break and the first tinge of green touches the fields, spring fever hits with the force of a pandemic.

My name is Kate Burkholder and I'm the chief of police in Painters Mill, Ohio. Founded in 1815, it's a pretty little township of about 5,300 souls that sits in the heart of Amish country. I was born Plain, but unlike the majority of Amish youths, I left the fold when I was eighteen. In nearby Columbus, I earned my GED and a degree in criminal justice, and I eventually found my way into law enforcement. But after I'd been in the big city a few years, my roots began to call, and when the town council courted me for the position of chief I returned and never looked back.

This morning, I'm in the barn with my significant other, John Tomasetti, who is an agent with the Ohio Bureau of Criminal Investigation. We met in the course of a murder investigation shortly after I became chief, and after a rocky start we began the most unlikely of relationships. Much to our surprise, it grew into something genuine and lasting, and for the first time in my adult life I'm unabashedly happy.

We're replacing some of the siding on the exterior of the barn. Tomasetti made a trip to the lumberyard earlier for twenty tongue-and-groove timbers and a couple of gallons of paint. As we unload supplies from the truck, a dozen or so Buckeye hens peck and scratch at the dirt floor.

Our six-acre farm is a work in progress, mainly because we're do-it-yourselfers and as with most endeavors in this life, there's a learning curve. We're hoping to replace the siding this coming weekend. Next weekend, we prime and paint. The weekend after that, weather permitting, we might just get started on the garden.

"I hear you finally got another dispatcher hired," Tomasetti says as he slides a board from the truck bed and drops it onto the stack on the ground.

"She started last week," I tell him. "Going to be a good fit."

"Bet Mona's happy about that."

Thinking of my former dispatcher—who is now Painters Mill's first full-time female officer—I smile. "She's not the only one," I say. "The chief actually gets to take the occasional day off."

He's standing in the truck bed now, holding a gallon of paint in each hand, looking down at me. "I like her already."

I drop the final board onto the stack and look up at him. "Anyone ever tell you you look good in those leather gloves?" I ask.

"I get that a lot," he says.

He's in the process of stepping down when my cell phone vibrates against my hip. I glance at the screen to see DISPATCH pop up on the display. I answer with, "Hey, Lois."

"Chief." Lois Monroe is my first-shift dispatcher. She's a self-assured woman, a grandmother, a crossword-puzzle whiz kid, and an experienced dispatcher. Judging by her tone, something has her rattled.

"Mona took a call from the manager out at the Willowdell Motel. She just radioed in saying there's a dead body in one of the rooms."

In the back of my mind I wonder if the death is from natural causes—a heart attack or slip-fall—or, worse-case scenario, a drug overdose. A phenomenon that's happening far too often these days, even in small towns like Painters Mill.

"Any idea what happened?" I ask.

"She says it's a homicide, Chief, and she sounds shook. Says it's a bad scene."

It's not the kind of call I'm used to taking.

"I'm on my way," I say. "Tell Mona to secure the scene. Protect any possible evidence. No one goes in or out. Get an ambulance out there and call the coroner."

It takes me twenty minutes to reach the motel. I took the time to throw on my uniform and equipment belt, and made the drive from Wooster in record time.

The Willowdell Motel is a Painters Mill icon of sorts. The sign in front touts MID-CENTURY MODERN with CLEAN ROOMS and a SPARKLING POOL in an effort to lure tourists looking to spend a few days relaxing in Amish country. The locals don't see the place with such optimism, especially when the pool isn't quite so sparkling, the façade is in dire need of fresh paint, and the rooms haven't been renovated since the 1980s.

I pull into the gravel lot to find Mona's cruiser parked next to the office, the overheads flashing. She's exited the vehicle and is standing outside room 9 talking to a heavyset man wearing camo pants and a golf shirt. I've met him at some point, but I don't recall his name.

Likely, the manager. I park the Explorer next to her cruiser and pick up my radio mike. "Ten-twenty-three," I say, letting Dispatch know I've arrived on scene.

I get out and approach them. Mona glances my way, looks unduly relieved to see me. She's twenty-six years old and has been a full-time officer for a few weeks. She's as enamored with law enforcement now as she was on her first day on the job. Despite her lack of experience, she's a good cop; she's motivated, has good instincts, and she's willing to work any shift, which is a plus when you only have five officers in the department.

I take her measure as we exchange a handshake. She's pale-faced; her hand is shaking and cold in mine. Mona is no shrinking violet. Like most of my officers, she prefers action over boredom, and she's never investigated a crime that didn't intrigue her in some way. This morning, she's stone-faced and I'm pretty sure I see a fleck of vomit on her sleeve.

"What do you have?" I ask.

"Deceased female." She motions with her eyes to room 9. "She's on the floor. Chief, there's blood everywhere. I have no idea what happened." She glances over her shoulder at the man who's straining to hear our every word, and lowers her voice. "It looks like there was one hell of a struggle. I can't tell if she was stabbed or shot or . . . something else."

I turn my attention to the man. "You the manager?"

"Doug Henry." He taps the MANAGER badge clipped to his shirt. "I'm the one called 911."

"Any idea what happened?" I ask. "Did you see anything?"

"Well, checkout is at eleven. Maid isn't here today, so I gotta clean. I called the room around ten thirty. No one picked up, so I waited until eleven and knocked on the door. When she didn't answer, I used my key." He blows out a long breath. "I ain't never seen anything like that in my life and I used to work down to the slaughterhouse. There's blood everywhere. Stuff knocked over. I got the hell out of there and called you guys."

"Who is the room registered to?" I ask.

"Last name is Schwartz," he tells me.

It's a common name in this part of Ohio, both Amish and English. If memory serves me, we have at least two families here in Painters Mill with that last name. "First name?"

"I can go look it up for you," he offers.

"I'd appreciate it." I turn my attention to Mona. "You clear the room?"

Grimacing, she shakes her head. "Once I saw her, I figured this was more than I could handle and got out."

"Anyone else been in the room?"

"Just me."

"Coroner and ambulance en route?"

She nods. "Sheriff's Office, too."

I start toward room 9. "Let's clear the room," I tell her. "Make sure there's no one else inside. Quick in and out."

I go through the door first. "Stay cognizant of evidence. Don't touch anything."

"Roger that."

It takes a moment for my eyes to adjust to the dimly lit interior. I smell the blood before I see it. The dark, unpleasant smell of metal and sulfur. A few feet away, a red-black pool the size of a dinner plate is soaked into the carpet. A smear on the bedspread. Spatter on the headboard and wall. A finer spray on the ceiling. On the other side of the bed, I see the victim's hands.

"Clear the bathroom," I tell Mona. "Eyes open."

I feel the familiar quiver in my gut as I move to the bed—that primal aversion to violent death. No matter how many times I see it, I always get that shaky feeling in the pit of my stomach, that shortness of breath. I round the foot of the bed and get my first look at the body. The victim is female. Lying on her stomach. Legs splayed. One arm beneath her. The other arm is outstretched, clawlike hand clutching carpet, as if she'd been trying to drag herself to the door. She's wearing a pink T-shirt and panties. Socks.

I wish for better light as I approach. I pull my mini Maglite from my utility belt, flick it on. The beam tells a horrific tale. A lamp lies on the floor, shade crushed, the cord ripped from the wall. Whatever happened to this woman, she fought back, didn't make it easy for the son of a bitch to do this to her.

Good girl, a little voice whispers in the back of my brain.

"Bathroom is clear," comes Mona's voice.

"Blood?"

"No."

I glance over my shoulder, see her silhouetted against the light slanting in from the door. My mind has jumped ahead to the preservation of evidence; I'm keenly aware that I'm in the process of contaminating that evidence. No way around it.

"Go outside and get the scene taped off," I tell her, hearing the stress in my voice. "No one comes in. No vehicles except the coroner."

"Ten-four."

I'm no stranger to violence or the unspeakable things human beings are capable of doing to each other. Even so, for an instant I can't catch my breath.

The woman's head is turned away from me, her chin tilted at an unnatural angle. I see strawberry-blond hair matted with blood, the scalp laid open, a small red mouth at the back of her head. Green-blue fingernail polish. Gold bracelet. Pretty hands. And I'm reminded that just hours ago, this woman cared about such mundane things as a manicure and jewelry.

Careful not to disturb the scene, I sidle around to the other side of the woman. I know immediately she's dead. The left side of her face has been destroyed. Cheekbone caved in. Eyeball dislodged from its socket. Nose an unrecognizable flap of skin. Tongue protruding through broken teeth. A string of blood and drool dribbling onto the carpet to form a puddle the size of a fist.

I shift the beam of my flashlight to her face. Recognition flickers uneasily in my gut, the stir of some long-forgotten memory. A punch of dread follows, because at that moment I do not want to know her. But I do and the rush of nausea that follows sends me back a step.

Bending, I put my hands on my knees, and blow out a breath. "Damn."

I choke out a sound I don't recognize, end it with a cough. Giving myself a quick mental shake, I straighten, look around the room. A high-end purse with leather fringe has been tossed haphazardly onto the chair. An overnight bag sits on the floor in front of the cubbyhole closet. I go to the chair, pluck a pen from my pocket, and use it to flip open the flap. Inside, I see a leather wallet, a cosmetic case, a comb, perfume. I pull out the wallet. I notice several twenty-dollar bills as I open it and I know that whoever did this didn't do it for money.

Her driver's license stares at me from its clear-faced pocket. The floor tilts beneath my feet when I see the name. Rachael Schwartz. The dread bubbling inside me burgeons as I stare down at the photo of the pretty young woman with strawberry-blond hair and her trademark almost-smile. It's the kind of smile that shouts *I'm going places and if you can't keep up you will be left behind!* But then that was Rachael. Hard to handle. High emotion and higher drama. Even as a kid, she was prone to making mistakes and then defending her position even when she was wrong, which was often. If you hurt her or angered her, she lashed out with inordinate ferocity. Faults aside, her love was fierce and pure. I know all of those things because I was one of the few Amish who understood her, though I never said as much aloud.

Closing my eyes, I bank the rise of emotion, shove it back into its hole. "Son of a bitch," I whisper.

I knew Rachael Schwartz since she was in diapers. She was seven years younger than me, the middle child of a Swartzentruber family here in Painters Mill. The Swartzentruber sect is an Old Order subgroup and its members adhere to the timeworn traditions in the strictest sense. They eschew much of the technology other sects allow, such as the use of gravel for long lanes, indoor plumbing, and even the use of a slow-moving-vehicle sign for their buggies. The Schwartzes had five kids and I babysat them a few times when I was a teenager. Her *mamm* and *datt* still live in the old farmhouse off of Hogpath Road.

I lost track of Rachael over the years. I heard she left Painters Mill at some point, before I returned here as chief. She was the only girl I'd ever met who was worse at being Amish than me.

Using my cell, I snap a photo of the license in case I need to reference the information later.

"Chief?"

I startle, turn to face Mona, hoping my face doesn't reflect the riot of emotions banging around inside me. "You get the crime scene tape up?" I ask.

"Yes, ma'am." Something flickers in her eyes. She cocks her head. "You know her?"

I sigh, shake my head. "Not well, but . . ." I don't know how to finish the sentence, so I let the words trail off.

Mona gives me a moment; then her gaze flicks to the purse. "Anything?"

"Driver's license. Cash." I acknowledge the thought that's been nudging at the back of my mind. "No cell phone. Have you seen one?"

"No."

I use the pen to go through the scant items inside, then drop the wallet back into the purse.

By the time I've finished, I've got my head on straight. I start toward Mona. "I'm going to call BCI," I say, referring to the Ohio Bureau of Criminal Investigation. "Get a CSU out here. In the interim, we need to canvass, starting with the motel rooms. Check with the manager to see which ones are occupied. Start with the rooms closest to this one and work your way out. Talk to everyone. See if they saw or heard anything unusual."

"You got it."

We exit the room. On the sidewalk outside the door, I stop, draw a deep breath, let it out, draw in another. "Get Glock out here, too," I say, referring to Rupert "Glock" Maddox, my most experienced officer. "We got four vehicles here in the parking lot. I'll find out which one belongs to her and we'll get it cordoned off, too."

"Got it, Chief."

Pulling out my cell, I call Dispatch. Usually, we communicate via radio. Because I don't want Rachael's name floating around on the airwaves in case someone is listening to a police scanner, I opt for my cell.

"Run Rachael Schwartz through LEADS," I tell Lois, referring to the Law Enforcement Automated Data System, which is a database administered by the Ohio State Highway Patrol and allows law enforcement to share criminal justice information. "Check for warrants. Phone number. Known associates. Whatever you can find." I glance down at the photo on my phone and recite the address off her license. "Check property records, too. Find out who owns the property where she lives."

"Roger that."

I hit END and turn to the motel manager, who's standing a few feet away, smoking a cigarette. "She dead?" he asks.

I nod. "Can you tell me which rooms are occupied?"

"Two. Four. Seven. And nine."

I nod at Mona and she starts toward the room two doors down.

"Do you know which vehicle belongs to Schwartz?" I ask the manager.

He looks down at the paper in his hand. "Let's see if she included the info on her check-in form. Here we go." He motions toward the Lexus parked a couple of spaces down from the room. "Right there."

"Was she alone?" I ask.

"I didn't see anyone else. No other name on the form. And she only requested one key."

I nod, look around, spot the security camera tucked under the eave a few yards away. "Are your security cameras working?"

"Far as I know."

"I need to take a look," I say. "Can you get the recordings for me?"

"I think so."

"What time did she check in?"

He glances down at the form in his hand. "A little after eight P.M. yesterday."

I nod. "Would you mind sticking around for a while in case I have some more questions?"

"I'll be here until five."

I thank him and hit the speed dial for Tomasetti.

CHAPTER 3

"I figured you wouldn't be able to go long without hearing the sound of my voice."

I manage a pretty decent rendition of a laugh. But Tomasetti's an astute man—or maybe I'm not as good at my seasoned-cop equanimity as I think, because he asks, "What's wrong?"

"There's been a homicide," I tell him. "At the motel."

A beat of silence and then, "What do you need?"

"A CSU, for starters."

"Shooting? Stabbing? Domestic? What do you have?"

"Not sure. Beating, I think. Hard to tell because there's a lot of trauma. Victim is female. Thirty years old."

"I'll get someone down there ASAP." He waits, reluctant to end the call, knowing there's more. "What else, Kate?"

"Tomasetti, this girl . . . she was Amish once. I mean, years ago. I heard she left." I stumble over my words, jumble them, take a moment and clear my throat. "I knew her. I mean, when she was a kid. Growing up."

"Any idea who might've done it?"

"No. I haven't seen her in years." I look around, hating it that my thoughts are in disarray, that some distant connection is getting in the way. "Whoever did this . . . it's bad. There was an incredible amount of violence."

"Killer knew her."

"Probably." I scrub a hand over my face. "I need to tell her parents."

"Hang tight. I'll be there as soon as I can."

I've just ended the call when the crunch of tires in gravel draws my gaze. I look up to see a Holmes County Sheriff's Office cruiser pull into the lot, overheads flashing, and park behind my Explorer. I've met Dane "Fletch" Fletcher a dozen times in the years I've been chief. We've worked traffic accidents together. Defused a couple of domestic disputes. A bar fight at the Brass Rail. Last summer, we participated in a fundraiser for the 4-H club and spent most of the day in a dunk tank while squealing preteens threw a softball to hit the drop button. He's a decent cop with a laid-back personality and a sense of humor I appreciate a little more than I should.

"Hey, Fletch," I say, crossing to him.

He greets me with a handshake. "Heard you've got a dead body on your hands."

I lay out what little I know. "BCI is on the way."

"Hell of a way to close out the week. County is here to help if you need us, Kate."

The Willowdell Motel is inside the township limits of Painters Mill. But I work closely with the sheriff's office. We have a good relationship, and depending on manpower and workload, our boundaries sometimes overlap.

He scratches his head, his eyes on the open door of room 9. "Victim?"

I give him the rundown on Rachael Schwartz, sticking to the facts, tucking all those other gnarly emotions back into their hole.

"Formerly Amish, huh?" He rubs his hand over his chin. "Damn. Back to visit the family?"

"Maybe." I sigh, look around. "I did a cursory search of the room. There's a purse with an ID. Money still inside, so this wasn't a robbery. I didn't find a cell. We'll get a closer look once BCI gets here." I'm relieved when my thoughts begin to settle, my cop's mind clicking back into place.

I work a pair of gloves from the pouch on my utility belt and slip them on as I approach the Lexus parked a few yards from room 9. It's a newish sedan with a gleaming red finish and sleek lines that speak of affluence and prosperity.

I'm aware of the deputy behind me, craning his neck to see inside the vehicle. "Nice wheels for an Amish lady," he comments.

"Formerly Amish."

I'm reluctant to touch anything, but in the forefront of my mind the knowledge that a killer is walking free in my town pushes me to do just that. I open the driver's-side door. The interior is warm and smells of leather and perfume, all of it laced with the vague aroma of fast food. There's a wadded-up McDonald's bag on the floor of the back seat. A pretty floral jacket draped over the passenger seatback. A pair of royal-blue high heels lie on the passenger-side floor. Leaning in, careful not to touch anything else, I open the console. Inside, I see a couple of audiobooks, a pack of Marlboros, loose change, and a travel-size bottle of ibuprofen. No cell phone. I'm about to close the console when I spot the folded piece of paper tucked into the cellophane cover of the cigarette pack. Using my cell, I take a couple of photos. Then I pluck the note from the pack and unfold it. A single address is written in blue ink and underlined twice.

1325 SUPERIOR STREET
WOOSTER

"Hello," I say. I set the note on the seat, pull out my cell, and snap another photo.

"What's that?"

I turn to find Fletch standing behind me, craning his head. "Not sure," I tell him. "An address."

He squints at the paper. "Huh."

Fletch is a good enough cop to know that the fewer people inside the crime scene tape, the better. I nudge him to give me some space. "Do you have cones and tape?" I ask, referring to typical traffic equipment.

He catches my drift. "You want me to cordon off the parking lot?"

"That would be a big help. On the outside chance we can pick up tread marks or footwear imprints."

"Whatever you need, Chief."

Leaving the note on the seat, I circle around to the front of the vehicle and do a similar search of the passenger side, but find nothing of interest.

I've just closed the door when the coroner's Escalade pulls up and parks a few yards away.

I pull out my cell and call Dispatch.

"Hey, Chief."

"I need you to look up an address." I pull out my cell, call up the photo of the note, and recite the address. "Find out who lives there and get their information. Run them through LEADS and check for warrants."

"Give me two minutes."

"Thanks."

I end the call and look around. Mona and Glock are talking to a tattooed-up couple who'd spent the night in a room two doors down. They can't seem to stop looking at the door to room 9. Even from twenty feet away, I see shock and curiosity on their faces.

Because Painters Mill is a small town, it's not unusual for me to be acquainted with the people I deal with in the course of my job, whether they're victim or perpetrator or somewhere in between. This is different. I didn't know Rachael Schwartz well. In fact, I hadn't thought of her in years. Not since hearing about the tell-all book she wrote about the Amish two or three years ago, anyway. Even then, it was only a passing thought. A shake of the head. I didn't read the book.

But I knew her as a child—and she made an impression. She was a lively, outspoken girl, both of which set her apart from other Amish kids. She was precocious, questioning of authority, and argumentative—all of which worked to her detriment. As she entered her teens those traits burgeoned into disrespect for her elders and disdain for her brethren, which caused tremendous problems for everyone involved, but especially for Rachael.

Last I heard—likely in the course of a conversation with one of the local Amish—Rachael had left the fold and fled Painters Mill some twelve or thirteen years ago. Where did she go? Aside from authoring the book, how did she spend the last years of her life? Why was she back in town? Who hated her with such passion that they beat her to an unrecognizable heap?

The questions nag, like an irritated nerve beneath a rotting tooth. And I know in the coming days, I'm going to do everything in my power to get the answers I need, even if I don't like what comes back at me.

CHAPTER 4

Rhoda and Dan Schwartz live on a narrow dirt track a mile or so off of Hogpath Road just outside Painters Mill. The couple is a pillar of the Amish community and has been for as long as I can remember. Now that her children are grown and married, Rhoda has gone back to teaching school at the two-room schoolhouse down the road. Dan runs the dairy farm with the help of his eldest son. They're decent, hardworking people, good neighbors. All of that said, they were quick to condemn me when I got into trouble as a teenager. I wonder if their intolerance played a role in their daughter's leaving the fold.

The death of a child is the worst news a parent can receive. It's the kind of slow agony they take with them to the grave. It changes the order of their world. Steals the joy from their lives, their hope for the future. Generally speaking, the Amish are stoic when faced with grief, in part because of their faith and their belief in eternal life. Even so, when it comes to the loss of a child, there is nothing that will spare them that brutal punch of pain.

Dread lies in my gut like a stone as I make the turn and barrel up the lane. The Schwartz farmhouse is an old two-story structure that's been added onto several times over the decades. The brick façade is crumbling in places. The front porch isn't quite straight. But the white paint is fresh and the garden in the side yard with its picket fence and freshly turned earth is magazine-cover perfect.

I park in the gravel area at the back of the house next to an old manure spreader and follow the flagstone walkway to the front. I find Rhoda on the wraparound porch. She's on her knees, half a dozen clay pots scattered on sheets of *The Budget* newspaper, and a bag of potting soil leaning against the column. She's a pleasant-looking woman of about fifty, her silver-brown hair tucked into her *kapp*, and a quick smile that reveals dimples she passed on to her daughter.

"Hi, Rhoda," I say as I ascend the steps.

She looks up from her work. "Katie Burkholder! Well, I'll be." She gets to her feet, brushes her hands on her skirt. "*Wie bischt du heit?*" How are you today?

Her expression is friendly and open, but she's surprised to see me, wondering why I'm here, in uniform. I'm loath to tear her world apart and I experience a wave of hatred for the son of a bitch who took her daughter's life.

She reaches for my hand and squeezes. "How's your family, Katie?" She's got short nails, her palms callused. "Is that sister of yours *ime familye weg* again?" The Amish have an aversion to the word "pregnant," instead using their own phrase, "in the family way." "That Sarah, always holding us in suspense."

I look into her eyes and for the first time I notice she also passed their blue-green irises on to Rachael, too, and an uneasy sensation of her coming grief tightens my chest.

"I'm afraid this is an official visit, Rhoda." I squeeze her hand. "Is Dan home?"

Her smile falters. Something in my expression or tone has given her pause. She cocks her head, the initial tinge of worry entering her eyes. "Is everything all right?"

"Where's Dan?" I repeat.

"He's inside," she tells me. "I made fried bologna sandwiches for lunch. I suspect he's sneaking a second one about now. If you'd like to stay, we can get caught up on things."

She's nervous and blabbering now. She knows I've news to bear, that it's not good. A hundred scenarios are surely running through her mind, as if she'd always known her daughter's antics would catch up with her one day and lead to this moment.

"The man eats like a horse, I tell you," she says in *Deitsch*.

I want to wrap my arms around her, silence her chatter, hold her while she comes apart, absorb some of the pain I'm about to inflict. But there's no way I can do any of those things, so I brush past her and open the door. "Mr. Schwartz?" I call out. "Dan, it's Kate Burkholder."

Dan Schwartz appears in the doorway that separates the living room from the kitchen, a sandwich in hand. He's wearing a straw flat-brimmed hat. Blue work shirt. Brown trousers. Suspenders. His face splits into a grin at the sight of me. He's still missing the eyetooth I recall from my youth. He's never gotten it fixed.

"*Wie geht's alleweil?*" How goes it now? At the sight of me and his wife, his expression falls. "*Was der schinner is letz?*" What in the world is wrong?

"It's Rachael," I tell them. "She's dead. I'm sorry."

"What?" Choking out a desperate-sounding laugh, Rhoda raises her hand, takes a step back, as if she's realized I'm a carrier of some deadly contagion. "*Sell is nix as baeffzes.*" That's nothing but trifling talk.

23

Dan reaches for his wife, misses, stumbles closer and grasps her hand in his. He says nothing. But I see the slash of pain lay him open. While the Amish live by their belief in the divine order of things and life beyond death, they are human beings first and foremost, and their pain rips a hole in my heart.

"Rachael?" Rhoda brings her hand to her face, places it over her mouth as if to prevent the scream building inside her from bursting out. "No. That can't be. I would have known."

"Are you sure?" Dan asks me.

"She's gone," I tell them. "Last night. I'm sorry."

"But . . . how?" he asks. "She's young. What happened to her?"

I almost ask them to sit down, realize I'm procrastinating, a feeble attempt to spare them that second brutal punch. But I know that delaying bad news is one thing a cop can never do. When notifying next of kin, you tell them. Straightforward. No frills. No beating around the bush. You lay down the facts. You express your sympathy. You distance yourself enough to ask the questions that need to be asked.

Because I don't have the official cause or manner of death, I tell them what I can. "All I know is that her body was found around eleven o'clock this morning."

The Amish man raises his gaze to mine. Tears shimmer in his eyes, but he doesn't let them fall. "Was it an accident? A car?" His mouth tightens. "Or drugs? What?"

I'm not doing a very good job of relaying the facts. My mind is clouded by my own emotions, the things I saw, the things I know about their daughter. "She was found in a room at the Willowdell Motel," I tell him. "We don't know exactly what happened, but there was some physical trauma. The police are investigating."

Rhoda Schwartz presses both hands to her cheeks. Tears well in her eyes and spill. "*Mein Gott.*" My God.

Dan looks at me, blinking rapidly, trying to absorb. "What kind of trauma?"

I can tell by the way he's looking at me that he already suspects that his daughter's antics, her lifestyle, finally caught up with her.

"I believe Rachael was murdered," I tell them.

"Someone . . . took her life?" Rhoda chokes out a sound that's part sob, part whimper. "Who would do such a thing? Why would they do that?"

Dan looks away, silent. The muscles in his jaws work. His eyes glitter with tears, but still they do not fall.

After a moment, he raises his gaze to mine. "Rachael was here? In Painters Mill?"

"You didn't know she was in town?" I let my gaze slide from Dan to Rhoda, the question aimed at both of them.

Both shake their heads.

"Do you have any idea why she was here?" I ask.

Rhoda doesn't even seem to hear the question. She's turned away, wrapped her arms around herself, blind and deaf, cocooned in her own misery. From where I stand, I can see her shoulders shaking as she silently sobs.

"We didn't know," Dan tells me.

"When's the last time you saw her?" I ask.

Dan lowers his gaze to the floor, so I turn my attention to Rhoda.

The woman looks at me as if she'd forgotten I was in the room. Her face has gone pale. Her nose glows red. She blinks as if bringing me back into view. "Right before Christmas, a year ago, I think."

That Rachael hadn't seen her parents in almost a year and a half tells me a great deal about the relationship. "Last time you talked to her, did she mention any problems? Was she troubled in any way?"

The Amish woman shakes her head. "She seemed same as always. A little lost maybe. But you know how that goes. She left the fold. That's what happens."

"Do you stay in touch with her?" I ask. "Did she call or write?"

"I talked to her on her birthday," the Amish woman tells me. "I called her. From the pay phone shack down the road there. Been a year ago now."

"How did she seem last time you talked to her?" I ask. "Did she mention what was going on in her life? Was she having any problems? Anything unusual or worrisome?"

"She was fine." The Amish woman's face screws up. Leaning forward, she buries her face in her hands.

I give her a moment and press on. "How was your relationship with her overall?"

"As well as can be expected," Rhoda tells me. "Bishop Troyer put her under the *bann,* you know. I never lost hope that she'd find her way back to us, back to the Amish way."

For the first time I see guilt on their faces, mingling with the grief, as if they've just realized they should have softened their stance and stayed closer to their daughter in spite of the rules.

"Did she stay in touch with anyone else here in Painters Mill?" I ask.

"She was always close with Loretta Bontrager," Rhoda tells me.

I don't know Loretta personally, but the image of a quiet little Amish girl drifts through my memory. Back then, her last name was Weaver and she was the polar opposite of Rachael. While Rachael was loud and outspoken, Loretta was reserved and shy. No one could quite figure out how they became best friends. Loretta still lives in Painters Mill; I see her around town on occasion. She's married now with children of her own.

I pull the notebook from my pocket and write down her name.

"They've been friends since they were little things," Dan says.

"Don't know if they see each other much anymore," Rhoda adds. "But if Rachael kept in touch with anyone here in Painters Mill besides us, it would be Loretta."

I nod, my mind already moving in the next direction. "Was there anyone else she was close to?"

"We wouldn't know about that," Dan tells me.

"Did she have a boyfriend?" I ask.

Dan drops his gaze, deferring to his wife.

"She was private about such things," the Amish woman says quietly.

I nod, realizing she likely doesn't know, and I shift gears. "Did she ever mention any problems with anyone? Any arguments?"

The man shakes his head, his eyes on the floor, mouth working.

But it's Rhoda who answers the question. "If she did, she never spoke of it. Not to us."

"Probably didn't want to worry us, you know," Dan adds. "She was thoughtful that way."

"Thoughtful" is the one word I wouldn't use to describe Rachael Schwartz. "Do you know any of her friends in Cleveland?" I ask.

The couple exchange a look.

Dan shakes his head. "We don't know anything about her life there." Disapproval rings hard in his voice.

"Do you have any idea where she worked?" I ask. "How she was making a living?"

"Worked at some fancy restaurant," Rhoda tells me.

"Do you know the name of it?"

"No." Shaking her head, Rhoda looks down at her hands. "And she wrote that book, you know. All those lies." She clucks her mouth. "Amish men having their way with women in the back seat of their buggies. Good Lord."

"Chafed a lot of hides here in Painters Mill." Dan grimaces, shame

27

darkening his features. "We knew nothing good would come of her being in the city."

"Evil goings-on," Rhoda adds. "We tried to tell her, but she was a headstrong girl, didn't listen. You know how she was." She shakes her head. "She would have been safer here. Gotten married. Had a family. Stayed close to God."

I don't point out to them that from all indications Rachael was murdered right here in Painters Mill, likely by someone who knew her. Someone filled with rage, a complete lack of control, no conscience to speak of, and the capacity to do it again.

CHAPTER 5

The Willowdell Motel is crawling with law enforcement when I arrive. In an effort to preserve any possible tire tread evidence, all official vehicles have relocated to the road shoulder in front of the motel. I see Glock's cruiser. An SUV from the Holmes County Sheriff's Office. An Ohio State Highway Patrol Dodge Charger. The only vehicles inside the perimeter are the BCI crime scene unit truck and the Holmes County Coroner's van.

I pick up my radio and hail Dispatch. "Anything come back on Schwartz?"

"Two DUIs in the last four years," Lois tells me. "Both out of Cuyahoga County. She pled no contest both times. Hot-check charge six years ago. Paid a fine. Last summer she was arrested for domestic violence. Charge was later dropped."

A ping sounds in the back of my brain. "Does Prince Charming have a name?"

"Jared Moskowski. Thirty-two years old. No record. Never been

29

arrested." She rattles off a Cleveland address. "Get this: Moskowski was the complainant on the domestic," she says.

Most often in the course of a domestic dispute, it's the female who gets roughed up by a male partner and makes the call. Knowing what I do about Rachael Schwartz, I'm not surprised that she was at least as much an instigator as a victim. Even so, I'll make sure Tomasetti takes a hard look at Moskowski.

I'm about to thank her and end the call when she pipes back up. "Oh, and I got a line on that address you gave me."

"Shoot."

"It's not a residence, but a business. A bar called The Pub."

"You're a font of interesting information this afternoon," I tell her.

"Internet connection helps a little."

As I park behind Glock's cruiser, I wonder if Rachael is still involved with Moskowski. I wonder if their relationship is volatile. I think about the bar in Wooster and I wonder why Rachael would write down the address when she lives in Cleveland, which is about an hour's drive away. Did she have plans to meet someone? Or did she meet with them on the drive to Painters Mill from Cleveland? Was there an argument? Did that someone follow her to Painters Mill and confront her in that motel room?

I spot Tomasetti's Tahoe several yards away and start toward it. I find him leaning against the hood, talking on his cell. Upon noticing my approach, he ends the call.

"You talked to the family?" he asks.

I nod, wondering if traces of the conversation are still evident on my face. "They took it pretty hard."

He's looking at me a little too closely, his eyes seeing more than I want him to see. "Hard on you, too, evidently."

"And here I thought I was getting pretty good at my tough-guy façade." I make the statement lightly, but it doesn't ring true.

"How well did you know her?"

"I didn't, really. Not as an adult." I struggle to put my finger on the flicker of pain in my chest. "The first time I saw Rachael Schwartz, she was still in diapers."

"Long time."

"She was too damn young to die."

I'm exasperated that I can't hold his gaze. Maybe because I know he sees all the things I'd rather not deal with at the moment. That my emotions are too close to the surface. He watches me, saying nothing, and in that instant, the silence strips me bare.

"I knew her when she was a kid. That's what's so tough about this. Of all the Schwartz kids, Rachael is the one that . . . made an impression. She was vivacious. A mischief-maker. She loved to laugh. Trouble was never too far away." I don't know why I'm telling him all of that, but it feels important and the words come out in a rush.

"Connections," he says.

"Too many probably."

He sighs. "Looks like trouble found *her* this time."

"You going to assist with the case?" I ask. "I mean, officially?"

"I'm your guy."

I look toward the motel room. In my mind's eye, I see the way Rachael Schwartz looked dead on the floor. The extent of damage to her body. Her face.

"Tomasetti, the level of violence . . ."

"Yeah."

"It was . . . over-the-top. Personal, I think, and passionate."

I tell him about the domestic dispute, but he already knows. "I got an address for Moskowski," he tells me. "Detectives are on their way to pick him up."

Typically, and since this is my case, I'd be part of the interview process. But because this investigation involves multiple agencies, and Moskowski lives in Cleveland, which is light-years out of my jurisdiction, Tomasetti will be the one to conduct the initial Q and A.

I hold his gaze, wrestling with what needs to be said and what doesn't. "Rachael Schwartz . . . she wasn't exactly the poster child for an Amish girl."

He cocks his head, knowing there's more, waits.

"She got into trouble a lot. I mean, growing up. She made a lot of mistakes. Broke the rules. If her penchant for finding trouble followed her into adulthood . . ." I'm mixing potentially helpful information with extraneous crap, so I take a moment, dial it back. "I'm not saying she was a bad person. She wasn't. Just sort of . . . full-bore."

"I've been around long enough to know that most people are little bit of both," he says gently.

"I don't want her to be just another young woman who ended up dead because she made some bad decisions. She wasn't perfect, but she deserved the chance to live her life."

He watches a state trooper get into his vehicle and pull out, gives me a moment to settle. It's a small thing. But it's one of a thousand reasons why I love him. John Tomasetti knows my weaknesses. All of them. He gets it. He gets me. And he's good at letting things be.

"Are we talking about a specific bad decision?" he asks.

"Domestic violence incident aside." I tell him about the book. "It made quite a stir here in Painters Mill. Some people weren't happy with her."

"Anyone in particular?"

"The Amish. Others, I'm sure. I'll do a little digging and let you know when I get a name."

He nods. "So she's likely made a few enemies over the years."

"Probably."

He nods toward the motel. "The manager came through with the CCTV. It's not good. Too dark. Too far away. Angle is bad." He shrugs. "I put our IT guys on it, so we'll see."

Movement at the door of room 9 draws my attention. A technician with the coroner's office clad in protective gear is wheeling a gurney from the van to the walkway outside the room.

"Before I go . . ." I tell him about the piece of paper in the vehicle with the scrawled address. "It's a bar in Wooster. The Pub. I thought I'd run up that way as soon as I get some time."

His eyes narrow on mine. "Wooster is about the midway point between Cleveland and Painters Mill. You thinking she met someone on her way down?"

"Maybe."

I'm only giving him part of my attention now. Doc Coblentz is standing just inside the doorway of the motel room, typing something into his iPad. The last thing I want to do is go back in there. But my need for information—my need to hear the coroner's preliminary thoughts—overrides my misgivings.

"I've got to go."

He looks past me, watches the technician kick down the brake on the gurney. "You've got this, right?"

The smile I give him feels tight and phony on my face, so I lose it, let him see the truth—that this has me a hell of a lot more shaken than I want to be.

"I just want to get this right," I tell him.

"You will."

There are too many people around for a kiss goodbye or any such nonsense, so I brush my fingertips across his hand and start for the door.

I nod at the deputy as I duck beneath the crime scene tape. My boots crunch against gravel as I walk toward room 9. I pause at the doorway and find Doc Coblentz standing over Rachael Schwartz's body. Clad in protective gear—face mask, disposable gown, a hair cap even though he's bald, and shoe covers—he looks like a cross between the Michelin man and the Pillsbury doughboy.

His technician, also clad in protective gear, punches something into an iPad.

"Doc," I say.

Doc Coblentz turns, looks at me over the top of his eyeglasses, and I can't help but notice that even in the face of such a heinous crime, his expression is serene. Unlike me, he's not shaken or angry or outraged. Not for the first time I wonder how he does it, dealing with the dead as often as he does, and I'm reminded that he is first and foremost a man of medicine. A pediatrician—a healer of children. When it comes to his role as coroner, he is a scientist with a puzzle to solve.

"Come on in, Kate," he says. "I'm about to release the scene to all those anxious-looking BCI boys out there and all their high-tech gadgets."

I cross to him, trying not to notice the stink of blood and urine and other smells I don't want to think about. "Can you tell me what happened to her?" I ask.

"I can speculate."

"I'll take whatever you can give me."

He looks down at the victim and sighs. "Preliminarily, and simply judging by the trauma, I would say she was beaten to death."

"Fists? Weapon?"

"Blunt object more than likely."

I force myself to look at the body, grapple to put what I see into words. "What about the . . . wounds?" I ask. "Is it possible she was also stabbed or slashed?"

"Force of impact," he tells me. "Which basically means she was struck with such force that it broke the skin, laid it open. As far as I can see, there are no incised wounds. Or gunshot wounds for that matter. As I'm sure you're aware, my assessment could change once I get her on the table."

I nod, shuddering inwardly. "Any idea of the time of death?"

"Well, she's in full rigor, which sets in at about two hours after death and completes at about eight hours. Depending on several factors, in this case the ambient temp and rate of decomp, full rigor ends after eighteen to twenty hours."

I calculate the equation, recall the manager telling me she checked in at about eight P.M. last night. "So, it's safe to say this probably happened sometime during the night."

The coroner shrugs. "Or very early this morning."

I look around, take in the obvious signs of a struggle. I think about the cash, the possibility that this was drug related, and I ask, "Can you tell if she was moved? After she was killed?"

Doc Coblentz nods at the technician, who has come over to stand next to us. In tandem, both men kneel and ease their gloved hands beneath the victim's shoulder and hip and lift her several inches. Beneath her, the carpet is wet with urine. I squat for a better look. My eyes are drawn immediately to the purple-black flesh that had been pressed against the carpeted floor.

"As you can see," the doc says, "she's almost into full lividity. Once the heart stops beating, gravity sets in and the blood settles to the lowest part of the body and pools. That happens at approximately twelve hours." The men ease the body back to the floor. "I would venture to say she died shortly before or after she fell or was pushed or placed here on the floor."

"Any chance you can narrow down the time of death, Doc?"

He makes a sound that's part growl, part sigh. "Tough to do at this

35

point, Kate. Once I get her to the morgue, I'll get a core body temp. That said, and taking all of the usual caveats into consideration, judging by the extent of rigor and livor, I'm guessing she died somewhere between eleven P.M. and five A.M."

A hundred more questions fly at my brain, but I set them aside for later because I know he won't be able to give me definitive answers. I straighten, and start toward the door. For the first time I'm aware that my face is hot, the back of my neck damp with sweat. The room feels small and claustrophobic. The air is thick and stinking of bodily fluids.

Outside, I swallow the spit that's pooled at the back of my throat and take a deep breath of fresh air.

I don't speak to anyone as I make my way toward the Explorer. I can't get the picture of Rachael Schwartz's brutalized body out of my head. Her skin laid open. Her face destroyed. Eye bulging from its socket. Her body broken beyond words.

I reach the Explorer, yank open the door, and slide behind the wheel, take a moment to compose myself. With a murder investigation spooling and the clock ticking, I need to be focused on my job. On finding the person responsible and bringing him to justice. Instead, my thoughts are scattered. I'm outraged and saddened and furious at once. That a woman I knew as a child is dead. That it happened in the town whose residents I swore to serve and protect.

"Not on my watch," I whisper.

Putting the vehicle in gear, I pull out of the gravel lot and head toward town.

CHAPTER 6

I met Rachael Schwartz for the first time when she was a newborn. The birth of a baby is a momentous occasion for all families, but it's an especially big event when you're Amish. After the new mom has had a few days to rest, the Amish women in the community come calling to see the new addition. Most bring a covered dish or two, help out with any chores that need to be done, and share a cup of *siess kaffi* or sweet coffee.

At the age of seven, I wasn't particularly interested in babies, but I recall my *mamm* dragging me over to the Schwartz farm, where I spent an hour watching her coddle and coo over a crying, red-faced infant that smelled of sour milk and stomach gas. Rachael didn't make a good first impression.

In a peripheral sort of way, I watched her grow up. Because of our age difference, we didn't play together or spend time. But all Amish children attend worship and mingle afterward—and squeeze in some playtime if possible. As her personality developed, I took notice, because for once someone else was getting into trouble instead of me.

The Amish generally have no use for babysitters. Most of the time and regardless of the occasion they take the baby with them, whether it's to worship, a wedding, or a funeral. When I was thirteen, Rhoda and Dan Schwartz had to travel to Pennsylvania. My *mamm* offered up my babysitting services, perhaps in the hope of reinforcing my own understanding of responsibility and Amish gender roles. Babysitting a herd of kids was not my idea of time well spent. But I hadn't yet discovered the power of argument, and so, by well-meaning parents hoping the experience might somehow help me find my missing maternal instinct, I was thrown to the wolves. It should have been pure misery for a girl like me—a tomboy who didn't quite conform or know how to fit in. How unlikely that another girl who was every bit as fallible as me would turn an unbearably mundane babysitting assignment into something unexpected.

Generally speaking, Amish kids are pretty well behaved, with a good work ethic and an early-to-bed-early-to-rise routine that make them easy to manage. Rachael was a rule-breaker with a penchant for trouble and a talent for fun.

She was the girl whose dress was perpetually stained, her *kapp* never quite straight, her gap-toothed smile beaming mischief. She was perpetual motion meets chaos. The kid who talked too much and had a temper when she didn't get her way—and might even mete out some revenge if you crossed her. But she was also a curious child who asked too many questions, especially about topics she didn't necessarily need to know, and she was rarely satisfied with the answers she got. The one who preferred baseball to dolls, and whose favorite food was strawberry ice cream. She was a prankster. Sometimes those pranks weren't very nice. I was a victim myself a time or two, but I quickly realized: You could get mad, but you couldn't stay that way, because Rachael always found a way to make you laugh, even when you didn't want to.

Rhoda and Dan were going to be gone for three days, which meant this hell-world I'd stepped into was going to last a while. It was on that second day I learned just how alike Rachael and I really were.

I was in the kitchen, making bologna sandwiches, when eight-year-old Danny burst in, breathless and sweating, his voice infused with panic. "Rachael got her head cut off!" he cried. "I think she's drowning!"

That got my attention. I dropped the spatula, ran to him, knelt in front of him. "What happened?" I asked. "Where is she?"

"She rolled down the hill!" the boy cried. "The barrel hit a tree and it bounced over the bob-wire and went in the crick!"

My babysitting skills may have been lacking, but I was responsible enough to experience a moment of terror. I grabbed his hand. "Show me!"

We dashed out the back door, ran to the barn, through the stalls and equipment area, and exited through the rear pens. From there, we sprinted across the pasture, huffing and puffing. Danny yelped when he lost his hat, but he didn't go back for it. Another fifty yards and the land swept down at a steep angle. At the base of the hill, two Amish boys were climbing over a five-strand barbed-wire fence. A fifty-five-gallon drum was wedged between the strands. Beyond, the green-blue water of Painters Creek snaked eastward, its murky surface dappled with sunlight slanting down through the trees.

"Where is she?" I cried as I started down the hill, running too fast, especially with an eight-year-old boy in tow.

"She flew out of the barrel!" he cried.

The answer didn't make any sense, so I kept going. Having heard us, the boys, on the other side of the fence now, spun toward me. Breathless with panic. Faces sweaty and red.

"*Vo is Rachael?*" I called out to them. Where is Rachael?

"*Sie fall im vassah!*" her older brother shouted. She fell in the water.

I noticed that one end of the barrel had been cut off and removed. And a horrific picture emerged. The boys had been getting inside the barrel and rolling down the hill, which was far too steep for such a game. Somehow, six-year-old Rachael had gotten involved.

I reached the fence and vaulted it without slowing, my eyes skimming the water's surface. "I don't see her!"

"She rolled down the hill in the barrel!" The neighbor boy, Samuel Miller, stuttered every word. "It hit the fence and she fell out! Went in the water!"

I stumbled down the steep bank, tripping over the tangle of tree roots. A couple of feet from the water's edge, I slipped in mud and plunged into the water. A crush of cold. The smell of fish and mud. Deep water. Over my head. I surfaced, sputtering.

"Rachael!" Treading water, I looked around, felt around for her with my legs.

"Where is she?" Even as I shouted the words, I heard a cough. I swiveled, spotted the small form crawling onto the rocky shoal on the opposite bank. Rachael, blue dress soaked and torn. On her hands and knees. Her *kapp* tugged down over one ear. One shoe missing.

I dog-paddled toward her. My feet made contact with the rocky bottom and I rushed to her. "Rachael!"

She sat on the rocks, her legs splayed in front of her. Her face was eggshell pale. Eyes huge. Expression shaken. A scrape on her chin. A drop of watery blood dangled beneath her nose.

I thought about the barbed wire and envisioned a gaping wound in need of stitches. Every single awful scenario scrolled through my mind at a dizzying speed.

"Are you hurt?" I heaved myself from the water and started toward her, my dress dripping, shoes squeaking with every step.

The girl looked up at me and blinked. I braced, expecting a wail and tears. Instead, she wiped blood from her nose with a hand that was rock steady. A grin overtook her face. A laugh burst from her mouth.

"You're not going to tattle on me, are you, Katie?" She frowned at the smear of blood on her hand. "I want to do it again."

CHAPTER 7

Ben and Loretta Bontrager own a good-size dairy operation on a sixty-two-acre spread a few miles outside Painters Mill. I've known Loretta since she was a youngster, too shy to speak, and hiding behind the skirt of her *mamm*'s dress. She was the polar opposite of Rachael and yet somehow the two girls became best friends. While Rachael was the gregarious live wire, Loretta was the quiet and obedient follower.

Aside from the occasional wave in town, I haven't spoken to Loretta in years. I met her husband, Ben, for the first time two years ago when he ran into some problems for selling unpasteurized milk, which is illegal in the state of Ohio. He readily agreed to cease operations and there was never a need for me to come back. Until now.

I've just turned in to the lane of the Bontrager farm when I glance across the pasture to my right and spot the horse and rider. It's common to see people riding horses here in Painters Mill. We've got a few cowboys, the local 4-H club; even Amish kids partake on occasion. This particular equestrian rides like poetry and takes the horse into a circle at an easy lope. Horse and rider are one, a ballad of perfect balance and animal beauty that's so captivating, I stop the Explorer to take it in.

After a moment, the rider spots me, slows the animal, and trots toward me. I almost can't believe my eyes when I realize this rider is not only Amish, but female. She's bareback, sneaker-clad feet dangling. Her skirt is hiked up to her knees and I see a pair of trousers underneath. She clutches a tuft of mane with one hand, and with the other grips the reins, which look like old leather lines that have been cut short for riding. The horse's head is high, nostrils flared, foam at the corners of its mouth.

"Nicely done," I call out to her.

The girl runs her hand over the animal's shoulder, but not before I see the flash of pride in her eyes. "He's a good horse," she tells me.

I get out and walk over to the fence that runs alongside the lane. She's eleven or twelve years old, with big brown eyes, a sprinkling of freckles on a sunburned nose, and dark hair tucked messily into a *kapp*. A tiny bow peeks out at me from the base of the head covering, and I smile. That bow, which is not approved by the *Ordnung*, is a symbol of a girl's individuality, a sign of independence, and a small way to set herself apart from her *mamm*.

The horse is a Standardbred, the most common breed used for buggies. Most are worked so much in the course of day-to-day transportation, they're rarely used for riding. Most are never trained for anything but driving.

"You're a good rider," I tell her.

The girl lifts a shoulder, lets it drop, looks down at her dangling foot.

"Who trained him to ride under saddle like that?" I ask.

"I reckon I did."

She mumbles the response in a way that tells me it's an achievement

43

she probably shouldn't admit to, and I wonder if she's been warned to stay off the horse. It wouldn't be the first time an Amish girl was disallowed to partake in an activity a boy would have every right in which to excel.

"You should enter him in the Annie Oakley Days horse show," I tell her.

Her eyes light up. I see pride in their depths, and I hope she holds on to that as she grows into adulthood.

"What's your name?" I ask.

"Fannie Bontrager."

"Ben and Loretta are your parents?"

"*Ja.*"

"Are they home?"

Nodding, she points toward the house.

I round the front of the Explorer and open the door. Look across the hood at her. "Enjoy the rest of your ride, Fannie."

Beaming a grin, she wheels the horse around, and lopes away.

Shaking my head, I get back into the Explorer and continue on.

The Bontrager farmhouse is a two-story frame structure with fresh white paint, double redbrick chimneys, and a gleaming metal roof. I drive past a ramshackle German-style bank barn and a muddy pen where a gaggle of Holstein cows encircle a round bale of hay. I park at the rear of the house and take a narrow concrete sidewalk to the front porch. I've barely knocked when the door swings open.

Loretta Bontrager wears a gray dress with a matching *halsduch,* or "cape"; an organdy *kapp;* and a pair of nondescript oxfords. She's got a dishcloth in one hand, a soapy sponge in the other, her attention lingering on whatever she'd been cleaning.

She does a double take at the sight of me. "Katie Burkholder?" Stepping aside, she ushers me inside. "What a surprise."

I go through the door and extend my hand. "It's been a while."

"I'll say." She drops the sponge into a bucket full of suds, dries her hands with the dish towel, and grasps my hand. "Time has a way of slipping by, doesn't it? Too fast if you ask me."

"I met your daughter on my way up the lane," I tell her.

"Probably on that horse again, eh?"

"She's a good rider."

"Like her *datt*, I guess." She shakes her head. "Keeping her off that horse is like trying to keep the wool off a sheep."

She cocks her head, polite, wondering why I'm here. "*Witt du kaffi?*" Would you like coffee?

"I can't stay," I tell her.

Something in my voice must have alerted her that I'm not here for a friendly chat and she goes still.

"Loretta, I'm afraid I've got some bad news. It's Rachael Schwartz. She's dead."

The Amish woman's smile falters as if for an instant she thinks the words are some cruel joke. "What?" She sways, reaches out and sets her hand against the wall. "But . . . *Rachael*? Gone? How can that be?"

"I'm sorry. I know you were close."

She steadies herself, lets her hand slide from the wall, and faces me. "Rachael," she whispers. "She's so young and healthy. How?"

"She was murdered," I tell her. "Sometime last night."

"Oh . . . no." The words come out on a gasp. "Someone—" She cuts off the sentence as if she can't bring herself to finish. "Do her *mamm* and *datt* know?"

"I just talked to them."

She makes a sound that's part sympathy, part pain. "Poor Rhoda and Dan. My heart is broken for them." Tears shimmer in her eyes when she raises her gaze to mine. "I can't understand this, Katie. Who would do such a thing? And *why?*"

"I don't know. We're looking into it." I pause, give her a moment. "I understand you kept in touch with her. I was hoping you might be able to shed some light on her life. The people she knew. Do you have a few minutes to answer some questions?"

"Of course." But she looks as if she's grappling for strength that isn't there, for the control she can't quite reach. "Whatever you need . . . however I can help, just ask."

I pull my notebook from my pocket. "When's the last time you saw her?"

She looks down at the floor, thinking, and then raises her gaze to mine. "Over a year, I think. We met a couple of times at a little diner between Painters Mill and Cleveland, just to stay in touch and get caught up on things. I missed her so much after she moved away." She shakes her head. "I must have sent her a hundred letters that first year, but you know Rachael. She wasn't much of a letter writer."

"Did you visit her in Cleveland?"

She shakes her head. "I had Fannie by then and it was tough to get away with a new baby and all. You know how it is."

"When's the last time you talked to her?" I ask.

"A few months, I think."

"Did she mention any problems? Anything unusual or troubling in her life? Arguments or disagreements with anyone? A boyfriend maybe?"

The Amish woman considers a moment, then tightens her mouth. "She didn't mention any problems. But you know how Rachael was. Such a happy-go-lucky girl." Her brows furrow. "The only thing that stands out about the last time I talked to her is that she seemed a little . . . lost. Lonely. Homesick, maybe."

"How so?"

"Reminiscing, I guess. Asking about her parents and such. Like she missed them." She emits a sound of dismay. "Like they would have anything to do with her."

My cop's antennae go up. "Bad blood?" I ask.

She waves off the notion. "Nothing like that. It's just that Dan and Rhoda were tough on her. You know how the Amish are. Hardest on the ones they love the most."

I nod, remembering my own rebellion against the rules and the hard line my parents took to rein me in. "Did she have a good relationship with her parents?"

"They never accepted her leaving. They wanted her to come back. Get married. Have lots of children." A wistful smile plays at the corners of her mouth. "Of course, Rachael didn't want any of those things." Loretta shrugs. "It makes me sad to say it, Katie, especially now. But I think they saw her as fallen. Like maybe she was so far gone there was no way to bring her back."

Neither Rhoda nor Dan had mentioned that aspect of their relationship with their daughter. Their grief had been genuine and deep. Even so, I was Amish once. I've been a cop long enough to know that sometimes it's those troubled, passionate bonds that push people to the edge of their tolerance.

"Did she stay in touch with anyone else here in Painters Mill?"

"Not that I know of."

"Did you know she was in town?"

Her eyes widen. "She was here? You mean—" She bites off the word. I see her mind work through the implications. "Katie . . . it happened *here*? In Painters Mill?"

"I believe so."

"Oh, dear Lord." Raising her hands to her face, she swipes at the

47

tears with her fingertips. "I always thought of the city as a place of sin. A place that wasn't always good or safe for her. To think it happened *here*." She presses a hand against her chest. "Did you get them?" she asks. "The person who did it?"

"We haven't made an arrest yet."

"That's a scary thing. I mean, knowing they're still out there."

I nod. "Loretta, can you think of anyone else Rachael might've come here to see?"

"Other than her parents . . ." Her expression turns troubled. "She wasn't exactly on the best terms with the Amish community."

I know where she's going, but I say nothing, wait for her to continue.

"The book, you know. She wrote all those terrible things about the Amish. Some of them thought badly of her. A few washed their hands of her completely. The elders knew she wasn't going to come back. Katie, no one said as much, but I don't think they *wanted* her back."

Misconceptions about *meidung* or excommunication abound. Most non-Amish people believe the *bann* is a form of punishment. It's not. Shunning is intended to be redemptive and bring fallen individuals back into the fold. In most cases, it works because when you're Amish, your family is the center of your universe. Without them, you are cast adrift in a world you're not prepared to handle.

"Did anyone in particular want her permanently excommunicated?" I ask.

"It was gossip mostly. You know how the Amish are. Rachael didn't talk about it. But I know it hurt her." Loretta smiles, reflective, but fresh tears glitter in her eyes. "You remember how she was. *En frei geisht.*" A free spirit. "She loved to laugh. She loved to love. She loved people. She loved life with all of its gifts. It was hard not to love her. But when she got mad . . ." She hefts a laugh. "You knew it. She did everything with such . . . *eahnsht.*" Zeal. "One of the reasons she didn't fit in, I suppose. She just couldn't follow the rules. That was why she left, you know. That was why I worried about her."

"Because she was a *druvvel-machah*?" I ask. Troublemaker.

"Because she never held back. Rachael was full speed ahead at a hundred miles an hour, even if she didn't know exactly where she was going. She was vocal and her opinions weren't always popular, especially among the Amish. Then she wrote that book and it just made everything worse."

I recall the stir it made here in Painters Mill. It was some kind of tell-all that was touted as nonfiction. For those of us who are familiar with the Amish, it was glaringly obvious the book was little more than a sensationalized hit piece rife with fiction.

I ask for her take anyway. "How so?"

"Well, she trashed that clan down Killbuck way. The Anabaptist group. They call themselves Amish, but they're not. *Maulgrischt*," she says, using the *Deitsch* term for "pretend Christian."

I'm familiar with Amos Gingerich and his followers. I see them on occasion at the farmers' market, selling vegetables, woodworking novelties, and plants and trees from a small nursery they run on their property. They call themselves the Killbuck Amish. They don't adhere to any *Ordnung* that I know of. The Amish refuse to claim them. In fact, a good number of the group's members are those who've been excommunicated from other church districts. Gingerich takes them in and, rumor has it, indoctrinates them into a community that's more cultlike than Amish. Last I heard there were thirty or so members who live in a communelike compound, a praxis more in tune with the Hutterites than Amish. While most members get around via horse and buggy, the community shares a single vehicle and has several phones on the farm.

The citizens of Painters Mill ignore them for the most part, but rumors abound. Things like the men taking more than one wife. That the children are at risk. A few years ago, the sheriff's office and Children Services got involved because someone claimed the kids were being separated from their parents and forced to work. The investigation that followed was inconclusive, but it put them on my cop's radar.

"Katie, you asked me if anyone ever threatened Rachael." She gives a single resolute nod. "You might take a look at Amos Gingerich. I think he threatened her once."

I take out my notebook and write down the name. "What kind of threat?"

"Well, you know she stayed with them awhile. After she was put under the *bann*. She didn't leave on good terms." She lowers her voice. "Rachael told me he mentioned some of the awful stories in *Martyrs Mirror*—you know, the way they tortured and killed the Christians way back when. It gave me the shivers, but Rachael just laughed. She wasn't too worried about it. I didn't think of it again until now."

Martyrs Mirror is a fixture in most Amish homes. My parents weren't readers, but my *mamm* kept a copy on a table in the living room. Over a thousand pages in length, the ancient tome details the horrors committed against Christians, especially the Anabaptists. I read the book as a kid—stories of men and women being burned at the stake, decapitated, drowned, and buried alive. The brutality and injustice left an impression, not only about faith and martyrdom, but the kinds of cruelties human beings are capable of.

"Do you know why he threatened her?" I ask.

She grimaces. "Rachael devoted an entire chapter to Gingerich and the Killbuck clan. She trashed them. Called him a polygamist—and accused him of worse."

"Like what?"

"I don't know it to be true, but she told me some of the men were taking wives as young as fourteen and fifteen years of age. Too young, you know. I told her to let it go. Go on with her life and forget about them. But Rachael was headstrong. Said those girls deserved to be heard. She told me later that her publisher made her change the names, to keep the lawyers out of it, I guess, but everyone knew. Amos Gingerich was not happy about it."

I think about the scrap of paper in her car with the address scribbled on it. "Do you know if Rachael knew anyone in Wooster? Or from the Wooster area?"

Her brows draw together. "Not that I recall."

"What about men? Did she have a man in her life? A boyfriend that you know of?"

Up until now, Loretta has been aghast and struggling to accept the news of her friend's death. Her reactions have been genuine, her demeanor stunned. My question effectively shuts her down, and my cop's gut takes note. Something there, I think, and I wait.

"Rachael is . . . was the best friend I ever had. I loved her like a sister. I don't want to say anything unkind." For a moment, the Amish woman wrestles with some internal foe, then raises her gaze to mine. "She was a wild one, Katie. As a teenager, she liked boys. As a woman, she liked her men. Maybe a little too much."

"Anyone in particular?" I ask.

The Amish woman presses her lips together. "She knew I didn't approve, so she didn't talk too much about it. But there were men. A lot of them."

"Do you have a name?"

She shakes her head. "All I know is that there was always a man in her life and every single one of them seemed to be wrong for her."

CHAPTER 8

Summer 2008

Loretta had never disobeyed her parents. Not once in all of her sixteen years. She'd never lied to them. Never shirked her responsibilities. Never conceived the notion of misleading them in any way. Tonight, all of that was going to change.

She'd laughed the first time she heard the expression "Amish rager." A few of the older Amish boys were talking about it at a singing she'd attended last year. She'd only caught snatches of the conversation. From what she gathered, a rager was a huge outdoor party, held in a barn or field, and isolated from the prying eyes of the adults. There was music and alcohol and, sometimes, the English showed up. It was the kind of gathering that would entail a lot of rule breaking that would undoubtedly get back to parents—and maybe even the bishop. At the time, such an idea had seemed profane and forbidden—something she would never get involved in.

What a difference a year made. Loretta was sixteen now—almost grown up—and her initial disdain for the idea of attending a rager had transformed into something closer to curiosity. Leave it to her best friend to bring that far-off temptation into sharp focus and test all the sensibilities she'd lived by the entirety of her life.

Last church Sunday, when the preaching service was over and all the adults were talking, Rachael had come to her, breathless and flushed, her eyes alight.

"There's a rager this weekend," she whispered, as they'd set out knives, cups, and saucers.

Rachael was so pretty. She was long-limbed with a sun-kissed complexion, and thick lashes over eyes the color of a summer storm. She already had a womanly figure, unlike Loretta, who was built like a broomstick. Her smile was as bright as the sun—and so contagious you couldn't help but smile back, even when you knew she was going to get you into trouble. This afternoon she was vibrating with energy Loretta knew would lead to no good.

"That's just plain silly," Loretta told her as she set a paper napkin on the table. "Mamm and Datt will never allow it."

Rachael rolled her eyes. "You're such a *bottelhinkel*." It was the *Deitsch* term for a worn-out hen that was ready for the stewpot. "We're not going to tell them!"

The thought of attending a rager appealed more than Loretta wanted to admit. But she knew it was an invitation for trouble. "Are you sure it's a good idea?" she said.

Looking left and right, Rachael took her hand and pulled her to the hall, out of earshot of the older women who were bringing out pies. "Ben Bontrager is going to be there."

Loretta's heart quivered at the mention of Ben Bontrager. She'd been half in love with him since she was six years old. He didn't know it yet, but she was going to marry him. They were going to live on a big farm and have dozens of children and too many animals to count.

"I don't think I can go," Loretta said.

"You have to!" Rachael whispered. "Ben is on *rumspringa*. I heard there are going to be some loose English girls there. You can't let him . . . you know."

Loretta wasn't dense; she knew boys were different from girls. They couldn't always control their urges. The thought of Ben giving in to some floozy *Englischer* crushed her.

"What do I tell Mamm and Datt?" she asked.

"Don't tell them anything, silly girl."

"How will I get out of the house without them knowing?"

Looking past her to make sure no one was listening, Rachael lowered her voice. "Sneak out your bedroom window. It's right over the porch. I'll meet you at the end of the lane at midnight. We'll go to the rager, stay for an hour, just long enough for you to see Ben, and then we'll go home. No one will ever know."

No one will ever know.

Famous last words.

A week ago, sneaking out of the house had seemed like such an exciting idea. Now, Loretta wasn't so sure.

Lying in her bed, she checked the alarm clock on the table for the hundredth time. It was eleven forty-five. The house had been quiet for some time. Her parents had retired to their room hours ago. Loretta knew her *mamm* liked to read before she went to sleep. But the light was out now. Time to go.

Rising, Loretta reached for her pillow and arranged it beneath the covers so if someone peeked in, they'd see the silhouette of her sleeping form. Satisfied, she crossed to the window. Her hands shook as she slid it open. The warm summer night greeted her as she stepped over the sill and onto the roof over the porch.

Careful not to make a sound, she lowered herself onto her rear and crab-walked down the slick metal to the nearest branch. Rising, she used the branch for balance and worked her way to the fork in the trunk. From there, she climbed down and jumped the last four feet.

The thump of her shoes hitting the ground seemed inordinately loud in the silence of the night. Certain someone must have heard, she looked around, heart pounding. But there was no one there. No lantern light inside. No movement in the kitchen window. Nothing but the sound of the bullfrogs from the pond and crickets all around.

Loretta launched herself into a run. She cut through the yard, the dew wet on her shoes. Upon reaching the gravel lane, she cut right and sprinted toward the road. Her feet pounded the gravel, her breaths echoed off the blackberry bushes that grew alongside the lane. She was nearly to the end when the shadowy figure stepped out in front of her.

Loretta yelped.

"Shhh!"

At the sight of her friend, relief flooded her with such force that her legs went weak. "You scared the jeepers out of me!"

Giggling, Rachael grabbed her hand. "Quiet or someone will hear you."

Rachael was wearing English clothes. Jeans. Tank top. Fancy sandals that showed her toes—which were painted pink. Suddenly, Loretta felt frumpy. "I look like a *bottelhinkel.*"

Stepping back, Rachael set her chin on her fingers and gave her a critical look. "At least we can fix your hair." Without waiting for her assent, Rachael untied the strings of her *kapp,* and removed it. Tucking it into the bushes so Loretta could pick it up later, she removed the bobby pins from Loretta's hair, then used her fingertips to muss it.

"There. Now you're gorgeous!"

"My hair looks like straw."

"Phooey." Rachael motioned toward the road. "Come on. We don't want to be late."

Only when they were well past the mailbox did Loretta notice the buggy. Her steps faltered as recognition kicked. "Who's that?" she asked, knowing full well who it was.

"He's just going to drive us," Rachael said.

The boy in question leaned against the wheel of his buggy, smoking a cigarette, watching them. "About damn time," he drawled.

Levi Yoder was twenty years old. A nice-looking Amish boy from a good family. But Loretta had heard the stories. He'd been caught smoking and drinking. Worst of all, he'd been caught going out with loose English girls. Just last Sunday at worship, she'd caught him looking at her. Beneath all that good-Amish-boy charm, he had a dark side.

"You didn't mention someone driving us," she whispered.

Before Rachael could respond, Levi tossed the cigarette onto the road and approached them. "Told you she'd chicken out," he said.

"No one's chickening out," Rachael snapped, a challenge in her voice. He grinned.

Loretta didn't like him, but she had to admit he looked good in English clothes. Blue jeans. T-shirt. Cowboy boots. He'd let his hair grow and if she wasn't mistaken, he was sprouting a goatee.

A shiver spread through her when his eyes landed on her. "You going to introduce me to your friend?" he asked Rachael.

"Nope." Rachael started for the buggy. "She has zero interest and you're just our ride."

He pressed his hand to his chest. "Cut a guy off at the knees why don't you?"

Feeling conspicuous, Loretta followed her friend.

56

Levi reached into the buggy and tore two cans of beer from a six-pack. He handed one to Rachael, who took it without thanking him as she climbed in.

Loretta reached the buggy and he held out a can of beer. "I remember you now. You're Rhoda and Dan's girl. The little skinny thing, never says a word."

Face burning, she looked down at her dress. She didn't know what to say or how to react. All she knew was that she didn't like the way he was looking at her.

"Here you go." Taking her hand, he helped her into the buggy.

Loretta slid onto the seat beside her friend.

Levi leaned in and eased the beer into her hand. "You grew up nice," he murmured.

"Cut it out, Levi," Rachael said. "We need smokes, too."

Climbing into the buggy, he pulled the pack from his shirt pocket, tapped one out, offered it to Rachael. "You're wound tight tonight, aren't you?"

She laughed. "You have no idea, Amish boy. Let's go. We don't have much time."

CHAPTER 9

There's one bookstore in Painters Mill. Beerman's Books has been a Main Street fixture for as long as I can remember. The owner, Barbara Beerman, has run the place since I was a kid. When my *mamm* came into town to pick up fabric at the store next door, I would sneak in to browse the kinds of books my parents didn't want me to read. I wasn't exactly a bookworm, but I loved being transported to exotic places. If I could break the rules in the process, all the better.

Beerman's Books is two blocks down from the police station. It's a small, narrow space that smells of patchouli and bergamot, books and dust, and coffee from the station next to the "reading nook," which is basically an antique chair, lamp, and side table where bookish types can kick back and read before buying.

The bell on the door jingles cheerfully when I enter. Barbara looks up from her place at the counter, an ancient-looking tome open in front of her. "Hi, Chief Burkholder. What can I do for you?"

I cross to the counter, aware of the resident cat skulking between the shelves. "I'm looking for the book written by Rachael Schwartz," I tell her.

"Ah. You and everyone else. I heard about the murder. Do you guys know who did it yet?"

"We're working on it."

She nods. "Well, we have her book." She pushes herself to her feet and rounds the counter. "The tourists love it so much we have a tough time keeping it in stock."

"Have you read it?" I ask.

"The day it was released. Talk about tell-all. Rachael Schwartz didn't pull any punches."

"So I've heard."

"Apparently, she wasn't fond of her brethren."

"Did she name names?" I ask.

She shakes her head. "There's an author note in the beginning of the book saying the names were changed to 'protect' the identities of people depicted. The Amish aren't the most litigious people, but the publisher was worried about potential lawsuits nonetheless, I suppose." She leads me to an aisle and starts down it. "That said, Painters Mill is a small town. A few days after the book was released an Amish guy came in and bought all six books. Said he was going to burn them." She clucks. "I told him I would order more, but he didn't seem to care."

Midway down the aisle, she bends and pulls out a good-size trade paperback. "Here we go." Straightening, she looks at the spine. "*AMISH NIGHTMARE: How I Escaped the Clutches of Righteousness.*"

"I'll take two copies," I tell her.

"Double the fun." She grins. "I'll ring you up."

The things I've learned about Rachael Schwartz in the last hours nag at me on the drive back to the Willowdell Motel. By all indications, she lived her life with a no-holds-barred abandon. She wasn't afraid to push boundaries or get too close to the edge. She wasn't afraid to step on toes. In fact, she seemed to thrive on controversy even though it caused her some degree of unhappiness. She was social, with a multitude of relationships, not all of which were auspicious. I think about the level of violence of the attack and I wonder who hated her enough to beat her with such savagery. Conventional wisdom tells me it was someone she knew. Did he follow her here from Cleveland? Or did she meet her killer here in Painters Mill?

It's late afternoon when I pull into the parking lot of the motel. As usual when I'm dealing with a serious case, I feel the ever-present tick of the clock, reminding me how crucial these first hours are in terms of solving of the crime. Five hours have passed since the discovery of Schwartz's body, and the parking lot is still abuzz with law enforcement vehicles. The BCI crime scene unit truck is parked outside room 9, the rear door standing open. A technician clad in white Tyvek carries a cardboard box from the room and loads it onto the truck. I spot Tomasetti standing next to his Tahoe talking on his cell and I head that way.

He drops the phone into his jacket pocket as I approach. "You're a sight for sore eyes," I tell him.

"That's what all the female chiefs of police tell me," he replies.

There are too many people around for a too-personal greeting, so we settle for a quick touching of hands. "Anything new?" I ask.

"CSU is about to wrap it up. They got some prints we'll expedite through AFIS. A lot of blood evidence. If we're lucky, some of it will belong to the perpetrator and we'll get some DNA."

"Weapon?"

"We searched the room. Dumpster in the back lot. Treed area in the rear. It's not here."

"Did you find a cell phone?"

"Behind the night table. Probably got knocked off during the struggle. I couriered it to the lab in London," he tells me, referring to the BCI lab near Columbus. "We'll go through it with a fine-tooth comb."

"I don't know anything about her life in Cleveland," I say. "Anything on known associates?"

"Detectives are on scene at her residence now." He glances down at his cell phone, where he's jotted notes. "She lives in a townhome in the Edgewater district. Lake view. Heated floors. Swanky."

"Finances?"

"Still looking."

We fall silent, the information churning. "She live alone?" I ask.

He hits a button on his phone, swipes the screen. "She lives with Andrea June Matson. Thirty-two years old. No record. Evidently, they're business partners and own a restaurant downtown. The Keyhole. Matson is currently unaccounted for, but we're looking."

"Any problems between them?"

"Cops have never been called to the residence or the restaurant, but detectives are canvassing now and will be talking to friends and family to see what pops."

"How did you find Matson?"

"I answered Schwartz's cell when it rang," he tells me. "It was Matson on the other end. She didn't like it when I couldn't put Schwartz on the phone and hung up on me. Evidently, she didn't believe me when I told her I was with BCI. Get this: The last call Schwartz made was to Matson. That was around midnight. We're triangulating towers now."

"I want to talk to her," I say.

"You and everyone else. I put out an APB. We'll get her." He cocks his head. "Anything on your end?"

I hit the highlights of my conversations with Rachael's parents and Loretta Bontrager and tell him about the book.

"Sounds like she lived an interesting life," he responds.

"Maybe a little too interesting," I tell him. "Anything on Moskowski?"

"They picked him up without incident." He glances at his watch. "I need to get up to Cleveland."

Part of me wants to be there for the interview, not only with Moskowski, but with Matson. While a lover is always at the top of a cop's suspect list, a business partner comes in on a fast second. Those two people aside, Rachael Schwartz left plenty of unresolved problems right here in Painters Mill.

"Chief Burkholder!"

Both of us look up to see Steve Ressler jogging toward us. He's a tall red-haired man clad in khaki slacks that are a couple of inches too short, a blue polo shirt tight enough to show ribs, and glow-in-the-dark white sneakers. Steve is the publisher of *The Advocate,* Painters Mill's weekly newspaper. The paper has a decent circulation, mainly because Ressler is good at what he does. He's old-school and covers stories with journalistic integrity and an unfailing adherence to the facts, even when they're hard to come by. He's a type A personality, a stickler for deadlines, and he rarely accepts "no comment" for an answer.

"What can you tell me about the murder, Chief? Do you have anyone in custody? Do you have a suspect?" The questions fly in a flurry, his eyes darting to the motel room door where the coroner technician rolls a gurney laden with a black body bag.

"All I can tell you is that we have a deceased female. Her name is Rachael Schwartz."

He scribbles the name furiously. "Can you confirm it was a murder?"

he asks. "Suicide? I heard it was murder. If that's the case, should the residents of Painters Mill be concerned for their safety?"

"The coroner has not ruled on manner or cause of death yet."

He gives me a spare-me-the-pat-rejoinder roll of his eyes. "Can you confirm that the victim was Amish?"

"Formerly Amish."

More scribbling. "Anything else you can tell me, Chief?"

"Just that the Ohio Bureau of Criminal Investigation will be assisting my department. I'll put out a press release shortly."

"Don't keep me waiting too long," Ressler says as he walks away.

The crush of gravel beneath tires draws my attention. I look up to see a sleek Audi sedan barrel into the lot. Going too fast. Not some lost tourist looking for a room or a local curious about all the law enforcement vehicles. Tomasetti notices, too, and without speaking we watch the vehicle skid to a stop a scant foot from the crime scene tape. The driver's-side door flies open and a stylishly dressed woman clambers out, big sunglasses, cell phone pressed to her ear, and looks around as if not quite sure where she's landed.

Mona, whom I charged with securing the scene, strides toward the woman. "Ma'am? Can I help you?"

"What's going on here?" The woman lifts the crime scene tape and ducks under it.

"Ma'am. Stop." Mona rushes to her. "You can't do that!"

In tandem, Tomasetti and I start toward them.

"Excuse me?" Spotting us, the woman calls out, "I'm looking for Rachael Schwartz."

"That's either a reporter or Matson," Tomasetti murmurs.

"My money's on Matson," I tell him. "Journalists can't afford clothes like that."

"Or the car."

Mona grasps the woman's arm, stopping her. "This is a crime scene, ma'am. You need to wait outside the caution tape."

"I'm looking for Rachael Schwartz." The woman's voice shakes. She's noticed all the law enforcement vehicles—and the coroner's van. "I need to know what's going on."

She's wearing a black skirt and jacket that contrast nicely with artfully highlighted blond hair. Silky pink blouse that's open at the throat. A body that regularly sees the inside of a gym.

"The police are investigating an incident." Gripping her arm, Mona ushers her toward the crime scene tape.

"Incident? What incident?" The woman twists away. "I think Rachael was staying at this motel." She thrusts a painted nail toward the door of room 9. "What in the hell is going on in there?"

Tomasetti and I reach them. I hold up my badge and identify myself. "Ma'am, what's your name?" I ask.

She looks at me as if I'm some insect that's landed on her arm and she's thinking about crushing me with a slap. "Are you in charge? For God's sake! Someone tell me what the hell is going on. I need to see Rachael Schwartz and I need to see her right now."

She's agitated, edging toward hysterics. She doesn't seem to notice when Tomasetti takes her arm. "Come with me," he says as he guides her toward the perimeter tape.

Mona hooks a finger around the yellow tape and holds it up as the three of us duck beneath it.

Realizing what's happening, the woman chokes out a sound of dismay and twists away. "Please tell me something didn't happen to her."

I take her other arm. I'm aware of Tomasetti standing on the other side of her, not touching her. Mona stands guard at the caution tape, watching us. Backup if we need it.

"What's your name?" I repeat.

"Andrea . . . Andy Matson." She stutters the name, her attention fastened to the doorway of room 9. "Please tell me she's not hurt."

"What's your relationship with Rachael Schwartz?" I ask.

"She's my business partner. My roommate. For God's sake, she's my best friend." She tries to wrench her arm from my grip, but I don't let her go.

"I've been trying to reach her all day. Rachael *always* answers her phone. Last time I called, some dude picked up. Said he was with BCI. I knew something was wrong . . . so I just got in my car and drove." The words tumble out in a rush.

Breathless, she thrusts her hand toward the motel, where the technician with the coroner's office is closing the double doors of the van. "I arrive to see that!"

She tears her eyes from the van, divides her attention between me and Tomasetti. "You guys are scaring the hell out of me."

"Rachael Schwartz is dead," I tell her.

"Dead?" She recoils as if I struck her. "But . . . that's crazy. She can't be . . . I just saw her yesterday. I talked to her last night. She was fine." She pauses to catch her breath. "What happened to her?"

"The coroner hasn't made an official determination yet, but we believe someone gained access to her room sometime during the night and killed her."

"Oh my God." Breaths hissing, she bends at the hip, sets her hands on her knees. "Rachael. Shit. Shit."

"Do you need to sit down?" I ask.

She spits on the ground, shakes her head.

I give her a moment, watching her for any telltale signs of deception, but she gives me nothing.

Feeling the tick of the clock, I touch her shoulder. "Ms. Matson, I know this is a bad time, but I need to ask you some questions."

Straightening, she blows out a breath, her expression dark, mascara beginning to run. "Who did it?"

"We don't know. We're looking. It would be a big help if you could help us fill in some blanks."

Her reaction seems genuine. Shock, after all, is difficult to fake. But I've been around long enough to know certain individuals are masterful at deception. It's too early in the game for me to tell, so I proceed with caution.

"When's the last time you saw her?" I ask.

"Yesterday morning. I passed her in the hall when she was on her way to get coffee. I was on my way to the shower."

"When's the last time you talked to her?" Tomasetti asks.

"Last night. On the phone. Late." She sets her thumb and forefinger to the bridge of her nose. "I gave her hell because I didn't know she was spending the night here. I'm like, oh, thanks for telling me."

As if remembering harsh words between them, she closes her eyes. "I was a shit. I didn't know that would be the last time we . . ." She doesn't finish the sentence.

"Was Rachael having any problems with anyone?" I ask. "Any arguments or disagreements? Did she have any volatile relationships?"

"Who *wasn't* she having problems with?" Choking out a sound that's part laugh, part sob, she lowers her face into her hands. "Every relationship she had was volatile. That's just the way she was."

Tomasetti makes a sound of irritation. "Straight answers would be a big help about now."

She raises her head. Misery boils in her eyes. "Look, all I'm saying is that for better or for worse, Rachael spoke her mind. Didn't hold back. That was one of the things I loved about her. I mean, the girl was on fire and burning hot, you know? She lived and breathed controversy. Anyone who disagreed with her? She ate them for lunch." She makes the statement with a fondness that tells me she's probably a bit of a rabble-rouser herself. "I told her one day it was going to catch up with her, but she just laughed."

"Who was she close to?" I pull out my notebook and pen.

"Jared Moskowski."

I feel Tomasetti's eyes on me, but I don't look at him. "Boyfriend?"

"Fuck buddy," she says. "And he's a jealous, insecure, and petty son of a bitch. Rachael was too much for him to handle and he knew it."

"Did they fight?"

"All the time."

"Did he ever hit her?" Tomasetti asks. "Or physically abuse her?"

"Not that I saw, but their relationship was . . . screwed up." She shrugs. "He wasn't man enough to handle her."

"Did they fight about anything in particular?" I ask.

"The frickin' weather, for God's sake. All I know is they didn't get along. They were always pissed at each other." She presses her lips together. "I don't know why she was so crazy about him."

She turns her eyes on me, outrage flashing, her mouth tight. "Did he do it?"

I ignore the question. "Is there anyone else Rachael didn't get along with?"

The woman's brows draw together. "I guess you know she used to be Amish. She's from Painters Mill. Her parents are religious fanatics and shunned her or whatever the hell they do." Resentment rings hard in the laugh that follows. "For God's sake, even the Amish were pissed at her."

"What about you?" Tomasetti asks.

She looks at him as if the question is a personal affront. "Are you kidding me?" Her gaze flicks to me. "She's dead and you two bozos are looking at me? That's rich."

"You can answer the question here, or we can do it at the police station," I tell her. "Your choice."

"Look, Rachael and I were friends. *Real* friends. We were roommates. Business partners. So yeah, there was some occasional conflict." Her eyes fasten onto mine, unshed tears glittering. "I'll be the first to tell you she was difficult. But I loved her anyway. She was like a sister to me, and you're a damn fool if you waste any time looking at me."

"How did you meet her?"

"I was the style editor at a boutique magazine in Cleveland and wrote a piece on how Rachael went from Amish girl to restaurateur. We met for drinks, got to talking. It didn't take long for me to realize she was one of the most ambitious and fascinating women I'd ever met." She smiles as if remembering. "I told her that her story would make a compelling book." She lifts her shoulders, lets them drop. "She had the story. I knew how to write. The rest is history."

"You cowrote the book?" I ask.

"I *wrote* the book," she corrects.

"Your name isn't on the cover," Tomasetti points out.

Her smile turns brittle. "Well, it should have been, but then that was Rachael for you. She wanted the limelight. I ended up in the acknowledgments."

"Big of her," he says. "Did you get angry about that?"

Matson rolls her eyes. "I got over it. By then we were friends. I didn't want anything so petty to get between us."

I keep moving. "Did she know anyone in Wooster? Did she ever go there? To meet anyone?"

"Wooster?" She shakes her head. "Never heard her mention it."

"We're going to need a DNA sample," Tomasetti tells her. "Prints too."

Her eyes narrow, so I add, "We need to rule you out so we don't waste anyone's time."

"Sure. Whatever." She shakes her head. "I can't believe this is happening. I can't believe she's gone."

Tomasetti taps the screen of his cell phone. "Where can we reach you if we need to get in touch?"

She rattles off a cell phone number and I punch it into my phone.

"If you go back to Cleveland, you need to keep yourself available in case we need to talk to you again," I say.

Her mouth tightens again. "I'm not going anywhere until I get some answers. How's that for guilty?"

"That'll do just fine," Tomasetti says.

CHAPTER 10

It's fully dark by the time the scene is cleared and the BCI crime scene truck pulls out. The motel manager called in a professional crew to clean the room, but they won't start until morning. According to Tomasetti, the agents retrieved a plethora of potential evidence, including DNA, fibers, blood evidence, hair, fingerprints, and footwear marks. They were able to cast a single decent tire imprint in the parking lot, ostensibly from a vehicle that had parked next to Rachael Schwartz's Lexus at some point. Everything was couriered to the police lab in London, Ohio. Fingerprint data should come back quickly. And while we won't get DNA results right away, we will likely find out soon if any of the blood is secondary—which could indicate the killer injured himself in the course of the attack. Conceivably, we could have a second set of DNA.

Tomasetti left for Cleveland to question Jared Moskowski. I'm standing at the doorway to room 9, procrastinating going inside. From where I stand, I can still discern the faint smell of blood. I can't help but think that last night at this time, Rachael Schwartz was enmeshed in the mundane of everyday life. What she would have for dinner. If she had time for a manicure. Wondering what to wear. She had a future and dreams and people who loved her. People she loved in return. Who saw fit to take all of that away?

Every light in the room burns, illuminating a still-macabre scene. As usual, the CSU left behind quite a mess. Many of the surfaces are covered with fingerprint powder. Drawers have been left open or pulled out and set on the floor. The bedsheets are gone. Bloodstains on the mattress and the single remaining pillow. Several squares have been cut out of the carpet and removed, likely to retrieve blood evidence. One of the curtains has been removed, probably for the same reason.

I think about Rachael as I enter the room. I take in the carnage and try to imagine a scene I don't want in my head. Rachael Schwartz may have been raised Amish, but she'd been English long enough to be well versed in the ways of the world. Not the kind of woman who would leave her door unlocked at night, even in a town like Painters Mill. More than likely, a knock sounded, after hours. Had she been sleeping? Surfing the internet on her cell? I look at the door, spot the peephole. Did she make use of it? Recognize the person on the other side? Or was she half asleep and simply opened the door?

I walk to the bathroom and look around. A high-tech curling iron sits on the counter. Her blow dryer. Her overnight case and handbag were transported to the lab to be gone through. Eventually, all of it will be released to her family. I leave the bathroom and cross to the bed. A small square of material has been cut out of the mattress. The hole is surrounded by blood that's soaked into the fabric. More blood on the wall, small droplets the color of red brick.

From all indications, Rachael was in bed and heard a knock at the door. She got up to answer. She greeted him. Words were exchanged.

71

An argument? She turned away, and he struck her from behind. Midway to the night table, she fell as her killer struck her repeatedly in a frenzied, violent attack. She made it to the night table. Scrambled across the bed. Fell to the floor on the other side. Tried to crawl to the door. But the assault kept coming. . . .

"You knew him, didn't you?" I whisper.

She'd fought her attacker. Fought for her life. I think about the position of her body. Facing the door. Arm outstretched, fingers clutching. And I suspect in the final minutes of her life, she'd known her life was going to end.

"Why did he do this to you?" I say aloud.

The only answer is the buzzing of the lamp and the strum of a hundred more unanswered questions running through my brain.

It's ten P.M. when I pull out of the gravel lot of the Willowdell Motel and head toward home. I'm beyond tired, in need of a shower and food and a few hours of sleep. With a killer on the loose and the unanswered questions coming at me like rapid fire, I don't think I'll get much in the way of shut-eye.

Why was Rachael Schwartz in Painters Mill? According to the people who knew her—Loretta Bontrager and her parents—she hadn't been back in months. No one knew she was in town. Who was she here to see? I think about the note with the scrawled address in her car. The farm where Tomasetti and I live is just south of Wooster. Too wired to sleep, I figure my time might be better spent stopping by the bar to see if anyone remembers seeing Rachael Schwartz. I drive past the township road that will take me home and continue north on Ohio 83. On the outskirts of Wooster, I pull over at Fisher Auditorium, punch the address into my GPS, and I head that way.

The Pub is located on the northwest side of town. It's a freestanding redbrick building set in a gravel lot littered with potholes and mud puddles. The no-name gas station next door is brightly lit, its green and white neon sign touting cigarettes, beer, and diesel. Farther down the street, the railroad-crossing lights flash red, the arms coming down to block traffic. It's prime time for a semirural dive bar like this one, but there are only four vehicles in the lot. I drive around to the rear. A Ford Escort is parked a few yards from the door. A blue dumpster sits at a cockeyed angle in the side lot, trash bags overflowing, a couple of cats scrounging for food.

I idle back around to the front lot and park next to an older F-150. The distant whistle of the train sounds as I head toward the front door.

There are two kinds of bars, in my mind. There's the kind where a police uniform will garner you a free cup of coffee and, if you're lucky, a burger. And then there's the kind where the sight of a cop clears the room. I know the instant I walk in that this one falls into the former group.

An old Traffic song "The Low Spark of High Heeled Boys" thrums from sleek speakers mounted on the beadboard ceiling. Two men in coveralls and caps sit at the bar, beer mugs sweating in front of them. Neither of them pays me any heed when I pass. A third man with a beard and camo jacket sits alone at the end of the bar, watching the Cavaliers trounce the Golden State Warriors on a TV mounted on the wall. Two women wearing tight jeans and equally tight shirts alternate between checking their phones and shooting pool. The bartender is a burly man in his forties, checked shirt with sleeves rolled up to his elbows, white apron tied at his waist, hair pulled into a ponytail at his nape. His eyes latch on to mine as I sidle up to the bar.

"What can I get you?" he asks.

"You have any decaf made?" I ask.

"Naw," he says. "Got a Keurig in the back, though. Makes a pretty decent cup. Cream? Sugar?"

"Black," I tell him. "Thanks."

He returns a short while later, cup and saucer in hand. "We don't get too many cops in here. They prefer the sports bar down on the south side." He tilts his head, reading the emblem on my uniform jacket. "You're a ways from home."

I pick up the coffee and sip. It's strong with a nice kick of bitter. "Good coffee."

"I like it."

I introduce myself. His name is Jack Boucher. He's owned the place for nine months. Turned his first profit last week.

"I'm working on a case." I pull the photo of Rachael Schwartz from my pocket and set it on the bar between us. "Have you seen her?"

He pulls reading glasses from his shirt pocket and squints at the photo. "She missing or something?"

"Actually, this is a murder investigation."

"Holy shit. Wow." He looks harder at the photo. "Pretty girl. Kind of classy looking." He shakes his head. "She ain't been in here that I know of. I would have remembered her."

He's still looking at the photo, so I leave it on the bar top. "Is it possible she came in when you were off?"

"I'm here seven days a week. Came in early for the lunch shift a couple times, so I could have missed her, if she came in later."

"Anyone else here I can talk to?" I ask.

"I got a gal bartends nights when I'm not here," he tells me. "Got a part-time cook, too. They both went home a couple hours ago."

"Will they be here tomorrow?"

"Dixie comes in around eleven. She's my cook. Rona, my bartender, gets here about four o'clock."

I nod. "You got a business card?"

"Yup." He snags a napkin off the bar and a pen from his breast pocket. "Right here." Grinning, he jots a number. "That's the landline. Whoever's running the place will pick up."

I take another sip of coffee. "You guys have security cameras?"

"I got one on the rear door. We were broken into a couple months ago." He shakes his head. "Damn camera's on the fritz, though."

I look around at the patrons. "Are any of these folks regulars?"

"Most of them are in here just about every night," he tells me. " 'Cept them girls playing pool. We get a regular lunch rush, too. People who work in the area mostly. You're more than welcome to talk to anyone you want."

"If you remember anything about this woman, will you give me a call?" I hand him my card.

"You know it."

I pick up the photo. "Thanks for the coffee."

"Good luck with your case, Chief Burkholder. I hope you find the cretin that done it."

CHAPTER 11

The nights tormented him. The endless hours of darkness and sleeplessness, when the not-knowing and the fear were a cancer eating him from the inside out and he could do nothing but ponder what he now knew was inevitable. It was no longer a matter of if he would be found out, but when, by whom, and how much it would cost him. Worst of all, there wasn't a damn thing he could do to stop it.

And so tonight, like the night before and the one before that, he sat at the desk in his dimly lit office and worked through every possible scenario. He thought about everything that had happened. Everything he'd done—both past and present. Most of all he thought about what he *hadn't* done, and he wondered if it was too late to remedy any of it now.

Rachael Schwartz had destroyed a lot of lives in the short time she'd been on this earth. She was a user and a taker with a streak of nasty that ran right down the center of her back. She loved herself above all else and had no compunction about slicing the throat of anyone who crossed her. And then she'd laugh as she watched them bleed out.

How ironic that she would ruin his life after she was dead.

He hadn't spared her so much as a passing thought in over a decade. Then out of the blue came the phone call that brought all of those old mistakes rushing back. *I have proof,* she'd claimed. With a few words, she took his carefully constructed life apart, left it in pieces at his feet. After all this time, she wanted a piece of him. She wanted what she believed was rightfully hers and goddamn anyone who got in her way, including him. Especially him. She'd threatened his marriage. His career. The well-being of his children. Any semblance of a future. Probably even his freedom. She did all of it with a vicious glee and a cold proficiency the years had honed to a razor's edge.

Now she was gone. He should be relieved, her memory nothing more than a black stain on his past. But he knew this wasn't over. In fact, the nightmare was just beginning and he was right in the center of it. How many people had she confided in over the years? Who else could potentially come forward? Had she been bluffing when she bragged about having put together some kind of "insurance policy" in case something happened to her? Even dead, the rotten bitch would see to it that he paid a price for what he'd done.

He wished to God he'd never laid eyes on her.

He'd never been the type of man to sit on the sidelines and let things play out, especially when there was so much at stake. There wasn't much he could do to save himself. The time for damage control had long since passed. Soon, the wolves would be scratching at the door. It was only a matter of time before they got in and tore him to shreds.

Cursing beneath his breath, he picked up the tumbler of bourbon, swirled the ice, and he sipped. He thought about his life. How far he'd come. The things he'd accomplished. And he knew there was one thing he had going for him. The only thing that might keep the wolves at bay. Rachael Schwartz had deserved her fate—and he wasn't the only one who thought so. She had a pattern of fucking people over, using people, abusing her friendships. People like her made a lot of enemies—and he sure as hell wasn't the only one who'd benefited from her death. All he had to do was find them. Work them into the equation. At the very least, it would take some of the pressure off of him. Buy him some time. It was a starting point, anyway.

God only knew where it would go from there.

He was not going down for what he'd done. He sure as hell wasn't going down for something he *didn't* do. If that meant finding a scapegoat, then so be it. It wouldn't be the first time and it probably wouldn't be the last.

Holding that thought, he turned off the lamp, rose from the desk, and headed for the door.

CHAPTER 12

Day 2

The one thing that's always in short supply in the course of a homicide investigation is sleep. Not because there's too much to do or too many things happening at once, but because any cop worth his salt knows how crucial those first forty-eight hours are in terms of a solve. The truth of the matter is nothing happens fast when you're running against the clock. As Tomasetti is so fond of saying, "Hurry up and wait."

After leaving the bar last night, I couldn't sleep and spent the wee hours reading *AMISH NIGHTMARE: How I Escaped the Clutches of Righteousness*. I read with the goal of extracting some theory or motive or person of interest, but the tome was mostly sensationalistic bullshit. The one name that *did* rise above the rest was Amos Gingerich, the so called "bishop" of the Killbuck Amish. I don't know if the conflict that was detailed in the book is fact or fiction, but at the very least, I need to pay Gingerich a visit.

It was after three AM when I finished and, even then, I couldn't stop thinking about the case. I'm a seasoned cop; I've seen more than my share of violent crimes. The brutality of this one makes me shiver. Who hated Rachael Schwartz enough to beat her to death with such viciousness that bones were broken and her eye was dislodged from its socket? And why?

For every question answered, a dozen more emerge. One question rises above the rest. No one could tell me why she was in Painters Mill. Her parents didn't know. Loretta Bontrager didn't know. Neither did her business partner and self-proclaimed best friend.

Someone knew.

Rachael Schwartz was just thirty years old. She was a daughter. A best friend. A businesswoman. A lover. She made people laugh. Made them cry. From all indications, she made them angry, too. According to the people closest to her, she was a firebrand with a vindictive streak and thrived on making waves. Somewhere along the line, did she overstep some boundary that sent someone over the edge?

I think about my own knowledge of her. While that connection gives me some insight into her life, it's a little too close for comfort— and could lead me astray if I'm not careful. I knew her at a time in my life when I, too, was disgruntled with the Amish. I secretly admired that outspoken little tomboy. As much as I don't want to admit it, I cared for her because I understood a part of her others did not.

The mores an Amish person lives by are deeply ingrained at a young age. Close to eighty percent of Amish youths join the church after *rumspringa*. The vast majority never leave. One of the main differences between Rachael and me is that I left the fold of my own accord. Rachael Schwartz was ousted. And for the first time I realize I don't know exactly why.

It doesn't seem likely that there's an Amish connection to the murder. They are a pacifistic society, after all, and the way Rachael Schwartz was killed was incredibly violent. That said, the Amish are also human—prone to all the same weaknesses and frailties as the rest of us—so I make a mental note to find out why Rachael was excommunicated and who was involved.

The first hints of sunrise tinge the eastern sky purple as I leave the farm. I call Tomasetti as I make the turn onto Ohio 83 and head south.

"How did things go with Moskowski?" I ask.

"Cleveland PD detained him until I arrived. He claims he was home the night of the murder. Alone."

"No alibi," I murmur.

"None."

"What's your impression?"

"He's a slick son of a bitch. A player. Kept his cool with just the right amount of indignation that a bunch of dumb cops could pick him up and hold him against his will."

"How did he react to news of her death?"

"He seemed shocked. Interestingly, he didn't seem too broken up about the murder of a woman he claims to love. That said, he asked all the right questions, but then he's no dummy. He lawyered up."

"Of course he did," I mutter. "Do you know anything about the domestic she was arrested for? According to LEADS he was the RP."

"According to the report, Schwartz was highly intoxicated and slapped Moskowski in the course of an argument. He called the cops. She was arrested, spent the night in jail, but the charge was later dropped."

"Any idea what the argument was about?"

"Moskowski says she accused him of sleeping with someone else. He claims Schwartz was jealous and said it was a pattern with her." He rattles off a name I don't recognize. "The alleged other woman lives here in Cleveland, so I'm on my way to talk to her now. See if everything checks out."

"Did you find anything of interest at Schwartz's residence?" I ask.

"We got her laptop. A couple of boxes of paperwork. Some correspondence. We're going through all of it now." A thoughtful pause and then, "I did a cursory look through some of it. Interestingly, there were some letters from Amos Gingerich. Evidently, he wasn't happy with the tell-all she published."

"Did he threaten her?"

"Veiled. Talked a lot about martyrs."

I recall my conversation with Loretta Bontrager and her comments about Gingerich and *Martyrs Mirror.* "Can you send me copies of the letters?"

"I'll do it." He pauses. "One more thing that may or may not be related to any of this. It appears Rachael Schwartz and Andrea Matson lived above their means. I checked the books on the restaurant they own, and they barely make a profit. And yet they live in one of the most exclusive neighborhoods in the city."

"So where are they getting their money?"

"Still digging," he says. "Anything new on your end?"

"Spinning my wheels mostly."

"It's still early."

I smile, missing him. "Do me a favor and don't stay away too long."

"Bet on it."

The police station is usually quiet at this hour. This morning, with a homicide investigation spooling and the grapevine on fire, my entire team of officers has already arrived for the day. I walk in to find Mona standing at her desk, headset clamped over hair that's slightly wild, the switchboard ringing off the hook. Next to her, my first-shift dispatcher,

Lois, has the handset at the crook of her neck and waves a stack of pink message slips at me.

I grin at both of them. "Morning."

Both women mouth a reply, listening to their callers.

"Briefing in ten," I tell them. "Round everyone up."

Lois gives me a thumbs-up.

At the coffee station, I upend the biggest cup I can find, pour to the brim, and flip through messages. Tom Skanks, owner of the Butterhorn Bakery down the street, wants to know if there's a serial killer on the loose in Painters Mill. Town councilwoman Janine Fourman reminds me that a violent murder in Painters Mill will adversely affect tourism, not just the shops but the restaurants and B and Bs. She suggests I immediately request assistance from a larger, more proficient law enforcement agency to assure this crime gets the expertise it deserves.

I sigh as I head to my office. I'm going through my notes, struggling to read my own handwriting, when Mona appears in the doorway. "Everyone's RTG, Chief." Ready to go.

A couple of years ago, it wouldn't have been unusual to see her in a bustier and short skirt, purple streak in her hair, and still smelling of cigarette smoke from the night before. She's come a long way since those days. Though she worked through the night, she's in full uniform this morning. Hair pulled back. Minimal makeup. She looks like a cop. Unlike me, she's brimming with energy.

Feeling . . . old, I set down my cup. "You got time to sit in?"

She grins. "That's affirm."

Grabbing my notes, I round my desk, and we head toward the "war room," which is basically a storage-closet-turned-meeting-room—design compliments of Mona. I take in each member of my small police force as I stride to the half podium set up at the end of the table. Rupert "Glock" Maddox sits next to it, a spiral-bound pad and a pen on the tabletop in front of him. He's a former marine, a Little League coach, a father of three, and the first African American to grace the ranks of the department.

Next to him, Roland "Pickles" Shumaker nurses a to-go cup of coffee from LaDonna's Diner. I catch a whiff of cigarette smoke and English Leather as I pass. He may be down to working just ten hours a week—which entails crosswalk duty at the elementary school—but his uniform is creased, his hair and goatee are colored a not-so-natural hue of brown, and his trademark Lucchese boots are polished to a mirror sheen. Pickles might be an old-timer, but I've seen his file—all sixty pages of it—and I know he earned every "above the call of duty" and "risked his own life" comment, and then some. He spent years working undercover narcotics and made one of the biggest busts in the history of Holmes County.

Chuck "Skid" Skidmore sits across from Pickles looking a little rough around the edges. He's our resident jokester, and eschews early mornings, which is why he prefers second shift. I hired him shortly after becoming chief. He'd been terminated from the Ann Arbor PD for drinking on the job. But I liked him; I thought he deserved a second chance, so I hired him with the caveat that if I ever caught him drinking while on duty he would be out the door. He's never let me, or himself, down.

T.J. Banks had always been the departmental rookie—until I promoted Mona. At twenty-eight years of age, he's serious about his job, doesn't mind working graveyard, and is the first to volunteer for overtime. Baby-faced and charming, he's invariably in the process of landing a new girlfriend or breaking up with his current squeeze.

Mona sits next to T.J., looking at something he's showing her on his cell, probably some cop story that includes a generous amount of embellishment. She's not buying into it, but letting him have his moment. *Good girl,* I think, and I take my place at the half podium.

"As all of you know, thirty-year-old Rachael Schwartz was murdered in her room at the Willowdell Motel night before last. Our department is primary. BCI is assisting, as is the Holmes County Sheriff's Office. The killer or killers have not yet been apprehended or identified. That means mandatory OT until we make an arrest."

I glance down at my scrawled notes. "Doc Coblentz hasn't officially ruled on cause or manner, but this is an obvious homicide. NOK have been notified," I say, referring to "next of kin." "I don't have to tell any of you to not discuss this case with anyone. Refer any media inquiries to me."

I pass the folder containing the crime scene photos, reports, notes, and every scrap of information I've amassed so far to Glock so he can take a look and pass it on.

"From all indications, the victim was beaten to death," I tell him. "The murder weapon was not found. We're not making that public. The coroner wouldn't commit, but we're likely talking about piece of pipe or club, or some other heavy, blunt object."

I look at Skid. "I want you and T.J. to drive back out to the motel and continue our search for the murder weapon. Expand our original search area. We looked yesterday, but had to quit when it got dark. Check the ditches on either side of the road, woods, fields, walk it all the way to the highway. Check any dumpsters in the area. There's a service station down the road. If they've got security cams, get me the video."

Skid casts a half smile at T.J. "I guess we won't have to go to the gym this week," he says.

"You're welcome," I tell him, and turn my attention to Glock and

Pickles. "I want you guys to reinterview everyone who was staying at or visiting the Willowdell Motel the twenty-four hours before and after the murder. There was one person who checked out before we arrived. Find them and talk to them."

Nodding, Pickles hitches up his belt, his chest puffed out. "We're on it."

I glance at Mona. "I want you to look at Rachael Schwartz's social media accounts. I skimmed some of them last night and she's active and controversial. Twitter. Facebook. Instagram. See if she had any ongoing feuds or disagreements. Anything that catches your eye, let me know and we'll follow up."

She gives me a two-finger salute.

"Lois." I look up at my dispatcher, who's standing in the doorway, headset on, listening for incoming calls. "I want a hotline set up. Five-hundred-dollar reward for information. I emailed you a press-release draft. Give me a quick edit, if you would." I smile. "And get it out to local media. Steve Ressler at *The Advocate*. Millersburg. Wooster. Radio station down in Dover."

"Got it," she says, scribbling.

I'm not sure where the reward money will come from. I'll figure it out if and when I need it.

"Get with the technology people that handle Painters Mill's website, too. Get the hotline number on it, front and center. Our social media accounts, too."

"Yep."

I look out at my team. "We're already getting calls. Residents are anxious. Make yourselves visible around town when you can, do your best to reassure folks."

"Tell Tom Skanks free apple fritters and coffee would go a long way to keep us first responders on our toes," Skid mutters.

"Don't forget that new place," Glock adds.

"Mocha Joe's," T.J. tells them, referring to a nice little upscale coffeehouse in town.

I try not to smile, but I don't quite manage. "I'll see what I can do."

My cell phone vibrates against my hip. I glance down to see HOLMES CNTY CORONER pop up on the display. I look out at my team. "My cell is on twenty-four seven," I tell them. "Day and night. Let's go to work."

CHAPTER 13

Loretta Bontrager couldn't remember the last time she was so excited. Seeing a new baby for the first time was a happy occasion. It was one of the joys of being Amish, especially for the women. She'd known Mary Sue Miller most of her life. They'd gone to school together, played hide-and-seek in Amos Yoder's cornfield as kids, been baptized at about the same time, and were married within weeks of each other. This was Mary's fourth child. Baby Perry had been born just a few days ago and Mary was finally rested up enough to share him with the community.

Children were a gift from God. Loretta couldn't wait to cuddle him. What a joy it was to hold a new baby. Like her *mamm* always said: Children are the only treasure you can take to heaven.

Though Loretta was genuinely happy for her friend and anxious to meet the newest member of the family, the occasion was marred by the death of Rachael Schwartz. Loretta simply couldn't stop thinking about her. She hadn't been able to eat or sleep. She'd been living in a fog since it happened and that wasn't the worst of it. At night, and despite her fervent prayers at bedtime, the nightmares came for her. Dark images that left her gasping and tearful, her heart filled with grief.

Loretta had been closer to Rachael than she was to her own sister. She'd broken the rules herself to stay in touch with Rachael after she'd left. Truth be told, Loretta had always worried about her. The way she lived her life. Her lack of faith. She knew things about Rachael. Things that scared her—even now. She'd prayed for her friend's well-being. Her happiness. Most of all, she prayed for her soul.

Now that Rachael was gone, Loretta worried not only about the horror of her death and the fate of her soul, but the secrets Rachael had taken with her to her grave.

"Mamm, I bumped the *bott boi* and a piece of crust broke off the side." Potpie.

At the sound of her daughter's voice, Loretta glanced over from her driving. Even embroiled in dark thoughts she had no business thinking on such a pretty spring morning, she smiled at the sight of her sweet face. "Let me see," she said.

Fannie lifted the foil covering and pointed. Sure enough, a chunk of the lard crust had chipped off the side of one of the sausage and potato pot pies she'd made a little before five A.M.

"Looks like a little mouse sampled a piece of that crust," Loretta said.

Fannie grinned. "It wasn't me."

"Well, in that case just press it back together," Loretta told her. "No one at Mary's house will even notice."

They were in the buggy and traveling at a good clip down the township road. Around them, the pastures were astoundingly green, the trees in the woods bursting into bud, and the entire countryside was rife with birdsong. After such a long and cold winter, Loretta appreciated the gentle day.

She glanced away from her driving. A smile touched her mouth as she watched the girl press the wayward piece of crust back into place. "If we had some milk, we could glue it," Loretta told her.

She was probably taking too much food over to Mary and her family. But having a baby was a busy and exhausting time. And Loretta loved them so much. She was hoping to help with a chore or two while she was there, if Mary would allow it.

She was so enmeshed in her thoughts, Loretta didn't notice the car blocking the road until she was nearly upon it.

"Whoa!" she called to the horse.

The animal stopped so abruptly its steel shoes slid on the asphalt.

"Mamm?"

Loretta felt her daughter's questioning gaze on her as she backed the horse up a couple of steps. She watched the driver's-side door open. Her heart sank when he stepped out. She sat stone-still, the leather lines taut in her hands.

Taking his time, the man started toward them.

"Tuck that foil back around the *bott boi,*" she said to Fannie, more to keep her occupied than because the potpie needed covering.

"Nice morning for a buggy ride," the *Englischer* said as he reached them.

Loretta said nothing. She could barely bring herself to look at him. Or breathe. She knew what he'd see in her eyes if she did. Fear. Knowledge. Secrets. She'd seen him around town dozens of times over the years, and she cringed every time. She knew it was wrong to have such thoughts, but she didn't like him.

She knew things about this man. Things she didn't want to know. She had no idea if he remembered her. If he knew she and Rachael had been friends. Regardless, she went out of her way to avoid him.

"Hi there, young lady," he said to Fannie.

The sight of him looking at her daughter unnerved Loretta. Before she could react, he reached into his pocket and withdrew a package of chocolate-covered peanuts. The kind you could buy at the grocery-store checkout. He extended his hand and offered it to the girl. "You like chocolate?" he asked. "These are my favorite."

Fannie nodded, her hand going up to take the candy. Quickly, Loretta snatched up the potpie, shoved it into her daughter's hands. "Take this and put it in the back seat," she said in *Deitsch*. "We don't want to lose any more of that delicious crust now, do we?"

Curious about the *Englischer,* the girl hesitated before taking the pie.

Loretta gave her a helpful little push. "Go on now. Get back there. Make sure the foil stays on that casserole, too. Hold it on your lap so it doesn't bounce around too much."

As the girl climbed into the back seat with the pie, Loretta forced her gaze to the man standing next to the buggy, trying in vain to ignore the chill lodged in her spine.

"What do you want?" she asked.

"Cute kid." He watched Fannie settle onto the back seat. "Going to be pretty when she grows up," he said. "Like you."

Loretta looked down at her hands, tried not to notice they were shaking, and loosened her grip on the leather lines.

"Kids are innocent when they're that age," he drawled. "What is she? Ten? Twelve?" When she didn't respond, he continued. "I got four at home. Two boys. Two girls. And another on the way. Boy do they keep me and my wife busy." He shrugged. "Childhood is an important time. For Amish kids, too, huh?"

She said nothing.

He continued as if he didn't expect a response. "You never want anything bad to happen to them when they're that age. Scars, you know. The girls especially. I think little girls need their moms even more than the boys, you know?"

"All children need their parents," she said, hating it that her voice was shaking, the words little more than a whisper. That he had the power to frighten her—that there wasn't anything she could do about it—disturbed her so much she could scarcely breathe.

"All I'm saying is that kids are a lot less likely to have trouble in their lives if their parents are around to raise them. You know, to guide them through their teen years and all."

Loretta didn't know what to say to that. He was talking in riddles and she wasn't sure what he meant or where the conversation was heading. All she knew was that she didn't want to talk to him. He hadn't threatened her, but the way he looked at her, the things he said, the way he said them, terrified her. She didn't want him to talk about her daughter. She didn't want Fannie exposed to him. She didn't feel safe on this back road alone with him.

She picked up the leather lines. "I have to go."

"Reason I stopped you." He leaned slightly closer. "Did you hear about what happened to your old friend?"

Loretta clucked and jiggled the lines to move the horse forward, but he grabbed the leather and held them taut so the horse remained stopped. "The one used to be Amish. The blonde. What was her name? Rachael?" He nodded. "Yeah, Rachael Schwartz. The pretty one."

She closed her eyes. She didn't want to think about Rachael or what had happened to her. She sure didn't want to discuss it with this pig of a man. "I don't want to talk about it. Not to you."

He turned his head, his eyes scanning the road behind her and in front of the buggy. She stared at his profile, seeing the muscles in his jaw work. Anger, she thought, and another layer of fear settled over her. When his eyes landed on hers, the light in them startled her.

"I heard she told some lies about me," he said. "Maybe she told you."

"I don't know what you're talking about."

"Well, in that case, why don't I bring you up to speed?" He leaned closer. "Whatever she said, it ain't true. Nothing happened. Do you understand?"

She stared at him, unable to speak, barely able to manage a jerk of her head.

"If you're smart." He lowered his voice to a hoarse whisper. "If you care about that pretty little girl in the back seat, you'll keep your goddamn mouth shut. Do you understand me?"

She swallowed, jerked her head. "I don't know anything."

"Your friend was a liar," he said. "She made things up. Ugly things that weren't true. We both know that, right? Everyone in this town knows it. Even the Amish know it, for God's sake. Whatever she told you is a damn lie. You need to forget it. Put it out of your head. You got that?"

Her heart pounded so hard she could barely hear his voice over the roar. Her throat was tight and so dry she almost couldn't get the words out. "She didn't tell me anything."

"I didn't think so." His eyes drifted to the girl in the back seat, then back to hers. "I'd hate to see something bad happen to you or, God forbid, your kid."

"Please," Loretta whispered.

Grinning, he released the lines and stepped away from the buggy. "You ladies be careful out there."

Loretta's hands were shaking so violently, she could barely snap the lines. "*Kumma druff!*" Come on now.

The horse startled and launched into a trot.

Loretta felt his eyes on her as she maneuvered the horse around his vehicle. She didn't dare look at him as she passed him, but she felt the threat.

93

CHAPTER 14

It's ten A.M. when I park outside the emergency room portico of Pomerene Hospital in Millersburg and take the sidewalk to the double glass doors. The volunteer at the reception desk waves as I cross to the elevator and punch the button. I return the greeting, but my smile feels grim. When the doors swish closed, I slide the tube of Blistex from my pocket and smear a dollop beneath my nose. By the time the doors open, I'm shored up and ready to face what comes next.

The reception area is nicely furnished with light blue walls, gray carpet, a pretty cherrywood desk, and a scattering of brightly patterned chairs.

"Hi, Chief Burkholder."

Carmen Anderson has worked in an administrative capacity for Doc Coblentz for several years now. She's professional, good at what she does, and cheerful despite the fact that she spends much of her day in such close proximity to the dead. This morning, she's wearing a floral wraparound dress with a red belt, black blazer, and not-quite-sensible pumps.

"Hi." I stop at her desk and sign in. "You know you're one of the best-dressed women in Painters Mill, right?"

Her smile is dazzling. "Why thank you, Chief." She chuckles. "I don't get many compliments down here."

We share a laugh as I set down the pen. "Doc in?"

"He's expecting you." She stands and motions toward the doors at the end of the hall marked MORGUE AUTHORIZED PERSONNEL.

I don't let myself think about my purpose here, focusing instead on the questions roiling in my head as I tread down the hall and push open the door. The autopsy room is straight ahead, along with the alcove where the biohazard supplies are stored for visiting officials. To my left, I see Doc Coblentz's glassed-in office. The miniblinds are open. The doctor is sitting at his cherrywood desk, a wrapper containing what looks like the remains of a fast-food breakfast on the blotter in front of him next to a to-go cup of coffee.

I've known Doc since becoming chief. He's one of five doctors in Painters Mill, and assumes the responsibilities of coroner on an as-needed basis, which isn't often. On those occasions when he *is* called upon, he tackles his duty with compassion and professionalism. His is a tough position fraught with high emotion and a drop-everything-and-get-it-done timeline. There's no room for error—and invariably some cop or lab hounding him for results. Doc's a laid-back individual with an inhuman work ethic and the curiosity of a scientist, both of which make him very good at what he does. Somehow, he manages to remain an optimist.

Setting down the coffee cup, he looks at me over the rims of his glasses. "I know you're in a hurry to get to the bottom of what happened to that young woman, so I cleared my schedule. I'm planning to do the autopsy this morning."

"Time and manner would be a big help," I tell him.

"Figured as much. I've got some preliminary observations you might find useful." Rising, he motions toward the alcove outside his office. "Shall we?"

I go to the alcove where Carmen has laid out an individually wrapped gown, disposable shoe covers, hair cap, face mask, and gloves. Doc waits in the hall while I gear up.

"You guys have any leads?" he asks.

"Not yet." I slide the covers over my shoes, tie the gown strings haphazardly, and step into the hall.

"You knew the victim?" Doc says.

I wonder how he knows that, if he heard it from someone or if I gave him some indication while we were at the scene yesterday. "Years ago." I say the words with calculated detachment, but I don't meet his gaze. I remind myself that this is not about me or my emotions. This is about Rachael Schwartz, the family that mourns her, the community that will bear the scar of her death, and the bastard who killed her.

"Tough when it hits close to home," he says.

"She was Amish," I say, keeping my answer as vague and impersonal as possible.

He makes a sound of understanding. "You make the notification?"

I nod, thinking of Rhoda and Dan, and I do my best to ignore the knot of discomfort that's tight and hard in my gut.

"A lot of people wonder how I do what I do. You know, autopsies and the like, dealing with the dead. Most are too polite to ask, but I see the questions. The truth of the matter is it's not as difficult as they think. It's not the dead who hurt. Their suffering is done."

I finally meet his gaze. "I guess we, the living, have the market cornered on that, don't we?"

His mouth pulls into a smile. "Precisely." He motions toward the double doors at the end of the hall. "Let's see what we can do to set you on track to get some justice for this young woman."

I'm aware of the buzz of the lights as I take the hall toward the doors. The only sound comes from the rustle of our protective clothing, the voice in my head telling me I'm a fool for being here when I could be knocking on doors and doing my job. But this is part of it and I've no intention of not following through. Not now. Not the next time or the next. Macabre as this pilgrimage is, it is my ritual. For better or worse, it is my introduction to the victim. I need to see her not as the girl I'd once known, but the woman whose life was cut short. It brings me one step closer to knowing her. Understanding what happened to her. It is my burden to bear. My tribute to the victim. To the family. If I'm lucky, it will bring me one step closer to getting inside the mind of a killer.

The autopsy room is too bright, the lights buzzing. Floor-to-ceiling subway tile covers the walls. Ahead, a stainless-steel gurney is draped with a sheet.

"I did a preliminary exam and went over every inch of her with a fine-tooth comb. I took samples and scrapings, took the requisite photos. Pulled blood and urine for a full tox screen. We couriered everything to the police lab in London, including the clothes she was wearing at the time of her death. This morning, my technician cleaned her up. For obvious reasons, I took a CT scan and X-rays." The doctor sighs. "I've seen a lot of injuries, a lot of deaths. Motor vehicle accidents. Farming mishaps. You name it. This woman suffered a tremendous amount of physical injury."

I resist the urge to shudder. "Says something about the killer," I say.

"That's your forte, not mine. Thank God for that." He shuffles to a clipboard hanging on the wall, flips the page, makes a note. "The victim arrived here at the morgue at four twelve P.M. Core body temperature was taken at four forty-six." He flips another page and frowns, mumbling. "Heat is lost at about one point five degrees per hour. Liver temp was seventy-seven point six." He turns to me. "My best estimation is that she died sometime between one and three A.M."

He rehangs the clipboard and crosses to me, looks at me over the tops of his bifocals. I look back, trying not to acknowledge the compassion I see in his eyes, not only for the woman lying on the gurney, but for me.

"You sure you're up to this?" he asks.

"You know I'm not going to give you a straight answer, right?"

His smile is subdued. "If it makes you feel any better, your aversion to all of this isn't necessarily a bad thing. Means you're human."

He peels away the sheet cover.

For an instant, I struggle to make sense of what I'm seeing. Too many stimuli hit my brain at once. I see white skin marred with the blue-black bruising of livor mortis. Breasts drooping to each side of a rib cage that isn't quite symmetrical. Hip bones and a flat belly with the silver pinpoint of a piercing at the navel. The dark triangle of hair at her pubis. Bare feet that are somehow undamaged. It's the pink polish on the toenails that turns me inside out and rouses the stir of outrage. And for the hundredth time I'm reminded that just a day and a half ago this young woman cared about such trivial, everyday things as a pedicure. She painted her nails and put on makeup. She went shopping and combed her hair. She laughed and breathed and touched the lives of the people around her. I take all of it in, the broken heap of what's left, and for an instant I'm frightened in some base and primal way.

A paper sheet covers the victim's head, a quarter-size stain of watery pink blood warning me that I don't want the doc to pull it away. The ends of damp blond hair stick to the stainless steel.

Then my cop's brain clicks into gear; the questions begin to boil, part habit, partly the side of me that wants to catch the sick fucker that did this to her. "Cause of death?"

"Preliminarily speaking, she likely died of nonpenetrating trauma. Of course, I won't officially rule on cause or manner until I've completed the autopsy." He shakes his head. "To be perfectly honest, Kate, the injuries are simply too numerous to quantify. Several of these injuries could have been fatal on their own. All of that said, I do have some specifics and the postmortem CT scan will help us break it down."

Reaching up, he angles the reflective overhead light. I'm aware of my heart thrumming against my ribs. The heat of the light. The hum of something unseen on the other side of the room.

Doc Coblentz pulls away the paper covering the victim's head. I see damp blond hair. The gaping red mouth of a scalp wound. A forehead that's been laid open to the bone. A cheek that's caved in. Her left eye bulges from its socket, unseeing and dull. Mouth open, tongue bulging. Front teeth missing. Her chin is simply . . . gone.

Something unpleasant jumps in my chest. I think of the little girl I used to babysit. The one that was loud and bold and challenged my authority. The one that liked to run and laugh and pick on the other kids . . .

"In looking at the CT scan," the doc begins, "I counted six impact sites on the skull alone. There are multiple cranial-bone fractures. Fracture of the occipital bone. Subdural and subarachnoid hemorrhages. The areas affected include the frontal, parietal, and temporal regions."

"Do you have any idea what the murder weapon was?" I ask.

He shakes his head. "I may be able to come up with a theory once

I'm able to look at the CT scan and take some measurements. If we're lucky, the scrapings I sent to the lab will come back with some foreign material that will tell us. Something like a flake of rust from a steel pipe. Wood splinters from a club or board. Something like that. At this point, I do not know."

I'm looking at the doc. He's staring back at me, uncertain, waiting. I force my eyes back to the victim. Calmer, I start to notice details I missed at first glance. Her right hand is purple. Her fingers twisted into unnatural shapes. The right side of her rib cage is misshapen, the ribs obviously broken.

"What about the rest of her?" I ask.

"Whoever did this struck her with indiscriminate brutality. Head. Body. Whatever he could reach. It was likely a frenzied attack." Using a swab, he indicates the swollen hand. "The middle phalanx on the right hand is fractured. Probably a defensive wound."

"She tried to protect herself," I say.

He nods. "Ulna is fractured." He shifts the swab from her forearm to her shoulder. "Clavicular fracture. Sternal fracture. Scapular fracture. Ribs four through six are fractured. There are likely internal injuries of the lateral thoracic walls and posterior thorax as well."

"Was there any indication of sexual assault?" I ask.

"There's no trauma, but as a manner of routine I took vaginal and anal swabs which will tell us if there's semen present."

I nod, trying not to look at what remains of Rachael Schwartz, but unable to look away. "Did this attack require physical strength?"

"I can't answer that definitively, but if I were to venture a guess, I would say a strong person did this. The magnitude of the force was considerable."

"Was any of this done postmortem?"

"As you know, bruising ceases once the heart stops. There are at least two locations where bones were fractured and yet there was little in the way of bruising. I would venture to say the beating continued after she was deceased, at least for a short while."

After leaving the morgue, I sit in the Explorer for several minutes, gathering the frayed edges of my composure, tucking them into some semblance of order, so I can get back to work. It's not easy. When I close my eyes, I see the horrific injuries that were done to Rachael Schwartz. The gaping wounds and broken bones. In my mind's eye, I see her as a nine-year-old Amish girl who smiled because I said something inappropriate. As a kid, Rachael wasn't quite sweet. She wasn't quite innocent. Charming, but not always genuine. If you were a parent, you were never quite sure if you wanted your own children to associate with her. But she loved life. She lived it to its fullest. Maybe with a little too much gusto—and, perhaps, at the expense of others. But she deserved the chance to live her life.

My face is hot, so I lower the window and force myself to listen to the call of a blue jay in the maple tree next to the parking lot. I focus on the breeze easing into the cab. I draw a deep breath, discern the smell of fresh-cut grass. The distant bark of a dog. After a few minutes, the jittery sensation in my stomach subsides. The darkness ebbs. My hands grow steady on the steering wheel. When I close my eyes, I recall everything I know about Rachael Schwartz not with the shock of a woman who is a little too close, but with the emotional distance of a cop determined to do her job.

Putting the Explorer in gear, I pull out of my parking spot and head toward Painters Mill.

CHAPTER 15

Summer 2008

The rager was in full swing when Loretta and Rachael arrived. Loretta had never seen so many people in one place. She sure as heck had never seen so many English cars. The pasture behind the barn had been transformed into a virtual parking lot, filled with as many cars and trucks as buggies. Two young Amish hostlers were carting around buckets and soliciting tips for watering the horses.

Levi parked his own buggy behind a pickup truck with giant tires and a big chrome tailpipe. Rachael was sitting next to Levi. Loretta was sitting on the outside seat and slid from the buggy the moment it came to a stop.

"Hold up." Reaching into the back seat, Levi tore two more beers off a six-pack and handed them to Rachael, but his eyes were on Loretta. "One for the road."

Grinning, Rachael took both cans and slid from the buggy without thanking him. "We need smokes, too, Amish boy."

Mouth pulled into an assessing half smile, he fished the pack out of his pocket, tapped out two smokes, and handed them to her. "I'll meet you back here in two hours," he said.

"Three," said Rachael.

Loretta elbowed her. "Two," she whispered.

Rachael rolled her eyes. "Two and a half."

Levi regarded them, his eyes lingering on Loretta a tad too long. "Don't be late. I gotta work tomorrow."

He secured the leather lines, then slid down from the buggy. Loretta watched as he handed a five-dollar bill to one of the hostlers. Relief slipped through her when he was finally gone.

"You're frowning."

Loretta turned to see her friend come up beside her. "I don't like him."

"Oh, Levi's all right," Rachael said. "He's just . . . finding his way, I think."

"He whips his horse too much," Loretta said, motioning toward the whip sticking out of the holder attached to the buggy. "Mamm told me the way people treat God's creatures speaks to the way they deal with people."

Two English boys, cans of Budweiser in hand, walked by. One of them, a tall boy with a scraggly beard and John Deere cap, turned and walked backward, his eyes on Rachael, and whistled.

Once they'd passed, Rachael looked at Loretta and they broke into laughter.

"*Er is schnuck,*" Rachael said. He's cute.

Feeling frumpy, Loretta looked down at her dress. "I'm not sure I fit in here."

"Hmmm." Rachael studied her clothes for a moment. "I think we can fix that."

"But Mamm will—"

"Never know."

Taking Loretta's hand, Rachael led her back to the buggy and they ducked into the shadows behind it, out of sight of the crowd. "Give me your *halsduch*," she said, referring to the capelike feature draped over her dress.

"I don't see how that's going to help," Loretta said.

Rachael held out her hand. "Trust me."

Frowning, Loretta lifted the triangular piece of cloth over her head and handed it to her friend.

Rachael tossed the *halsduch* into the buggy. "Roll up your sleeves. To your elbows." As Loretta obeyed, Rachael went to the buggy and returned with a box cutter.

"What's that for?" Loretta asked.

"Hold still or I'll cut your leg off." Kneeling, she set to work at the hem. "It's going to look great. You'll see."

Loretta closed her eyes tightly as her friend sawed at the fabric. She didn't know if she was more excited—or terrified. The one thing she did know was that she was going to let her do it despite the possibility of her *mamm* finding out.

"All done."

Loretta opened her eyes and looked down at her dress, mildly shocked by the sight of her knees. "Oh."

Rachael got to her feet, looking at her friend admiringly. "One more thing." Quickly, she removed the leather belt from the waistband of her jeans and leaned close to wrap it around her friend's waist. "There. Oh, that's nice. See?"

"I feel ridiculous."

"You have great legs. For a skinny Amish girl." Grinning, Rachael kicked off her English shoes. "Let's switch. These sandals will go great with that dress. Sneakers are fine with my jeans."

Loretta toed off her plain sneakers, then slid her feet into the sandals. This time when she looked down at her clothes, she smiled. "Almost pretty."

"Told you." Rachael gave her a big, smacking kiss on the cheek.

"My knees are knobby."

"Your knees are sexy, silly girl." Rachael snapped open her beer. "Bottoms up."

Loretta drank as fast as she could, ended up choking twice. Before she was completely finished, Rachael took her can and slung both of them into the open window of a parked car.

"Come on." Laughing, Rachael took her hand. "We've got a lot of partying to do and not much time to do it."

Hand in hand, they passed a big tent where two Amish girls had set up a table draped with a red and white cloth. The handwritten sign announced HOME-CURED HAM SANDWICH WITH CHOW-CHOW $3. A few yards down, an English man had set up beer kegs on a picnic table laden with napkins and plastic cups, and a sign that read: BEER FOR A BUCK. Just past him, an Amish boy was selling cigarettes for four dollars a pack.

Rachael rushed to the beer table. "Two beers!" she said, breathless with excitement.

The man looked from Rachael to Loretta and frowned. "How old are you?"

Loretta started to speak up, but Rachael cut her off. "We're twenty-one."

He frowned, but grabbed two plastic cups and filled them with beer. "Two bucks."

There were so many stimuli coming at her from so many directions, Loretta almost couldn't take all of it in. Generators rumbled somewhere on the periphery. Bright lights shone from a dozen or so tents and food trucks. There was the din of voices and the tinkle of laughter. The bass thump of the band in the throes of some old Lynyrd Skynyrd song.

Rachael handed Loretta a plastic glass filled with beer and then raised hers. "Let's do a toast this time," she said. "To our first rager."

Feeling grown-up and sophisticated, Loretta bumped her cup against her friend's. "And good friends."

Eyes locked, they drank. Loretta only managed half her cup. Rachael finished all of hers, licked the foam from her lips, and tossed the cup over her shoulder. "I love that song! Let's go see the band."

The closer they got to the music, the more crowded it became. Along the way, they passed a pickup truck with the tailgate down. A bearded *Englischer,* wearing denim overalls and sunglasses even though it was dark, sat on a lawn chair. The sign on the truck touted SHOTS FOR $2.

Rachael's eyes widened at the sight of it. Squealing in delight, she pulled Loretta over to it and ordered. "Two shots."

"But I'm not finished with my beer," Loretta told her.

"It's called a chaser, silly girl." She laid four dollar bills on the tailgate.

"For a bunch of Bible thumpers, you Amishers sure can put away the booze." He poured from an unlabeled bottle into two clear plastic cups. "All's I got left is moonshine."

"That'll do." Rachael watched him pour.

He thrust two cups at her. "Enjoy."

Turning her back to him, Rachael handed one of the cups to Loretta and raised her own. "Cheers!"

The two girls locked elbows and drank. There wasn't much in either cup and Loretta managed it in a single gulp. The alcohol burned all the way to her stomach.

"*Fasucha vi feiyeh!*" she said, coughing. Tastes like fire!

Rachael threw her head back and laughed. "One more."

Before Loretta could refuse, Rachael darted back to the truck. The surly man poured again.

"Better be careful with that," he said.

Ignoring him, Rachael handed one of the cups to Loretta.

"Are you sure about this?" Loretta asked.

"Last one," Rachael assured her.

The burn engulfed Loretta's throat with such heat that her eyes watered. This time, it migrated down to her belly, and her head began to swim.

Taking her hand, Rachael led Loretta closer to the band and into the crowd. Around her, the music pulsed like a living, breathing thing. She could feel the beat of the drums all the way to her bones. The voices seemed louder, but not quite clear. The colors around her brighter. And she wondered why the drinking of alcohol was against the rules. How could something that made you feel so good, the world around you so beautiful, be such a bad thing?

Around them, everyone was dancing and laughing. Loretta looked left and saw an English girl wearing blue jeans with only a bra, holding a bottle of beer above her head, rubbing her pelvis against an Amish boy Loretta had gone to school with. The sight embarrassed her, and yet she couldn't look away. The boy was so enthralled he didn't notice her. Probably a good thing, since she wasn't supposed to be here. The last thing she needed was someone telling her parents.

A few feet away, Rachael raised her hands over her head. Hair flying, she danced to the raucous music. Loretta thought she'd never seen her friend look so beautiful. Even one of the band members had noticed and grinned down at her from the stage as his fingers ripped across the strings of his guitar. Loretta didn't know how to dance, but the rhythm made her feel in synch with the music. She raised her hands and threw back her head and, somehow, she knew the words to the song and she belted them out. She saw the guitarist looking down at her from the stage and she smiled back at him, and in that moment, she was beautiful and desired. There were no rules holding her back, and this dusty field with its brash vendors and rowdy occupiers was the only place she ever wanted to be.

"I never want to leave!" she cried to her friend.

Rachael Schwartz threw her head back and howled.

CHAPTER 16

I'm no stranger to the intricacies of a homicide investigation. Knowing the relationships of the victim, past and present, is one of the most important factors to establish. There's no doubt in my mind that Rachael Schwartz likely knew her killer. Yet when I spoke with her parents, they claimed no knowledge of discord in her life. Not because none existed, I'm sure, but because they weren't close to her. Both Loretta Bontrager and Andy Matson indicated Rachael did, indeed, contend with a fair amount of conflict. She shared a tumultuous relationship with her lover, Jared Moskowski. According to Loretta, she may have had other lovers we've not yet identified. She'd been shunned by the Amish. While I've heard rumors, I don't know exactly why. Was it due to something specific she'd done? Or the end result of years of breaking the rules? Then, of course, there is the issue of the tell-all book. No one appreciates having their dirty laundry aired for everyone to see. How much friction was there between Rachael and the Killbuck clan?

It's late morning when I pull into the gravel two-track of Bishop

David Troyer's lane. As I drive around to the back of the house, I notice the bishop's horse is hitched to the buggy, telling me he or his wife is probably getting ready to leave. I park adjacent to a beat-up shed and take the sidewalk to the back door.

Through the window, I see the bishop in the mudroom, looking at me through the glass. He's using a walker these days. And while he seems a tad smaller in stature, his belly not quite so round, he is not diminished. His presence and those all-seeing eyes invariably make me feel like I'm fourteen years old again, and put before him for breaking some rule. I was terrified of him during my formative years. Strange as it sounds—though I'm a grown woman and a cop—a smidgen of that old fear still exists.

I push open the door and lean in. "*Guder mariye,*" I tell him. Good morning.

I've known David Troyer the entirety of my life, and he looks much the same as he did when I was a kid. A head of thick gray hair generously streaked with black, blunt cut above heavy brows. A salt-and-pepper beard that reaches nearly to his waist. As usual, he's dressed in black, but for the white shirt beneath the jacket and suspenders.

"Katie Burkholder," he says in a wet-gravel voice. No smile. Just those astute eyes digging into mine. "You are here about Rachael Schwartz?"

I nod. "Do you have a few minutes, Bishop?"

"*Kumma inseid.*" Come inside. He turns and starts toward the interior of the house.

I follow him through the mudroom and into the kitchen. I wait while he maneuvers the walker to one of four chairs and settles into it. His wife, Freda, stands at the sink, washing dishes. She looks at me over her shoulder and nods a greeting that isn't quite friendly. I do the same.

"I was on my way to see Dan and Rhoda," he tells me. "This is a dark time for them."

"I won't keep you." I take the chair across from him. "I'm trying to figure out what happened to her, Bishop. I'm wondering if you have any insights into her life. Her relationships. If she was dealing with any problems. If she had any ongoing disputes or conflicts."

His eyes settle on mine, large and rheumy behind the thick lenses of his glasses. While the years may have taken a swipe at his physical body, his intellect remains sharp, his spirituality intense.

"You know I've not seen her in years," he says.

"You knew her as a child," I say. "Growing up." I pause, hold his gaze. "You know her parents. The Amish community as a whole."

"You knew her, too, no?"

"When she was a kid."

"Then even *you* know her life was filled with conflict."

He makes the statement as if it's somehow a miracle I've figured out anything about anyone, a reference no doubt to my Englishness. I absorb the jab without reacting, keep moving. "I'm looking for details," I tell him. "Names. Circumstances."

"She disobeyed her parents at a very young age. Not once, but many times. They brought her to me dozens of times. This girl child. So full of life and with eyes for all the wrong things." The old man shrugs. "Usually a good talking-to does the trick, you know." A smile plays at the corners of his mouth. "Not so for this girl. I spoke with the *Diener*," he says, referring to the other elected officials, the deacon and two preachers. "We did what we could. We stressed the importance of the *Ordnung.*" The unwritten rules of the church district. "We reinforced the importance of *demut,* the Christian faith, the worth of separation, and the old ways." *Demut* is *Deitsch* for "humility," a cornerstone of the Amish mindset. "Katie, young Rachael *harricht gut, awwer er foligt schlecht.*" Heard well, but obeyed poorly. "Dan and Rhoda did their best to teach her *Gelassenheit.*"

The word holds myriad meanings for the Amish. Suffering. Tranquility. Surrender. He shrugs. "Even so, there was trouble. Drinking. Gallivanting around. Lying about it. Dan came to me, asked that she be baptized early. He thought it might help. She was only seventeen. I went to the *Diener.* They agreed."

I'd heard Rachael had been baptized early, without much of an opportunity to sow a few wild oats. I'd wondered why her *rumspringa* had been cut short. Now I know.

"They thought it would fix her. We thought it was worth a try. And so the summer before she was to be baptized, the ministers took her through *die gemee nooch geh.*"

Once a young Amish person has made the decision to join the church, *die gemee nooch geh* is the period of instruction in which the ministers teach the young person *wertrational,* the values and what it means to be Amish.

"Rachael went through all the instruction. The *Diener* gave her time to turn back." He sighs. "Rachael became a member of the *Gemein.*" The community. "But she didn't make the vow with the solemnity it deserves. Six months later, she was shunned and excommunicated."

In the church district here in Painters Mill, being shunned or placed under the *bann* is usually remedied by the correction of some "bad behavior." For example, if a baptized Amish person is caught driving a car or using technology that isn't allowed—and he gets rid of the car. Excommunication, on the other hand, is usually permanent—and rare.

"Why was she excommunicated?" I ask.

The old man looks down at his hands, laces his fingers. Watching him, I realize that even after the passage of so many years he's bothered by this particular subject. Because his efforts weren't enough to save her? Or something else?

"Bishop, I'm just trying to understand what happened to her," I say quietly. "To do that, I need some insight into her history, her past."

"Are you certain you want to know, Katie?"

I look at him, taken aback by the cryptic question. "If you know something about Rachael Schwartz that might help me figure out who did that to her, I need to know about it."

Sighing, he turns his attention to his wife. "*Ich braucha zo shvetza Chief Burkholder,*" he tells her. I need to speak with Chief Burkholder. "*Laynich.*" Alone.

"*Voll.*" Of course. Giving me a final look, the Amish woman sets the dish towel on the counter and leaves the room.

For a moment, the only sound is the birdsong coming in through the window above the sink. The bawling of a calf in the field.

The bishop raises his gaze to mine. "Rachael Schwartz was deviant. The type of woman to do things best saved for marriage."

"I need names."

"Some were English. The Amish . . ." He shrugs.

The hairs on the back of my neck prickle. "Was she a minor?" I ask. "Under sixteen?"

"Close to that age. I'm not sure." Another shrug. "These are things I heard."

"From whom?"

He raises his head, his eyes searching mine. "These questions . . . may be the kind that are best not answered."

"I don't have that luxury," I snap.

He's unfazed by my tone. My impatience. After a moment, he nods. "Perhaps you should ask your brother."

"Jacob?" I stare at him, aware that my face is hot, my heart beating fast and hard in my chest. "Ask him what exactly?"

"You want to know about Rachael Schwartz? Ask him."

"What does she have to do with my brother?" Defensiveness rings hard in my voice, despite my efforts to curb it.

"Jacob came to me. Years ago. For counsel."

"Counsel for wh—"

He raises his hand, slices the air, and cuts me off. "I'll not speak of it. Not now. Not ever. If you want to know, go to Jacob."

"Bishop, you can't drop something like that in my lap and then walk away without an explanation."

Grasping the rails of his walker, he pulls himself to a standing position. "I've nothing more to say to you, Kate Burkholder."

Perhaps you should ask your brother.

The bishop's words taunt me as I drive down the lane. Jacob's name is the last name I expected to hear in the same sentence as Rachael Schwartz. I simply can't get my head around the implications. Jacob and I were close as kids. I admired him. Looked up to him. Relied on him for guidance. I loved him with all my young heart. Until I was fourteen years old and a neighbor boy by the name of Daniel Lapp entered our safe and protected world and introduced me to the dark side of human nature. It wasn't my parents, but Jacob who judged me that day. It was he who blamed me. For what happened to me. For what I did about it. For the death of a man I'll never come to terms with. Our family was never the same. But it was my relationship with Jacob that was shattered. I still see him on occasion. I visit my sister-in-law and my niece and nephews. But Jacob and I rarely speak. We're strangers.

Jacob came to me. Years ago. For counsel.

I search my memory for some link between Rachael and Jacob, but there's nothing there. My brother is eleven years older than Rachael, give or take. Too much of an age gap for their paths to have crossed in terms of courting. In addition, Jacob has been married for years. Why in the name of God would he go to the bishop about Rachael Schwartz?

I'm heading in the direction of his farm when my cell phone dings. Glock's name pops up on my dash screen. I hit the ANSWER button. "Please tell me you're calling with some good news," I say without preamble.

"Try this on for size," he replies. "Lady walking her dogs found a baseball bat in the ditch off Holtzmuller Road. She thought it was odd, took a closer look, and found blood."

My interest surges. "Holtzmuller isn't too far from the Willowdell Motel. Where are you?"

"Holtzmuller and TR 13," he tells me.

"Keep the dog lady on scene. I'll be there in two minutes."

I rack the mike and cut the wheel, make a U-turn in the middle of the road. The engine groans as I crank it up to just over the speed limit. Hopefully, the bat is the break we need. At the very least, it gives me some time to figure out how to approach Jacob with questions he's probably not going to want to answer.

Holtzmuller Road crosses Township Road 13 four miles south of Painters Mill. It's a little-used stretch that's more two-track than asphalt and runs through a rural area of rolling hills and feeder creeks, pastures and fields. This afternoon, the grass and surrounding trees erupt with the color of an Irish countryside. I round a curve and spot Glock's cruiser parked on the shoulder, the overhead lights flashing. Fifty yards beyond his car, he stands in the middle of the road, talking to a woman dressed in tie-dyed yoga pants and a pink athletic bra. He had the foresight to protect the scene and set out half a dozen safety cones to block traffic. Two golden retrievers sniff around at their feet.

I roll up behind his cruiser, flip on my overheads, and start toward them.

Glock and the woman turn and watch me approach. The dogs bound over to me, tongues lolling, tails waving. I bend, run my hands over their soft coats.

"Hey, Chief." Glock and I exchange a handshake. He motions toward a single cone in the ditch twenty yards away. "Bat is over there. Hasn't been moved or touched."

Nodding, I offer my hand to the woman and introduce myself. "I hear your dogs made an interesting discovery."

"I almost didn't stop," she tells me. "But they wouldn't come when I called and they're usually so obedient." She motions in the general direction of the cone. "I stopped and walked over there for a look. I thought maybe an animal had been hit by a car and needed help. But it was a baseball bat. At first, I didn't think anything of it. But it's a perfectly fine bat, right?" She hefts a laugh. "I was going to take it home for my kids. Then I saw the blood. I remembered hearing about that woman who was killed, and it freaked me out." She pats the cell phone strapped to her hip. "So I called you guys."

"We're glad you did," I tell her. "How long ago did you find it?"

"Twenty minutes?" she says.

"Did you see anyone else out here?" I ask. "Any vehicles or buggies on the road?"

"Not a soul. That's why I run on this stretch. There's no traffic and I don't have to worry about the dogs."

I'm ever cognizant of the possibility of evidence as we speak. Tire-tread marks or footwear imprints. If we're lucky, we might be able to extract fingerprints or DNA.

"Officer Maddox will take your contact info in case we have any more questions."

"Glad to help."

While Glock takes her information, I walk toward the cone sticking out of the grass in the ditch. Avoiding the gravel shoulder, I wade through ankle-high grass. Sure enough, next to the cone—twenty feet from the road—a wooden baseball bat is tucked into the grass, hidden from sight. It's a full-size Louisville Slugger. Well used, the logo worn by time and use. Benign looking except for the copious amount of blood smeared on the business end of it.

I think about Rachael Schwartz, the damage done to her body, and I know in my gut this is no coincidence. Keeping a prudent distance from the bat, I squat, pull out my reading glasses, and lean as close as I dare. Even without magnification, I discern several long hairs, small chunks of blood and tissue, all of it smeared and dry.

Pulling out my cell phone, I call Tomasetti.

He picks up on the first ring with a growl of his name.

"I think we found the murder weapon," I tell him.

"Well, it's about damn time someone called with some good news. What do you have?"

I tell him. "I need a CSU. Can you expedite?"

"I'll have someone there inside an hour."

I give him the location. "We'll protect the scene. I haven't looked around much, but there's a gravel shoulder. Might be able to pick up tread."

"I'll make sure they have plaster," he says. "Keep me posted, will you?"

"You, too."

I'm clipping my cell back onto my belt when Glock approaches, his eyes on the bat.

"What do you think?" he asks.

"Definitely blood. If we can extract DNA or prints." I shrug. "Could be a break."

He looks around. "What are we? Three miles from the motel?"

"Thereabouts." I look around. Half a mile down the road, I see the woman and her dogs walking away. "So, if we're right and this is the murder weapon, the killer left the motel and came this way."

"Heading away from Painters Mill." Glock looks left and right. "So where the hell was he going?"

"There's not much traffic out this way. Farms mostly."

"So he might live out this way. Or he might've simply been looking for a place to ditch the bat. Grass is tall enough so that he probably figured no one would find it."

"Did you happen to notice any tire-tread marks?" I ask. "Footwear?"

"I did a cursory search when I arrived. I can take a more thorough look around if you want." He sighs. "Sure would like to find this prick."

While Glock walks the road, searching the gravel shoulder for marks, I pull out my cell and take photos of the bat. The CSU will do the same. They'll protect the blood evidence and then courier the bat to the BCI lab in London, Ohio, where any fingerprints, blood type, and DNA will be extracted. If we're lucky, there will be some identifying mark to indicate where the bat was manufactured and sold. If we can find the merchant, we might be able to find out who purchased it. DNA will take some time—a few days, depending on how busy the lab is and how hard Tomasetti can push for priority—but even if the lab can match the blood type we'll have a little more to go on, especially if any of the blood belongs to the killer.

"I got nothing, Chief."

I turn to see Glock approach. "Zero traffic out this way," he says. "He probably just stopped the car, got out, flung the bat into the grass."

I nod in agreement, but my mind has already taken me back to the situation with my brother. "I've got to drive down to Killbuck," I tell him. "Can you hang out here until the CSU arrives?"

"Yep." He cocks his head, slants me a look that's a little too concerned for comfort. "Want some company? That Gingerich dude is weird as hell."

"I expect some of these people might be more apt to open up if I'm alone."

"Gotcha." He grins. "I guess I do kind of have that whole outsider vibe going on."

I smile back. "Call if you need anything."

As I leave Holtzmuller Road and head east, it isn't the thought of Amos Gingerich that claws at my brain, but a brother I haven't seen for six months, a past I'm loath to revisit, and a terrible suspicion that if I'm not careful I could sever ties I've cherished my entire life.

CHAPTER 17

A sense of nostalgia grips me as I pull into the long gravel lane of my brother's farm. I take my time as I drive toward the house, trying to remember the last time I was here. *Too long,* my conscience reminds. Last month, I missed my nephew's birthday. I have no idea what's going on in their lives.

The apple trees in the orchard on my right are in full, brilliant bloom. It seems like yesterday when Datt and my grandfather planted those trees. It never ceases to shock me to see that they're fully mature and have been bearing fruit for decades now.

The house is plain and looks exactly the same as when I was a kid. There are no flower beds or landscaping, just a small garden in the side yard with ruler-straight rows of tiny corn and tomatoes. I idle around to the rear of the house and park next to a hitching post that wasn't there last time I was here. I sit for a moment, taking all of it in, and in that instant the longing for something I can't quite identify grips me with an almost physical pain. This farm and the people who've lived here are my history. The house where I grew up. Where so much happened. The barn and outbuildings where my sister, Sarah, and Jacob and I played hide-and-seek. The fields and pasture where I ran free without a care in the world. It speaks of a time when I never questioned the wisdom of my parents or the rules set forth by the Amish leadership. This small farm with its ramshackle outbuildings and old German bank barn was my world. My family was the center of my universe, vast and unblemished. I had been painfully innocent, never lonely or alone, and my perceptions had not yet been skewed or scarred by the injustices of life.

I get out of the Explorer and take the narrow sidewalk to house. A blue jay scolds me from his perch in the cherry tree in the yard as I step onto the porch, and I'm reminded that I'm an outsider here, not only to the land, but to my own family. I'm about to knock when my sister-in-law, Irene, pushes open the screen door.

"Katie!" She does a double take, her eyes wide. "My goodness. What a nice surprise!"

Irene is pretty in a girl-next-door kind of way, with flawless skin sprinkled with freckles and clear hazel eyes. She's wearing a blue dress with a white apron that's stained with what looks like grape juice, and an organdy *kapp,* black oxfords.

"Hi." I manage a smile that doesn't feel genuine. "Is Jacob around?"

"He's in the barn, replacing a wheel on that old manure spreader. It conked out yesterday. Fourth time this spring." Frowning, she motions toward the barn. "He'll be there a while, Katie. *Kumma inseid. Witt du kaffi?*" Come inside. Would you like coffee?

Amish decorum urges me to take her up on the offer. Spend a few minutes chatting and getting caught up on things. I should ask about my niece and nephews and all the things happening in their lives. I should make an effort to know her, find some common ground and put an end to the discomfort I experience every time I'm here. Of course, I don't.

"*Nay, dank,*" I say.

Had I been one of her Amish brethren, I'd likely get an argument. Or else she'd step onto the porch, take my hand, and usher me inside for a piece of pie that'll only be good one more day, or the coffee she just made. Not so for me. In all the years that I've known her, Irene has never uttered a cross word to me, but we have an understanding. She invites only because she knows I will decline. I don't know if my brother told her what happened that summer when I was fourteen, but she's never been comfortable around me and despite her best efforts, it shows.

Relief flashes in her eyes. "Next time then."

I nod. "Tell the kids hi."

"I will!" A too-bright smile. "Bye, Katie!"

The screen door slams as I start toward the barn and I shove aside a small pang of hurt. Ahead, the big sliding door stands open a couple of feet. I sidle through, give my eyes a moment to adjust to the dimly lit interior. The clank and pop of metal against metal takes me to a workshop off the main room. I enter to find my brother at the workbench, pounding a piece of steel into submission.

He's so intent on his work that he doesn't notice me. His mouth is pulled into a frown, partly from the exertion of the task, partly from what looks like frustration because the steel is refusing to bend to his will.

After a moment, as if sensing my presence, he glances up and does a quick double take. The small sledgehammer in his hand freezes in midair; then he lets go with a final, satisfying blow. *Clang!*

I put my hands on my hips, present a smile. "Are you beating that piece of steel? Or is the steel beating you?"

"Haven't decided yet."

I catch the hint of a smile in his eyes, and I wonder if he's happy to see me. I wonder if he remembers how things were between us when we were kids. How much I'd looked up to him. If he misses it. I wonder if he realizes he'd once looked at me with affection instead of the standoffishness I see today.

He sets down the hammer. "It's been a while."

"I know," I say. "Too long."

We stare at each other, sizing each other up, slipping into our respective suits of armor, putting up the defenses we need to get through this. He's too polite to ask why I'm here, but he knows me too well to assume it's for a friendly visit.

"I need to talk to you about Rachael Schwartz," I say.

Jacob is a stoic man. He's difficult to read and tends to internalize his thoughts and feelings. But I see the impact of the name. A minute quiver runs the length of his body. Suddenly, and uncharacteristically, he can't meet my gaze. Instead, he looks down at the length of steel, picks it up, puts it back down.

"I heard about what happened to her," he says.

"I didn't realize you knew her."

"I didn't, really."

"That's not what I heard."

Raising his gaze to mine, he picks up the piece of steel, turns it over, and clangs the hammer against it three times. I watch him work, wait for him to stop, to respond.

After a few minutes, he looks at the steel, gives a small nod and sets it down. "You talked to Bishop Troyer." It's a statement, not a question.

And it tells me that whatever it was that happened between him and Rachael, he told no one else.

"I'm trying to find out who did that to her, so I went to the bishop." I pause, struggling to get the words right, failing. "I was surprised to hear your name. I had no idea your paths had ever crossed." If my revealing my source causes a problem between the two men, they'll just have to work it out.

"It was a long time ago." He tosses the piece of steel into an old-fashioned slatted wood crate. "I can tell you it has no bearing on what happened to her."

"I need to make that judgment, Jacob."

Taking his time, he lifts a baton-size bolt from another box, uses pliers to pry the nut that's fused to it with rust. "I confessed."

"To what?"

He twists the pliers and the nut snaps loose. "It was a private thing." I wait.

When he raises his gaze to mine, I see anger in his eyes. "*Dich sinn mei shveshtah.*" You're my sister. "*Dich du net halda glawva.*" You do not hold the faith. "I'll not speak of it."

Irritation snaps through me, but I tamp it down. "I'm not here as your sister, Jacob. I'm here as a cop with a job to do. If something happened between you and Rachael Schwartz, you need to tell me. Right now."

"You think I did that to her?" he asks incredulously.

"No," I say, meaning it. My brother may be a lot of things, but being capable of beating a woman to death is not one of them. "But sometimes there are . . . patterns in a person's life. The more I know about Rachael Schwartz, the more likely I'll find her killer."

After a moment, he rounds the workbench, brushes past me, and goes to the door of the workshop. He glances out as if to make sure there's no one there, closes the door, and returns to the workbench. There, he sets both hands against the surface, and shakes his head.

"Rachael Schwartz was . . ." He looks around as if he's lost something, as if his surroundings will somehow help him find the right word. "*Narrisch.*" Insane.

I wait, let the silence work.

After a moment, he straightens, slides his hands into his pockets. "It happened right before she left. I was in the buggy, driving home. It was dark, nine or ten o'clock, I think. A summer storm had swept in." He shrugs. "I didn't see her. Almost ran over her. Out by the Tuscarawas Bridge. She was walking in the middle of the road, soaking wet. I knew Rhonda and Dan, so I stopped. I knew they wouldn't want their daughter walking in the dark and rain all by herself, so I asked her if she needed a ride home."

Jacob would have been twenty-eight years old and married. Rachael Schwartz left when she was seventeen.

"She got into the buggy . . . soaked to the skin and crying, shivering with cold." Shaking his head, he turns away from me, pretends to look at something on the shelf behind him. "I didn't know it at the time, but she was . . . *ksoffa.*" Intoxicated. "During the drive to her parents' farm, she . . ." He ducks his head, struggles to find the words, fails. "One minute she was sitting there, crying. The next she . . . I don't know what happened. She became *unshiklich.*" Improper.

It's the last thing I expected my brother to say. The last kind of situation I would ever suspect him of getting caught up in. "She made a pass at you?" I ask.

My brother looks at me, but doesn't hold my gaze. I see shame in his eyes. A hint of ruddiness in his cheeks. "She was . . . *iemeschwarm.*"

Like a swarm of bees. "It was . . . unfitting. For a girl to act that way. It was crazy."

Only then do I realize there's more to the story. Jacob won't meet my gaze. His discomfort—his shame—is tangible.

"I . . . was young. Weak. For a moment, the devil got ahold of me." He sighs. "I pushed her out of the buggy. She . . . fell down. On the road. She was . . . furious and screaming. It was as if the devil had crawled into her head. I didn't know this girl."

Grimacing, he shakes his head. "I left her there. In the rain and dark. I went home. I told no one." He sighs. "Only later did I find out she went to the bishop and told him . . . things that were not true."

"What did she tell him?" I ask.

The ruddiness in his cheeks blooms. "She told the bishop that we were of one flesh."

"Did you?"

"No." He forces his gaze to mine, his mouth pulled into a hard line. "Katie, I was married. I would not—" He cuts the sentence short, as if the final word is too forbidden to be spoken aloud. "She lied. To the bishop. To anyone who would listen. Caused many problems."

"What did the bishop do?"

"He came to me. I told him the truth." The color in his cheeks darkens and spreads. "I confessed to him. For . . . what I did. What I felt."

"He believed you?"

He gives a barely discernable nod. "He did not believe her, and rightfully so."

"Who else knows what happened?"

"No one."

I think about that a moment. "Do you know why she was upset and out walking so late and in the rain?"

"She didn't say."

"Do you know if there were any other incidents? With anyone else? Other men?"

"All I can tell you is that I never looked at her again. I never spoke to her. And I never, ever let myself be alone with her." He shakes his head. "A few months later, she was gone."

CHAPTER 18

The story Jacob told me about Rachael Schwartz follows me as I head south on Highway 62 toward Killbuck. I recall the passage in the book she wrote that's chillingly similar to the one Jacob just relayed. In the book, the man, whose name was not mentioned, refused to take no for an answer. He raped her in the back seat of his buggy and then threw her to the asphalt and left her. When she went to the bishop, he blamed her. None of the other Amish believed her because she was fallen. In the end, she was excommunicated.

Was that extract an embellishment of what occurred between her and Jacob? Or was there *another* incident in which she was sexually assaulted and no one believed her?

I'm not sure what to think. What to believe. About Rachael. Her motives. By sheer virtue that Jacob is my brother, I am biased. That said, as a cop—as a woman—I know there is no greater insult for a victim of sexual assault than to not be believed, to be dismissed or disparaged. But I know my brother. He's a straight shooter. He follows the rules, not because he has to, but because he subscribes to basic Amish tenets. I always believed that's one of the reasons he had such a difficult time dealing with what I did that summer.

The vast majority of Amish men are well behaved when it comes to their female counterparts. They're aware of appearances, particularly if they're married. That said, I'm not blind to the reality that Amish men are as mortal as their English counterparts. They step over the line. They behave badly. Sometimes they break the law. Am I too close—not only to my brother, but to the young Rachael Schwartz I'd once known—to see the truth?

It's afternoon when I enter the corporation limit of Killbuck. Amos Gingerich's settlement is located west of town on a county road that's riddled with potholes. The vegetation is lush and overgrown in this low-lying area. Massive trees crowd the shoulders of the road, the branches scraping the doors and roof of the Explorer.

Tomasetti made good on his promise to forward images of the letters Amos Gingerich sent Rachael Schwartz. His takeaway is spot-on. While the letters aren't overtly threatening, it's clear Gingerich wasn't happy with her. The question in my mind now is: Did he act on all the anger simmering between the lines?

Generally speaking, the Amish are pacifists and live by the canon of nonresistance. When under threat, they will not defend themselves or their property. If they have an unresolvable problem with a neighbor or town, they've been known to simply move away. In times of war, they are conscientious objectors and refuse to bear arms. I know the Amish charter by heart; I was raised with it and lived by it through my formative years. I may not agree with every aspect, but I am certain of one thing: The Amish are a good and decent society. They're hardworking, family oriented, religious, and they are good neighbors.

Amos Gingerich may have Anabaptist leanings, but I know enough about him to know he isn't Amish, and I would be wise to use extreme caution when dealing with him, especially since I opted to come alone.

Half a mile in, a wall of trees rises out of the ground and the road dead-ends. I bring the Explorer to a stop and sit there a moment, puzzled.

"Well, shit."

I'm in the process of turning around when I spot the narrow opening between two walnut trees that's shrouded with a tangle of wild raspberry bushes. The derelict remains of a mailbox slant up through hip-high bramble at a precarious angle. The number matches the address I have on file.

I pick up my police-radio mike. "I'm ten-twenty-three."

"Ten-four," comes Lois's voice. "Be careful down there, Chief."

"That's affirm."

I rack the mike and start down the lane, cringing when the branches scratch at the paint on my doors. The Explorer bumps over potholes and puddles, mud and gravel slinging into the wheel wells. I've traveled another half mile, wondering if I've made a wrong turn somewhere, when the trees fall away. The lane widens and I drive into a large clearing. A dozen or so small, clapboard buildings, the kind used for construction-site offices, form a half circle. The units are closely grouped, each with wood stairs and a porch adorned with a potted plant or lawn chair. To my left, I see a large swatch of what looks like a community garden, where two women wearing ankle-length dresses and winter bonnets hoe the soil between rows of tiny spring corn, caged tomato plants, and other, indistinguishable greens. Beyond, an old bank barn that was here long before the other structures lends a sense of character the rest of the place lacks. A couple of draft horses graze in a small pasture. In another pen, several pygmy goats stand on giant wooden spools, bleating. A black buggy—oddly adorned with an orange roof—is parked outside the barn. I take in the scene with the sense that it has been staged.

I idle across the clearing to a hitching post in front of the nearest residence and shut down the engine. The two women don't look up from their work as I get out of the Explorer, but I feel eyes on me as I make my way up the steps and cross to the door. I've barely knocked when the door cracks open several inches. I find myself looking at a woman, barely into her twenties. She's hugely pregnant and wearing a longish print dress, and a head covering that's neither Amish nor Mennonite.

Her eyes widen at the sight of my uniform. "Can I help you?" she asks.

I show her my badge. "I'm looking for Amos Gingerich," I tell her.

She blinks, her eyes darting left. "Amos?"

It's a dumb response. One designed to delay. She's not quick enough to think of a viable stall off the top of her head, and I resist the urge to roll my eyes.

"Amos Gingerich," I tell her. "I need to speak with him. Right now. Where is he?"

She visibly swallows, then raises her hand and points toward the old bank barn. Before I can say anything else, she shrinks back inside and closes the door.

"That wasn't too difficult, was it?" I mutter as I trot down the steps.

I reach the open area where my Explorer is parked and keep going at a brisk clip toward the barn. To my left lies the garden. It's a large chunk of land, an acre or so. The two women have stopped what they're doing. They lean on their hoes, watching me. I raise my hand to wave, but they don't return the gesture. I can't help but notice both women are pregnant.

The barn door stands open. I enter; the smells of cattle, horses, and freshly sawn wood lace the air. A few yards away, a man is bent over a table, working on something unseen. He's broad shouldered and dressed in black. A ponytail dangles to midback. I stand there a moment, taking his measure. He's well over six feet, two-fifty, with a muscular build. The flat-brimmed straw hat speaks of Amish leanings. The ponytail curtails any such misconception.

I'm about to announce my presence when he turns. Whether he heard my approach or merely sensed my presence, I can't tell, but when his eyes land on mine he's not surprised by me or the sight of my uniform.

He's got a thin, expressive mouth. A hook nose. Salt-and-pepper beard that reaches nearly to the waistband of his trousers. If he were Amish, the beard would tell me he's married and has been for some time. With this group, I'm not so sure. Pale eyes the color of an overcast sky. Amos Gingerich. I recognize him from the photos in Rachael's book.

"Ah, the police." Good-naturedly, he presses his hand to his chest. "Am I in trouble?"

Something about him I can't quite pinpoint unsettles me in spite of his friendly tone. His accent tells me he's not originally from this area. That *Deitsch* is likely not his first language.

"That depends." I approach him, tug my badge from my pocket, and introduce myself. "Amos Gingerich?"

He nods. "What can I do for you?"

Something disingenuous peeks out at me from behind his eyes, the curl of his mouth. "I'd like to ask you a few questions," I say.

Taking his time, he sets down the sander and plucks off his leather gloves. "This is about Rachael Schwartz?"

"So you've heard."

"Word of death travels fast, especially when you're Amish."

I don't point out that his Amishness is debatable. "You knew her?"

"She came to us, here in Killbuck. Stayed for a time."

"How long ago?"

"Eleven or twelve years, I think. She'd been put under the *bann* by the bishop in Painters Mill. She was a troubled young woman." He touches his chest. "Inside, you know. She was alone. Confused. She had nowhere to go and so we took her in. We offered her refuge and counsel. A place to live. We offered her hope."

"How long did she stay?"

"Six months or so."

"That's not very long."

He shakes his head. "She was a restless soul. Searching for something she couldn't name. After a time, she realized she could not abide by our ways."

"What ways is that?"

"I don't want to disparage her. That's not our way. But she was . . . difficult."

"How so?"

He shrugs. "She was . . . disruptive. As bishop, my community comes first. When I asked her to leave, she became angry."

"Was she angry with anyone in particular?"

"Me, of course. But she also turned on some of the womenfolk. Some of the girls she lived with. Accused them of spying." He dismisses the word with a wave of his hand. "Strange things like that." He shakes his head. "She tried to come back, get into our good graces. But I wouldn't have it. A couple of years later that book came out. I was shocked by all the vicious lies. It caused problems for our small community. It seems young Rachael sold her soul for money."

I think about the rumors of polygamy, of children at risk, and the accusations that Gingerich is more cult leader than bishop. I ask anyway. "What kinds of problems?"

"Reporters started sniffing around, accosting us here or in town, asking all sorts of questions. The police came, too, as did the social peo-ple with the government, wanting to know about the children." His mouth tightens. "Our property was vandalized. People in town called us names or refused to do business with us. It was an outrage."

"What did you do?"

"What *could* we do? Like so many of our forefathers we put our fate in the hands of God and we weathered the storm."

"Did you blame Rachael Schwartz for any of it?"

"I blame intolerance," he tells me. "Ignorance."

I let it go, shift gears. "Was Rachael close with anyone in particular here in this community?"

"She was only here for a short time. I don't believe she got too close to anyone, really."

"What about you?" I ask.

He tilts his head, the spark of something I can't readily identify in his eyes. Irritation? Amusement? "What about me?"

"Were you and Rachael close?" I ask.

"No closer than any bishop and a member of his congregation."

I nod, look around, let the silence ride a moment. "So, you read her book?"

"What I could stomach."

"Then you know Rachael claimed the two of you had a relation-ship."

"I'm aware of that untruth." Another flash of pseudo amusement, darker this time, laced with anger. "The book was full of blasphemous lies. About me. My brethren. Written by a disgruntled and confused woman who in the end sold her soul for whatever the publisher paid her."

"You must have been angry," I say.

He gives me a pitying look, but there's an unsettling glint in his eyes.

Buried beneath all that righteousness and calm lies a cunning and indescribable menace that chills me, despite the .38 strapped to my hip.

"I hold no anger toward anyone," he tells me. "That's not our way. Rachael Schwartz *hot net der glaase*." Didn't keep up the faith. "She made many unfounded and painful accusations. She tried to hurt those who only wanted to help. Yes, the police investigated, but then you already know that, don't you, Kate Burkholder?"

"I do."

A ghost of a smile touches his lips. "It was a painful time for all of us."

"When's the last time you had any contact with Rachael?" I ask.

"I haven't spoken to her since the day I asked her to leave."

"What about letters?" I ask.

"Ah." His mouth curls in such a way that I can't tell if it's a smile or a snarl or something in between. The one thing I do know is that it's an unpleasant mien and it's focused on me.

"You obviously know I wrote to her. Simply to ask her to stop lying about us. Leave us be in peace."

"Did it escape your mind that you also threatened her?"

"A false witness shall not be unpunished, and he that speaketh lies shall perish," he tells me. "In case you're not well versed, and I suspect you are not, that passage is from the Bible. I thought it might help her see the error of her ways. That's all."

"Where were you night before last?" I ask.

"Here, of course." He spreads his hands, encompassing the area around him.

"Can anyone substantiate that?"

"My wife. A few of the others here in our community." He recites two names.

I pull out my notebook and write them down.

When I look up, he's tilted his head, looking at me as if I'm some fascinating science project. Some small animal that's about to be dissected by a kid who enjoys cutting a little too much. "I understand you're fallen, too, Chief Burkholder. Perhaps you have something to confess as well."

For an instant, I'm startled that he knows I'm formerly Amish. Quickly, I settle, reminding myself that Painters Mill isn't far from Killbuck. That gossip has wings. And that he probably knew at some point I'd drive down and talk to him.

Taking my time, I drop the notepad and pen into my pocket. "I appreciate your time," I say.

And I walk away.

CHAPTER 19

I've just entered the corporation limit of Painters Mill when my cell lights up. Seeing HOLMES CNTY CORONER on the dash display, I hit ANSWER. "Hey, Doc."

"I've completed the autopsy of Rachael Schwartz. Report is in the works, but since time is of the essence, I thought you'd want to hear my findings," he says.

"Cause and manner of death?" I ask.

"She died from multiple cranial-bone fractures, subdural and sub-arachnoid hemorrhages of the frontal, parietal, and temporal regions. Any one of those injuries could have been fatal."

"In English?" I say.

"Skull fractures." He heaves a sigh and for the first time I get the impression that this particular autopsy has exhausted him in a way that has little to do with a lack of sleep or physical stamina.

"All of it from blunt-force trauma?"

"Yes," he replies. "Manner of death is homicide," he finishes.

"Were you able to narrow down the time of death?" I ask.

"Between one and three A.M. That's as close as we're going to get, Kate."

"What about the rape kit?"

"No semen."

I think about that, once again the question of motive swirling. "Is there a preliminary report you can send me, Doc?"

"I'll email you what I have. Won't be finalized until tomorrow. I won't close out until tox comes back in a couple weeks."

I'm about to thank him when he speaks again. "Kate . . ." He makes a sound that's partly the clearing of his throat, but for the first time since I've known him, there's emotion tucked away somewhere in that sound. "That girl had seven broken bones. Internal hemorrhaging. Facial injuries. In all the years I've served in the capacity of coroner, I've never seen so much trauma as the result of a beating."

I wait, vaguely aware that I'm holding my breath. That I'm moved by his reaction, the unusualness of it, and part of me knows this moment is important. Not only for me, but for Doc Coblentz.

"I don't know if what I'm about to tell you is relevant in terms of the perpetrator or if it will be helpful to you in any way as you investigate this crime, but even after this victim was down and unable to protect herself or move, her attacker continued to strike. Those blows continued long after the victim's heart stopped beating." He pauses and I hear the hiss and flow of his breaths. "Speaking not as the coroner, but as a citizen? You need to find this guy, Kate. You need to stop him and quickly. None of us will be safe until you do."

Before I can assure him that I plan to do exactly that, the connection ends.

Rachael Schwartz was no angel, but she didn't deserve the fate that met her. No one deserves to die like that, especially at the hand of another.

. . . even after this victim was down and unable to protect herself or move, her attacker continued to strike.

The overkill indicates a high level of emotion. Intense and personal hatred. An all-consuming rage. A complete loss of control. Who hated her enough to beat her with such violence that they broke seven bones? Inside their twisted mind, what had Rachael Schwartz done to deserve it?

I'm in my office at the police station. It's after four P.M. now. Glock came in earlier for his end-of-shift reports and Skid came on board to relieve him. Lois went home for the day and my new dispatcher, Margaret, has spent the last hour cleaning and rearranging the credenza behind her workstation. I've read Doc Coblentz's preliminary autopsy report twice now. The picture that emerges is a thing of nightmares. In the early stages of the attack, Rachael Schwartz had tried to protect herself. Defensive wounds indicate she fought back; she was a fighter, after all. When those efforts proved fruitless, she tried to escape. But by then she was too injured to get away. While she was down, crawling or pulling herself along the floor, unable to defend herself, her killer stood over her and beat her to death.

I'm thinking about the baseball bat found in the ditch, in the process of reading the report for the third time, looking for details I might've overlooked, when the bell on the exterior door jangles, telling me someone has entered the station. A moment later, Tomasetti appears in the doorway of my office. He's carrying a record storage box. His laptop case strap is slung over his shoulder. He looks tired. Glad to be here. The knot in my gut loosens at the sight of him.

"You lost?" I say.

"I'm looking for Mrs. Tomasetti," he says.

I stand, ridiculously pleased by his use of the as-of-yet-unofficial title, liking the way he's looking at me, the half smile curving his mouth. "I don't think that's a done deal just yet," I tell him.

"Say the word, and we'll make it happen," he says.

"Thinking about it."

I've lost track of how many times he's proposed. Of course I plan to marry him; he's the love of my life. Even so, I haven't given him the answer he deserves. While marriage is an institution I believe in, the notion of tying that knot scares the daylights out of me. He's been a good sport about it. I'm a work in progress.

He enters my office. "Shall I close the door?"

Temptation ripples through me. I look past him, catch a glimpse of Margaret gathering the carafe and mugs from the coffee station in the hall and shake my head. "Rain check?"

"Bet on it." He sets the box on my desk, the laptop on the floor, and sinks into the visitor chair across from me.

"How was Cleveland?" I ask.

"Productive," he tells me. "Division of Police and BCI went through the house where Schwartz lived with Matson. We went over everything with a fine-tooth comb. Dusted for prints. We took her laptop to the lab. Email. Hard drive. Techs are looking at her browsing history."

"Anything interesting?" I ask.

"A couple of things stand out. According to one of her friends I talked to, Rachael was regularly intimate with two men, in addition to Moskowski."

I sit up straighter. "Did you—"

"Both have alibis for the night of the murder, but we're taking a good hard look at both of them in case this was a murder-for-hire or jealous-lover kind of thing."

Not for the first time, I'm reminded that Rachael Schwartz lived her life full bore. She was impulsive with a predilection for risky behavior and damn anyone who didn't like it.

Bending, he pulls a couple of items from the box. "You have chain of custody on this." He tosses a brown envelope on my desk. "Old photos."

I open it. The photos inside are faded and stained. Poor quality. There are four of a spotted horse that means nothing. I shuffle through, come to the last photo. It's a picture of Rachael Schwartz and Loretta Bontrager when they were barely into their teens. Loretta has a kind, ordinary face mottled with freckles, and the guileless eyes of a child. Rachael was a lovely girl with a not-quite-innocent smile and eyes that, even then, were a little too direct.

He places a manila folder on my desk and slides it over to me. "This is one of the more interesting finds."

I replace the photos, open the folder, and find myself looking at copies of Schwartz's banking and financial statements. Checking account. Savings. A small investment account.

"Not much in the way of savings," I murmur as I skim. "Investment account is almost dry."

"According to her accountant, The Keyhole didn't always turn a profit. Some weeks she barely made payroll."

"She was living above her means."

Leaning forward, he reaches out and flips the page. "Checking account has been in the red several times in the last couple of years. Look at the balance now."

My eyes widen. "Almost twenty thousand dollars." I look at Tomasetti. "Any idea where the money came from?"

He runs his finger down the page and taps on a figure highlighted in yellow. I slide my reading glasses onto my nose. Sure enough, there was a deposit made two months ago in the amount of fourteen thousand dollars.

I look at Tomasetti. "That's a lot of money. Royalty payment?"

"Cash," he tells me.

"That's odd."

"It's been my experience that when people deal in cash like that, they usually have something to hide or else they don't want it traced."

"Is there any way we can figure out who it came from?" I ask.

"I'm working on getting landline records," he says. "Might take a day or two."

"Cell phone?" I ask.

"We went through the one found on scene," he tells me. "We identified every number, but they gave us nothing. According to the friend I talked to, Rachael had *two* cell phones. Only one has been accounted for."

I think of the cell phone found at the scene. I remember thinking there should have been at least one call to someone in Painters Mill. For the first time, that there wasn't such a call makes sense.

"She didn't drive down to Painters Mill to ogle the Amish," I tell him. "No one I've talked to knew she was here or even knew she was coming."

"Someone did," he says. "We both know this wasn't random."

My mind spins through possibilities. "Her killer knew about the second cell phone and took it."

"Because they'd been communicating with it."

"Burner?" I ask.

"Why would she do that?"

"Maybe she was into something she shouldn't have been into?"

"Like what?"

"I don't know." I rap my palm against the desktop.

He leans back in the chair and contemplates me. "Rachael wasn't the only one living above her means."

"Andy Matson?"

"Worth checking. At the very least, rattle her cage a little."

I smile. "Not bad for a BCI guy."

"Every now and then I get it right."

Rolling my eyes, I get to my feet. "I'll drive."

In light of her friend's unsolved murder, Andy Matson had wanted to stay in Painters Mill for a few days rather than make the drive back and forth to Cleveland, if only to "make sure these small-town Barney Fifes do their jobs." It's nothing I haven't heard before; I don't take offense. With the B and Bs booked—and the Willowdell Motel hitting a little too close to home—she's staying at Hotel Millersburg, which is half a block from the Holmes County Courthouse. She agrees to meet Tomasetti and me at a nearby coffee shop.

We find her in a booth at the rear, staring at her phone, a frothy latte and half-eaten croissant in front of her. She looks up as we approach.

"Any news?" she asks, giving us only part of her attention.

"We're following up on a few things," I say vaguely as Tomasetti and I slide into the booth opposite her.

"Like what?" she asks. "Do you have a suspect?"

I let her fidget and stew, the questions hang, while we order coffee.

When our server hustles away, I turn my attention to her. "What do you know about Rachael's finances?"

"Finances?" she echoes stupidly.

"You know," Tomasetti says. "Money. Accounts. Savings. Checking. Investments."

She blinks, looks from Tomasetti to me, as if suddenly she's not quite in such a hurry to talk.

I say her name firmly. "If you're as smart as I think you are, you'll answer the question in the next two seconds and you'll tell the truth."

Andy looks down at the cup and plate in front of her as if she's lost her appetite for both. "Why are you asking me about her finances?" she asks.

"Because we want an answer," I say evenly.

She sighs. "I guess you've realized there was something going on with her."

I say nothing. Tomasetti follows suit.

She squirms beneath our stares. "Look, the only thing I know for certain about Rachael's money situation is that she spent it like it was frickin' going out of style. I mean, she had expensive taste. In clothes. Liked to travel. She loved fancy restaurants. Nice hotels." Her brows knit. "What's odd about that is that she didn't *make* as much money as she spent. I mean, The Keyhole was doing *okay*, but there were weeks when we barely broke even. Sure, she had royalties from the book, but they were dwindling because it had been out for a couple years. She wasn't exactly rolling in the dough."

"And yet she shopped at Saks," Tomasetti says dryly. "She bought expensive art. Spent two weeks in Hawaii last year. Stuff like that."

"Did you ever ask her about it?" I ask.

"Once or twice. You know, just sort of kidding around." She shrugs. "She'd say it was from a bonus. Or for some catering gig that never seemed to materialize. Mostly, she just changed the subject or laughed it off."

Beside me, Tomasetti makes a sound of annoyance. "You can cut the bullshit. We have her financial records. We can get yours, too, if you prefer to do things that way."

Giving him a withering look, she picks up her cup, sets it down without drinking.

"Look," she says, "I loved Rachael. She was fun and alive and . . .

she was one of the most amazing people I've ever met. She just had this way about her. This . . . persuasive energy that won you over. And you guys are sitting there judging her and doing the whole assassination-of-character thing, treating her as if she was some common criminal."

She's getting herself worked up, so I give her a moment, keep my voice level. "We're not judging her," I say gently. "We're trying to find the person who murdered her."

"She wasn't perfect," she snaps. "Rachael was . . . Rachael. I loved her anyway. I accepted her. Flaws. All of it. But . . ." She struggles to find the right words. "I'm not badmouthing her, but . . . I think you both know by now that she wasn't always a good person."

"How so?" I ask.

"When she wanted something, she went for it."

Tomasetti rolls his eyes. "What the hell does that even mean?"

She looks around, as if to make sure no one is close enough to hear what she's about to say, and lowers her voice. "Look, I don't know this for a fact, but it crossed my mind that Rachael might be blackmailing someone."

"Who?" I ask.

"No clue."

Groaning, Tomasetti leans against his chair back. "Right."

"Why did you think that?" I ask.

"The money for one thing. She was always throwing it around. And she was secretive about where it came from." She lowers her voice to a whisper. "A couple weeks ago, I walked in, late, and she was on the phone, arguing with someone. I mean, they were really going at it. I heard her threaten them."

"Any idea who?" I press.

"I asked, but she just laughed and said it was this bartender she'd had to fire, and he was trying to get his job back." She shakes her head. "Poor guy was in love with her, but she just . . . laughed." Her brows draw together. "I remember looking at her and thinking: She's lying."

"What's his name?" Tomasetti asks.

"Joey Knowles."

He writes down the name.

"Was the caller male or female?" I ask.

"Not sure." She gives a sheepish smile. "Rach was pretty much an equal-opportunity asshole."

"In what way did she threaten the person she was talking to?" I ask.

"I only caught the tail end of the conversation. She said something like—and I'm paraphrasing—'play your cards right and no one will ever know.' "

"Why didn't you mention this sooner?" I ask.

She looks away. "Because I don't want people thinking she was a bad person who deserved what she got. She didn't."

Tomasetti isn't buying it. "How much did she give you?" he asks.

She opens her mouth. Closes it. Blinks a dozen times. All of it accompanied by a deep flush that spreads down her throat like a sunburn. "She didn't—"

"How much?" he snaps.

"She . . . gave me the down payment for my car," she tells him. "The Audi."

"Nice of her," he says. "Did you ask her where the money came from?"

"No." She looks down at the coffee and shakes her head. "You know, the whole look-a-gift-horse-in-the-mouth thing, I guess."

"What else haven't you told us?" he asks.

She hits him with a contemptuous glare and pushes the plate away. For a moment, I think she's going to get up and leave. Instead, she

146

looks from Tomasetti to me and heaves a sigh. "In case you haven't figured it out yet, I'm no angel either."

"We kind of got that," Tomasetti mutters.

"If there's something else we need to know," I say, "now is a good time to tell us."

"God." Andy looks down at the plate in front of her. For the span of a full minute, she says nothing. Then she sighs, curses. "I took two thousand dollars, okay? For God's sake, I found it in her office. I was . . . pissed. I mean, she owed me. I mean, for the book. Right? So I took it. And then I felt like shit. That's why I was trying to reach her. I mean, the day she died."

"You stole two thousand dollars from her?" Tomasetti asks.

"I guess I did," she says. "I mean, I would have paid it back, but . . ." She ends the sentence with a shrug. "All of this happened."

"How did you know she'd driven down to Painters Mill?" I ask.

"She left a note."

"Do you still have it?" I ask.

"Um. Gosh, I don't know. Maybe." She lifts the leather bag off the back of her chair, digs around inside. "It was just a scribbled few words. Kind of vague and snarky."

She pulls out a wadded piece of paper, smooths it out. A smile tugs at her mouth as she sets it on the tabletop and slides it over to me.

Off to PM to TCB. Dinner tomorrow @ Lola's. Booze on me!

"What's TCB?" I ask.

"Take care of business."

"Any idea what she meant by that?"

She lifts her shoulder, lets it drop. "Just that she had something to do there."

"What did you do with the two grand?" Tomasetti asks.

Her eyes skitter right. It's a subtle reaction, but enough for me to know she's thinking about lying. Instead of answering, she sets her elbows on the tabletop and rests her forehead in her hands. "I know how this is going to sound. I know what you're going to think."

"Just answer the damn question," he growls.

"I blew it, okay? Bought a few things." She raises her head, looks from Tomasetti to me. "Look, it's not like I didn't have a good reason to take it. Rachael owed me."

"She owed you money?" Tomasetti asks. "You mean for the book?"

"Last year, when Rachael was buying the house, she was short. My mom had just passed away and left me a little money." She shrugs. "I knew Rachael was good for it, so I let her borrow six grand."

"Do you have anything in writing?" I ask.

"We're not exactly write-it-down kind of people."

"When was she supposed to pay you back?" I ask.

"Months ago, but—" Her brows furrow. "Last time I asked her about it, she said she was going to pay me back soon. That she was about to come into some cash."

"How long ago was that?" I ask.

"Two weeks maybe?"

"Do you know the source of the money she was about to come into?"

"She led me to believe it had something do with the book." She looks down at the tabletop and shakes her head. "I'm not a thief. I was tired of being put off, so I took it and I went fucking shopping."

Her voice cracks with the last word and she takes a moment to compose herself. "When I calmed down, I felt awful. I spent the rest of the day trying to run her down. But when I couldn't get her on the cell, I got worried. Rachael *always* answers her cell. She's like . . . addicted to it." She looks at Tomasetti. "Then I get *you* on the other end and it freaked me out. I checked motels in Painters Mill. When I got there, I found all those cop cars and I just knew . . ."

Lowering her face into her hands, she bursts into tears.

Tomasetti looks at me and frowns.

I pass her a fresh paper napkin. "Andy, do you know who she was meeting with?"

"No clue."

"Did Rachael's parents know she was coming?" I pose the question even though, according to Rhoda and Dan Schwartz, they had no idea their daughter was in town.

"I don't know." She blots at her eyes, careful not to smear her makeup. "Look, I've got nothing against the Amish. To each their own, you know? But Rachael's parents treated her like shit. Rachael tried to stay in touch with them. She missed them, wanted them in her life. All they ever did was judge her. Put her down. They disapproved of everything she did. Rachael was never good enough."

I nod, thinking about my own family and the dynamics of familial relationships. "Did Rachael stay in touch with anyone else in Painters Mill?"

"She had a friend." A wrinkle forms between her brows. "Amish."

"Male or female?" I ask.

She shakes her head. "All I remember is that Rachael had a couple of intense conversations with this so-called friend of hers and they weren't very Amish-sounding. Conversations that upset her even more than all that judgment shit coming down from her holier-than-thou parents."

CHAPTER 20

The Amish have a saying about deception. It goes something like: *Dich kann gukka an en mann kischt avvah du kann net sayna sei hatz.* You can look at a man's face, but you can't see his heart.

"What do you think?" I ask.

Tomasetti and I are sitting in the Explorer, parked outside the coffeehouse where we met with Andy Matson.

"I think if she's a liar, she's pretty good at it." He shrugs. "I don't believe she beat Rachael Schwartz to death. If she was involved, she hired someone. If she did, there will be a money trail."

I nod in agreement. "We need to look at the blackmail angle."

He grimaces. "If Rachael Schwartz knew something about someone, I don't think she'd hesitate to use it to her advantage."

"Matson may be trying to shift our interest to someone else." Even as I toss out the theory, it doesn't ring true.

His cell chirps. He pulls it from his pocket and checks the display, takes a minute to scroll. "Well, I'll be damned," he says.

150

"If it's not good news, I don't want to hear it."

He grins. "I just got the PDF of Schwartz's credit card activity in the thirty days before she was killed. Get this: The final transaction was at a bar in Wooster the evening before she was murdered. At seven twenty-nine P.M."

"The Pub?" I say.

He arches a brow.

"The scribbled address on the note," I remind him. "I drove up there last night. No one remembered seeing her." I think about that a moment. "How much was the charge?"

"Thirty-nine dollars and change."

Something in my chest quickens. I see the same rise of interest in Tomasetti's eyes. "It's a burger-and-fries kind of bar," I tell him. "Not the kind of place where dinner costs more than fifteen bucks, even if you have a beer."

"She wasn't alone."

"I'd venture to say she treated someone to dinner."

"In that case." He motions toward the clock on my dash, which reads 7:00 P.M. "You game for a beer?"

"Tomasetti, you're going to have to buy me something a hell of a lot stronger than beer."

The Pub was nearly vacant last time I was here. Of course, it had been late, after ten P.M. Tonight, the parking lot is chock-full of vehicles. Tomasetti and I park next to a white Dodge Ram pickup truck with the logo of a Wooster-based landscaping company emblazoned on the door.

We enter to the scream and bang of some chain-saw rock number I don't recognize. Every stool at the bar is occupied, mostly by men who look as if they've just gotten off work, wearing everything from oil-stained coveralls to shirts and ties. At the pool table in the back, three men in their twenties sip drafts in sweating mugs, shoot balls, and watch the nearest booth, where four college-age girls raise shot glasses in a toast. The bartender is female, in her fifties, with blond hair piled atop her head and a face full of artfully applied makeup. She's wearing a short black skirt with a white button-down shirt and an apron set snug against a nicely shaped body.

She nods at me and Tomasetti as we seat ourselves in a booth. In less than a minute, she's standing next to our table, order book in hand. "Hey, thanks for coming in tonight. What can I get you folks?"

I identify myself and pull out the photo of Rachael Schwartz. "I'm wondering if you've seen this woman."

She bends, pulls clunky readers off her crown, and squints at the photo. "Oh my God. That's the girl who was killed down there in Painters Mill."

I nod. "Have you seen her?"

"In here?" She shakes her head. "I don't think so. She's a pretty little thing. Unless I was crazy busy, I probably would have remembered her." She uses her pen to scratch her head. "When was she in here?"

"Night before last," I tell her. "Were you working?"

"I was." She looks at the photo again, gives another shake of her head. "Wish I could be more help. I sure don't like the idea of some monster getting away with something like that." She gives an exaggerated shiver. "But I didn't see her. We have dollar drafts that evening and this place was hopping."

Tomasetti pulls the redacted copy of Rachael Schwartz's credit card record from his pocket and shows her the charge. "Would it be possible for you to find the ticket for this charge?" he asks.

"We got computerized cash registers last summer. I bet Jack can come up with something. He's off tonight."

"I met him last time I was here," I tell her. "I'll give him a call."

Tomasetti motions in the general direction of the bar and pool tables. "Do you mind if we ask around?"

"Hey, knock your socks off." She tucks the pen and order book into the pocket of her apron. "Hope you find the bastard."

Tomasetti takes the bar. I meander to the pool table at the rear. The players are a lively group. Not too drunk—yet—and tickled to be talking to a female chief of police about a murder. I dig out the photo of Rachael Schwartz, but none of the young men remember seeing her. It doesn't take long for me to realize this second trip to The Pub is as big a waste of time as the first.

"No one who knew Rachael recalls her knowing anyone in the Wooster area." Frustration presses down on me as Tomasetti and I walk to the Explorer.

"On the other hand," he says slowly, "Wooster isn't too far to drive if you're from Painters Mill and you don't want to be seen together."

Tomasetti opens the passenger door, but doesn't get in. His eyes are narrowed on the service station and convenience store next door. The one with the green and white neon sign touting cigarettes, beer, and diesel.

We exchange a look over the top of the Explorer. "I'm not going to get my hopes up," I tell him.

"Worth a shot."

We get in. Behind the wheel, I put the vehicle in gear and idle over to the convenience store, park in front. I'm not even out of the vehicle yet when I notice the security camera tucked beneath the eve of the building. A bulging eye casting a disapproving glare in the general direction of The Pub.

I grin at Tomasetti. "Sometimes you earn your keep."

"That's what I keep telling you." He grins back and we head inside.

A lanky young woman with a pierced brow, arms covered with tats,

sits on a stool behind the counter, watching a game show on TV. She eyes us suspiciously as we make our way to her.

"You the manager?" I ask.

She looks me up and down. "Who wants to know?"

Tomasetti lays his ID on the counter. "The Ohio Bureau of Criminal Investigation." He motions in the general direction of the camera. "Are your security cameras working?"

"As far as I know." She cocks her head, curious. "Something going on?"

"I need the video of that west-facing camera," he tells her. "For the day before yesterday, between noon and midnight. Can you get that for us?"

"I'll have to call the owner," she tells him.

"We'll wait."

Loretta Bontrager couldn't sleep. She hadn't slept a wink since Rachael was killed. When she was a girl, her *mamm* had chided her for *aykna bang hatz*. For being an "owner of a worried heart," and for fretting about things over which she had no control. Things that her Amish faith required her to leave to God.

Aykna bang hatz.

She couldn't stop thinking about Rachael. The closeness they'd shared as girls. The laughter and love—and secrets. The memories, both good and bad. It had been almost fourteen years since Rachael left Painters Mill. In all that time, Loretta hadn't forged another relationship that even came close to the one she'd had with Rachael. A confidante she could tell anything and not be silenced or shamed. Now, Rachael was gone. Everything they'd shared was lost. She would never again hear her voice or laughter.

Tonight, contemplating her friend's death tormented her. How she

must have suffered. The terror. And pain. Dear God, she couldn't bear to think of it and yet she couldn't stop.

It was nearly midnight now, and the old farmhouse was hushed. Usually, Loretta enjoyed her evening solitude, when Ben and Fannie were safe in their beds, and she had some quiet time for reflection and prayer. Tonight, the silence was a lonely companion that made her feel as if she was the last person on earth. She should have joined her husband in bed hours ago. She'd feigned tidying up the kitchen and writing a letter to her cousin in Shipshewana, but neither of those things was the truth. She knew she wouldn't sleep and she simply couldn't bear the darkness. Not when there was already so much of it inside her. Once she laid her head down on the pillow, the images of Rachael would come to her and the dark and quiet would become intolerable.

Even now, with the sink clean and the floors mopped, the letter written and sealed, her mind whirred with images she didn't want to see, thoughts she couldn't bear to ponder. For the last two nights, desperate for peace, she'd fallen to going out to the barn. Muck boots over her socks. Her barn coat over her nightgown. Lantern in hand.

It was there, among the animals, the smells of hay and earth, that she found peace. The pygmy goats had had their babies a couple of weeks ago. The kids were tiny things, soft and warm and such a comfort to hold. The old draft mare had foaled last month, too, and the filly was a lively sprite with her *mamm*'s sense of mischief. Even the chickens roosting on the beams above the stalls calmed her nerves.

Loretta went to the goat pen first. "*Kumma do, mei lamm.*" Come here, my lamb. Bending, she leaned over the low fence to pick up the brown and white baby, her favorite. The one that melted in her arms because she enjoyed having her tummy rubbed.

She'd just lowered her cheek to the animal's muzzle when the shadow darted toward her from the darkness. Gasping, Loretta dropped the baby next to its *mamm* and stumbled back. She spun to run, but strong hands fell onto her shoulders, fingers digging in with enough force to bruise.

"Don't say a word," hissed a male voice, warm breath in her ear. "Do not make a sound. Do you understand?"

Rough hands spun her around so that she was facing him, and then he shoved her. Loretta reeled backward. Her back slammed against the wall, her head snapping hard against the wood. Simultaneously, recognition kicked, followed by a tidal wave of panic.

"You," she cried.

Lips peeled back, teeth grinding, he moved close. "Shut the hell up," he hissed.

She tried to pry his arm away, but he was too strong. All the while a thousand thoughts assailed her brain. She'd underestimated him. She'd been a fool for thinking he wouldn't come for her. She'd thought she was safe. Now, he was going to kill her.

"You lied to me," he ground out.

"No!" she squeaked.

"I heard you been talking to the cops."

"I didn't. That was before—"

He set his forearm against her throat, pressed hard enough to cut off her words. He was breathing as if he'd just run a mile. So close she could smell the stink of alcohol on his breath.

Unable to speak or breathe or even form a coherent thought, she jerked her head.

He eased some of the pressure off her throat, but he didn't release her. "What did you tell them?"

"Nothing!" she choked.

He slammed his fist against the wall inches from her head. "Don't fucking lie to me!"

The fear was like barbed wire drawn tight around her ribs. Breaths coming too fast. Chest taut. "I'm not."

"What did Schwartz tell you about that night?"

"She didn't tell me anything!" she cried.

His mouth tightened. Rage and disbelief in his eyes. Thinking about hitting her. Instead, he pulled her toward him, shook her, then slammed her back against the wall again, harder this time. Raising his hand, he jabbed his finger against her cheek hard enough to bruise skin.

"You keep your fucking mouth shut about that night. Not a word to anyone. You got me?"

She couldn't stop nodding.

He ground his teeth, looking at her as if he didn't believe her. "Nothing happened. Do you understand me? You say anything about what you *think* happened, and I'll come back. Next time, I'll kill you. I'll kill your husband. I'll kill your fucking kid. And I'll burn your goddamn house to the ground. You got that?"

"Please don't hurt them." She twisted, tried to duck away.

He clamped his hand around her throat, pressed her hard against the wall. "I'm an inch away from slitting your throat right now, you lying bitch."

She stared at him. Heart pounding. Blood raging in her veins. Terror clouding her brain. Pure evil stared back at her.

"I don't know anything," she said.

"Good. Keep it that way. Don't speak my name. Don't even think it." He lifted his hand and jabbed his finger against the side of her head. Once. Twice. Three times. "That sinking in? You got it?"

His other hand was still around her throat, crushing her windpipe, her voice box. She tried to answer, but couldn't so she nodded.

He stepped back, but didn't release her throat. She stumbled forward, set her hands on his wrist, tried to pry off his grip with her fingers, but he was too strong. He swung her around. Teeth grinding, a sound of rage gurgling in his throat, he shoved her hard.

Loretta tottered backward, struck a wood column, and went down on her backside.

Snarling a profanity, he stepped toward her, jabbed his finger at her face. "If I hear you been talking to the cops again, it's over for you."

She scrabbled back. "I won't."

"Don't make me come back," he whispered.

She didn't want to look at him, but she did. She could see his hands shaking. His finger pointing, an inch from her face. Forehead shiny and red and beaded with sweat despite the chill. Veins protruding at his temples. Spit on his lips. Breaths rushing between clenched teeth.

"Okay," she whispered.

He straightened. Shook himself as if coming out of some strange dream state. Blinking, he stepped back, looked at her as if suddenly he didn't recognize her. As if he wasn't quite sure why he was here. Abruptly, he turned and ran from the barn, disappearing into the darkness like a phantom.

CHAPTER 21

It's midnight by the time Tomasetti and I arrive back in Painters Mill. The service station owner wasn't happy at having his evening interrupted, but he met us at the station, and after a few technical issues, he provided a disk containing the security camera footage of the previous twenty-four-hour period. We're lucky, because in a matter of days, all of it would have been recorded over and lost.

I enter the station to find my newest dispatcher, Margaret, standing at the reception desk, headset clamped over brown-and-silver curls, the Painters Mill PD's policy and procedure manual open on the credenza behind her. She's updating the master file, printing everything out, and replacing the pages that have changed, something that hasn't been done since I've been chief.

"You're working late tonight," she says cheerily.

Her desk is bedecked with framed photos of grandchildren—ski vacations, summer picnics, and dogs of every shape and size. A sweating glass of iced tea and a sample-size tube of hand cream take up

159

space next to her keyboard. Not only has she turned the reception area into her home away from home, but she runs it with a level of military discipline not before seen. My officers have learned to provide her with what she needs in a timely manner—or else receive a thorough dressing-down.

"How's the P and P manual coming along?" I ask.

"Still waiting for Jodie to email me the file with the job descriptions." She punctuates the statement with a direct look over the tops of her bifocals, brows up.

"I'll light a fire," I tell her.

I hear Tomasetti enter as I unlock the door to my office. He exchanges niceties with Margaret—a meeting of two strong personalities—and I smile as my laptop boots up. I'm sitting at my desk when he appears in the doorway.

"She runs a tight ship," he says in a low voice.

"Cross her and you'll be walking the plank."

"I've no doubt."

I slide the disk into the drive and bring up the file. Instead of taking the visitor chair across from me, he rounds my desk and comes up behind me so he'll have a better view. Using the mouse, I click PLAY. The grainy footage comes to life. The camera angle is bad; the parking lot and front entrance of The Pub are too far away for us to see much in the way of detail. The lighting is far from ideal, the angle worse. On the positive side, we have a clear line of sight without obstruction.

We're champing at the bit to discover even the most minute of clues, but finding anything useful on a twenty-four-hour run of CCTV is not a speedy process. After the first hour, Tomasetti pulls up one of the visitor chairs and settles in beside me. I roll through the footage as fast as I dare. Both of us have our necks craned, eyes squinting.

One hour turns into two. At two A.M., I turn over the mouse to him and go to reception to make coffee. I've barely finished when Tomasetti calls out. "Here we go."

I return to my office and come up behind him for a look.

He backs up the footage, clicks PLAY. It's darker now, dusk, the resolution fuzzy and disjointed. Headlights flash as a vehicle pulls into the parking lot of The Pub and parks at the side of the building. My pulse jumps when I recognize it as Rachael Schwartz's Lexus. She doesn't open the door or get out. A full minute passes with no movement. Then the female driver gets out, slams the door, leans against the car door. Though I can't see her face, I can tell by the way she moves that it's her. She's wearing dark skinny pants with a cold-shoulder top. Heels. A hat cocked at just the right angle. The outfit speaks of attitude, confidence, and style, and she has mastered all of it.

"She's talking to someone on her cell," Tomasetti murmurs.

He's put on readers at some point. Black frames. The sight warms me, makes me smile. "You look good in those cheaters, Tomasetti."

He doesn't look at me, but I see his mouth twitch. "I know."

"You're pretty full of yourself, aren't you?"

"Full of something."

We turn our attention back to the screen. Rachael is still leaning against the car, cell pressed to her ear, talking animatedly, gesturing. Smoking a cigarette now. Even though it's been years since I saw her—and she was just a kid—her mannerisms are familiar. In spite of the dim light and poor resolution, it's evident that she was a beautiful, animated woman.

"We need to find that cell phone," I murmur.

"Call records would be nice." He's looking intently at the screen. "She's not happy with whoever's on the other end."

My cop's interest stirs. Though we can't make out her expression or hear what she's saying, her body language tells us she's arguing with someone. "Looks like it."

I glance at the time in the lower corner of the screen, which indicates the footage was recorded at 6:42 P.M. According to her credit card record, she had dinner with an unknown individual and paid for it with her card, just an hour later. Is she talking to her murderer? Planning to meet him? Does the argument have anything to do with her murder?

"Who are you talking to, my girl?" I whisper.

Rachael ends the call abruptly. Shaking her head, she cuffs the roof of the car with the base of her palm, then yanks open the driver's-side door and slides inside. We watch and wait, but the car doesn't move. Anticipation hums in the air between us. Two minutes pass. Six. Tomasetti scrolls, I go to the coffee station and pour two cups. I've just set them on the desk next to my laptop when I see the flare of headlights on the screen.

"Here he comes," Tomasetti says.

The glare makes it impossible to distinguish the make or model of the vehicle, let alone the license plate number.

"Come on," Tomasetti hisses.

But the driver parks on the other side of Rachael's Lexus, so that all we can see is the roof and a portion of the hood. A dark sedan. Four-door. A male disembarks. Too dark to see his face. Average height. Muscular build. He moves with the ease of a self-assured man. Comfortable with who he is. Confident. No hesitation or uncertainty.

The door of the Lexus swings open. Rachael gets out, slams it behind her. She rounds the hood, meets the man on the other side, out of sight. The footage is too grainy to see his face or discern his expression. But even to my untrained eye, his body language speaks of tension. He's much larger than her. I recall the autopsy report. Rachael Schwartz was five feet six inches tall and weighed in at 120 pounds. This man is taller by six or eight inches and outweighs her by seventy or eighty pounds. In a physical confrontation, she wouldn't stand a chance.

They exchange words. Some gesturing. Hands on hips. The tension remains, but it's more subtle now. Two adversaries facing off, aware of appearances, indications of weakness. Some elusive element simmering beneath the surface. After a moment, the male motions toward the bar. Rachael turns and looks, then shrugs. Reluctant. He motions again. This time, she throws up her hands and they start that way.

In that instant, they face the camera dead-on.

"Show us your face, you prick." Tomasetti clicks the mouse, freezing the frame. He tries to enlarge it, but the resolution becomes too grainy. Cursing, he clicks again, moving them forward frame by frame. It doesn't help.

"Any chance you have a computer guy who can bring that into better focus?" I ask.

"We can damn well try. I know one of the computer forensic guys. I'll give him a call, see if he'll meet me first thing." He checks his watch. "Let's see if Schwartz and her pal leave together."

It takes us twenty minutes to find their departure. Sure enough, Rachael and her male counterpart walk out of The Pub an hour later. This time, we catch a glimpse of their faces. It's blurred, but something pings in my brain. Something about the male. The way he moves? The way he walks? The set of his shoulders? His clothes? What?

"Freeze it," I say abruptly.

Tomasetti clicks the mouse.

"I think there's something familiar about that guy." I reach over and usurp the mouse. Back up the footage. Play it forward. "I don't know. Something . . ."

"You've met him before?" he asks.

"I'm not sure. Maybe. Something in the way he moves. There. The way he swings his arms when he walks, the tilt of his head."

"Do you mean, see-him-at-the-grocery familiar? Or maybe you've seen him around town? Or have you met him? Arrested him?"

"I don't know." Frustration sizzling, I play it again, taking it apart frame by frame.

Tomasetti waits, dividing his attention between me and the video. I turn to him. "I need a clear shot of his face, damn it. I'm pretty sure I've seen him before. I don't know him, but I've seen him. Maybe talked to him. His mannerisms are familiar."

He reaches for my laptop, presses the button to eject the disk. "Let me get to work on this."

CHAPTER 22

I'm tired to my bones, already missing Tomasetti and nearly to the farm in Wooster when my police radio barks. "Chief, I've got a ten-fourteen." Margaret uses the police code for "prowler" and then rattles off an address that's familiar—and still fresh in my memory bank.

"Is that the Bontrager place?" I ask.

"RP is Ben Bontrager," she tells me, using the abbreviation for "reporting party." "I know you're on your way home, but since they're Amish I called you instead of Mona. Do you want me to send her since she's on duty?"

"That's okay. You did the right thing." I turn round in the parking lot of a Methodist church and head that way. "I'm ten-seven-six."

One of the things my years in law enforcement have taught me is that coincidences rarely occur, especially in the course of an investigation. I've been chief in Painters Mill for about eight years now. Aside from the selling-of-unpasteurized-milk incident, my department has never been called to the Bontrager farm. And yet just outside of

165

twenty-four hours after the murder of Rachael Schwartz, I receive a call to report a prowler. Coincidence?

"We'll see," I murmur as I crank up my speed to just over the limit and run my overhead lights. In minutes I pull into the lane of the Bontrager farm. The house is lit with the yellow glow of lantern light. I keep my eyes open for movement as I barrel up the lane. There are no vehicles in sight. No one outside. I park behind the buggy at the rear of the house. I'm on my way around to the front when the back door swings open.

"Chief Burkholder?"

I turn to see Ben Bontrager standing on the porch, holding the door open, a lantern in hand.

"What happened?" I ask.

"There was a man. In the barn. A stranger. He threatened my wife. Roughed her up some." Looking distressed, he opens the door wider and ushers me through. "*Kumma inseid.*" Come inside.

"Is anyone hurt?" I ask as I enter.

"No."

"Where's the man?"

"He ran away."

"Did you recognize him?"

"I didn't see him." But his eyes skate away from mine. "*Deah vayk.*" This way.

I speak into my lapel mike and ask for assistance. "Mona, ten-fourteen. I'm ten-twenty-three the Bontrager farm. Ten-seven-eight."

Her voice cracks over the radio. "Ten-seven-six."

Ben and I pass through a back porch that's been enclosed and is being used as a laundry/mudroom. An old-fashioned wringer-style washer squats in the corner. A hat rack where four *kapp*s and a man's straw hat are hung. A clothesline decorated with men's shirts bisects the room.

Open shelving laden with canning jars. A taxidermy deer head with twelve-point antlers stares at me from its place on the wall.

"You didn't have to come, you know."

I look toward the kitchen to see Loretta Bontrager standing in the doorway, looking at me as if I'm going to pull out my .38 and cut her down. She looks shaken and pale, her nose and eyes glowing red as if she'd been crying. Even from ten feet away I see the marks on her throat.

I cross the distance between us. "Are you hurt?" I ask. "Do you need an ambulance?"

"I'm fine." She does her best to scoff, but doesn't quite manage. The look she gives her husband is fraught with recrimination. "I told you not to call. It was nothing. I'm fine."

I point at the marks on her neck. "Who did that to you?"

Giving her husband a scornful look, she turns and walks into the kitchen.

Puzzled by her response, I follow. "Loretta, what happened?"

Ben brushes past me to stand next to his wife. He sets his hand on her shoulder, but she moves aside and it drops away. An odd mix of concern and confusion infuses his expression. I notice the trousers over his sleep shirt, telling me he'd been in bed and wakened.

Loretta sinks into a chair as if her legs aren't quite strong enough to support her. "It was nothing," she tells me. "Just . . . a man down on his luck and in need of help. That's all."

I look at Ben and raise my brows.

He meets my gaze, gives a shrug. "I woke and she wasn't in our bed. I found her in the barn, crying. I saw those marks on her neck, and she told me about the man. I thought we should tell someone." He turns his attention to his wife and his mouth tightens. "Men who are down on their luck do not leave marks like that on a woman."

When Loretta looks away from him, he adds, "*Fazayla see.*" Tell her.

The Amish woman looks down at her hands and shakes her head. "I haven't slept well since . . . what happened to Rachael. So I go to the barn sometimes to see the lambs. The babies, you know." Her mouth curves as if the thought gives her comfort. "I was holding one of the newborns when a man just . . . came out of nowhere. He grabbed me." Her eyes flick away and she lowers her head, presses her fingers against her forehead. "He . . . wanted money. I told him I didn't have any and . . . he . . ." She touches the marks at her throat. "I think he didn't believe me. He shoved me. Choked me." She shakes her head. "He'd been drinking. I could smell it on his breath. I offered to give him food, but he got angry and . . . he pushed me down and then he just . . . ran out the back."

It's not the kind of crime we have here in Painters Mill. In fact, in all the years I've been chief, I can recall only two muggings. Both times it happened in the parking lot of the Brass Rail Saloon at closing time and involved individuals who'd had too much to drink.

"Did you recognize him?" I ask. "Have you ever seen him before? Around town?"

"No." She shakes her head, but doesn't look at me. "It happened so fast. And by lantern light. I didn't get a very good look at his face."

"Did he have a weapon?"

"I don't think so."

"What did he look like?" I ask. "Was he English? Amish? White? Or black?"

"English." Her brows knit. "White." She blinks as if taking herself back to a nightmare she doesn't want to revisit. "He was just . . . average looking. Scruffy. Sandy hair. Strong, though."

"Age?"

"Maybe thirty-five? A little younger than Ben and I."

168

"Height? Weight?"

She looks at her husband. "Shorter than Ben. Heavier though."

The image of the man's silhouette on the CCTV video flashes unbidden in my mind's eye. "What was he wearing?" I ask.

She struggles for a moment, then shakes her head. "Blue jeans, I think. I was so shaken up I didn't really notice."

"Was he on foot?" I ask. "Did he have a vehicle?"

"I didn't see a vehicle, but he could have parked it somewhere, I guess."

"Do you have any idea where he went?" I ask. "Do you know which direction he went when he ran away?"

Another shake. "I just saw him go out the door. At the back of the barn, the underside where the pens are. Ben woke up and . . . he ran over to the neighbor's house and called 911."

Speaking into my shoulder mike, I hail Dispatch. "I need County to assist. Ten-eighty-eight." Suspicious activity. I recite the address for the Bontrager farm. "White male. Six feet. One-ninety. May be on foot."

"Roger that."

I look at Loretta, trying to isolate the source of the sense that something about this incident isn't quite right. It's not that I don't believe her. She's visibly shaken. I can plainly see the marks on her throat. The blooming bruise on her cheek. I've no doubt *someone* accosted her. But I don't believe it was some random stranger and I don't believe he was here for money. The one thing I'm relatively certain of is that I'm not getting the whole story.

That said, like much of rural America, Painters Mill has been hard hit by the opioid epidemic. It's not out of the realm of possibility that someone looking for easy money went to an Amish farm in search of cash. It's well known most Amish keep cash on hand. It's also known that they will not defend themselves or their property. Many Amish, in fact, would hand over their cash just to help someone in need.

I look at Loretta. "Do you mind if I take a look at those marks on your throat?"

Her sigh is barely discernible, but she complies, tilts her head to one side. The flesh is abraded, the outline of fingers and a thumb visible. By morning, she'll have bruises.

"You sure you don't want to get yourself checked out at the hospital?" I ask.

"I'm fine, Katie," she tells me. "Just shaken up is all. I didn't even want to call you, but Ben thought we should. I wasn't expecting anything like that to happen out in the barn of all places, especially this time of night."

"Did the man who attacked you say anything else?" I ask.

"No, he just . . . asked for money. That's all."

I nod, but that uneasy suspicion scratches at the back of my brain again. I nod, give her a moment to say more. When she doesn't, I ask, "Is there anything else you'd like to tell me?"

The couple exchange a look. Ben leans against the counter, his arms crossed at his chest, his expression closed and grim. Loretta won't make eye contact with me, instead looking down at the floor. "I think that's about it," she says.

"I'm going to take a look around." Digging into my pocket, I pull out my card and jot my cell phone number on the back. "If either of you realize there's more you need to tell me, give me a call."

I set the card on the counter and start toward the door.

CHAPTER 23

Summer 2008

Loretta didn't know how long they danced or how many songs the band played. Twice she became separated from Rachael, but found her way back. Once, she danced with an English girl with blue hair and eyes smeared with what looked like charcoal. But the girl had a nice smile and a big laugh, and Loretta thought she'd never had so much fun in her life.

But, of course, as her *mamm* liked to say, all good things must come to an end, and as she danced next to the stage, her head began to swim. Sweat broke out on the back of her neck. When she looked at the stage, it tilted left and right and then swirled around her like some out-of-control merry-go-round. Worse, she was starting to feel nauseous. She looked around for Rachael, to tell her she needed to go get some water, but her friend was dancing with an English boy. His arms were around her waist and the way he was looking at her filled Loretta with a longing she didn't quite understand. Rachael looked so happy, Loretta decided not to interrupt and headed out on her own.

By the time Loretta reached the edge of the crowd, her stomach was seesawing. She barely made it to the nearest tent before throwing up. When she was finished, she went to the booth of the guy selling water, bought a bottle, and decided to take it to the buggy and lie down.

She got lost twice on the way. By the time she reached the buggy her head was pounding. Legs jittery, she drank half the water, and then crawled into the buggy to lie down in the back. It was cooler there and almost quiet. If she could just be still for a little while, she might be able to go back and rejoin Rachael.

"*Der siffer hot zu viel geleppert.*" The drunkard had just sipped too much.

Loretta wasn't sure how long she'd dozed. A minute or two. She sat up to see Levi Yoder standing outside the buggy, looking at her.

"You okay?" he asked.

"I'm fine."

He was looking at her bare legs, so she tugged at her skirt, ran her hand over the fabric, wishing her friend hadn't cut it. "Where's Rachael?"

"I was going to ask you the same thing." He pulled out his cell phone, squinted down at it, then looked at her. "She's late."

Loretta didn't respond. Her head was still aching, but her stomach had calmed. It was just like Rachael to be late. How could she be so irresponsible? But Loretta figured it was as much her fault as her friend's.

"I reckon we're going to have to just sit here and wait for her."

He was looking at her oddly, his head tilted to one side. The kind of look a man had when he was thinking about buying a horse; he liked what he saw, but thought he might haggle a bit before making an offer.

"I'm going to go find her." Loretta started to climb out of the buggy, but Levi blocked her way.

"What's your hurry?" he drawled.

He held a can of beer in his hand. A cigarette dangled from the side of his mouth. She didn't like the way he was looking at her.

"I don't want to get into trouble," she said.

"If she doesn't show in a few minutes, I'll go look." He flicked the cigarette away.

"My parents don't know I left," she said. "I have to go." She didn't want him to know that about her; the less he knew, the better. But she couldn't think of a better excuse to get away from him.

"I'll get you home," he said. "Don't worry."

He was blocking her way out, making her feel claustrophobic and trapped.

"Bet your pal will show any moment." He set his beer on the floorboard and started to climb into the buggy.

Moving quickly, Loretta tried to slip past him. But he was faster. His hands closed around both her biceps. Lifting her, he slid her onto the back seat. "What's your hurry?"

"Let me out," she hissed.

He grinned. "I always thought you were a cute thing," he whispered.

"I have to go." Loretta had barely uttered the words when he pushed her back and came down on top of her.

"Aw, come on," he whispered. "Just a kiss."

She turned her head just in time to avoid his open mouth. She discerned the wetness of spit on her cheek. The weight of his body, crushing against hers with such force that she couldn't breathe.

"I always fancied you," he murmured.

She tried to push him away, but he was too heavy. She twisted beneath him, tried to kick, but she was pinned. Vaguely, she was aware of him reaching between them, working at the zipper of his jeans, trying to get out his thing, his other hand sliding between her legs.

Panic unfurled inside her. Her *mamm* had warned her about boys like Levi. Don't get yourself into a mess, she'd said. Of course, that was exactly what Loretta had done. It was all her fault. How could she ever have believed sneaking out was a good idea?

"Levi, stop it!" She gasped the words, squirming, trying to keep her legs together.

In the next instant he jolted as if lightning had come down from the sky to strike his back. "What the—"

Loretta looked over his shoulder, saw movement outside the door.

"Get the hell off her!"

Rachael.

Relief moved through her like an earthquake. Oxygen bursting into air-deprived lungs. Cool water on a feverish face.

Levi raised himself up off her. Loretta caught a glimpse of him pushing his thing back into his pants. A moment later, a loud *snap!* sounded behind him.

He screamed. "Yawwww! Fuck!"

"Get off her!"

Levi was climbing out of the buggy when another *crack!* sounded, like a firecracker. He lost his footing and fell to his knees in the dust.

Loretta scrambled to the door. Rachael stood a few feet away, buggy whip in hand, fury in her eyes. In that instant, Loretta knew that while Levi Yoder might be bigger and stronger, he didn't stand a chance against her friend.

"Come on!" Rachael cried. "Run!"

Loretta didn't hesitate. She scrambled from the buggy, stumbled over Levi even as he lurched to his feet. Rachael threw down the whip and they ran.

Levi hurled expletives at them as they fled into the darkness. By the time they reached the road, both girls were breathless and laughing so hard they couldn't speak.

That was the night Rachael Schwartz became Loretta's hero. She was the only person who'd ever stood up for her. The only girl who'd ever fought for her. She was the best friend Loretta had ever had and there was nothing on this earth that could ever tear them apart.

CHAPTER 24

Day 3

There is a rhythm to a small town. An ebb and flow of a community in constant motion. A certain way of doing things. Expectations to be met. There's a set dynamic among the citizens. Reputations to uphold or cut down. Rumors to be told, stories to be embellished upon or brought to an end. If you're a cop and you're not cognizant of all of those subtleties, you're not doing your job. Having lived in Painters Mill most of my life, I also know that sometimes it's those very same undercurrents that can make my job more difficult.

It was after four A.M. when I arrived home from the Bontrager place last night. Mona and I, along with a deputy from the Holmes County Sheriff's Office, searched the entire Bontrager farm from corncrib to barn to chicken house and all the way to the fence line at the back of the property. The only indication anyone had been there other than Ben and Loretta was a single muddy footprint in the pen behind the barn. I snapped a dozen photos of it, but the ground was too juicy to pick up any tread and the images aren't going to be helpful. There was no sign of a vehicle. Nothing dropped or inadvertently left behind. Because of the hour, we couldn't canvass. I left instructions with Glock to talk with the neighbors at first light. Considering the time of the attack and that most of the farms are a mile or so apart, I'm not holding my breath.

Tomasetti spent most of the night at the police lab in London, which is just west of Columbus. He crawled into bed a little before five A.M., just as I was making my way to the shower. He let me know the information technology people at BCI are working on improving the quality of the video or at least trying to come up with some decent stills. A process that will likely take a couple of days.

I arrive at the station at seven A.M. to find Margaret's Ford Taurus parked in its usual spot. A lone buggy sits next to the car. The horse—head down, rear leg cocked, snoozing—is tethered to the parking meter. If I'm not mistaken, the buggy belongs to the Bontragers. I wonder if one of them had an attack of conscience for not telling me the whole story about the intruder last night, and decided to make things right this morning.

I enter to find Margaret standing at the reception station, six P&P manuals stacked on the credenza behind her.

Ben and Loretta Bontrager sit stiffly on the sofa, looking uncomfortable and out of place. Previously, Ben was a talkative, mild-mannered man. This morning he's stone-cold silent with a fractious air. Loretta looks as if she spent the night sleepless and crying. Her face is the color of paste, dark circles beneath troubled eyes. The marks on her neck have bloomed into bruises. Their daughter sits between them, her head on her *mamm*'s shoulder, faceless doll in her lap, unaware that this isn't the kind of visit to be enjoyed.

Loretta gets to her feet when I enter, the knitting in her lap falling to the floor. I can tell by her expression this is the last place on earth she wants to be. Something has changed since I last spoke to her and the upshot isn't good.

"Good morning," I say.

"Morning, Chief." Margaret motions to the family. "Mr. and Mrs. Bontrager arrived a few minutes ago. They'd like to talk to you if you have a few minutes."

I turn my attention to the couple. "What can I do for you?"

The Amish woman stoops to pick up her knitting, nearly drops it again. She looks flustered and on edge. I can't help but notice that her hands are shaking when she tucks the spool of yarn into her sewing bag.

"I need to tell you something," she blurts. "About last night."

"All right." I motion toward my office.

Loretta looks at Margaret and offers a tremulous smile. "If you could keep an eye on Fannie for a few minutes?"

"Sure I can," Margaret says cheerfully. "I was just going to fix myself a nice cup of hot chocolate." She looks at Fannie. "Whipped cream or marshmallow, young lady?"

The Amish girl grins. "Both."

"*Heicha dei fraw.*" Obey the woman. Loretta eases her daughter toward Margaret, but her attention is already on me and what lies ahead.

At the coffee station, I pour three cups and hand both of them a cup. I unlock my office door and we go inside. I motion them to the visitor chairs and then take my own chair at my desk.

Before I can say anything, Loretta sets down her cup. "I wasn't completely honest with you last night, Chief Burkholder. I'm sorry. I should have . . . I should have . . . Ben thought I should come in as soon as possible and set things straight."

"We didn't want to get involved in all of this, Chief Burkholder," Ben adds. "But telling the truth . . . is the right thing to do, so we came."

"I'm glad you did." Interest piqued, I wait.

Loretta sits up straighter, folds her hands in her lap, looks down at her hands. "I know who came to the barn last night. I saw his face. I know him."

"Who?"

"Dane Fletcher," she tells me. "He's a police. A deputy. With the sheriff's office."

I barely hear anything past the name, over the gong of disbelief in my head. *Fletch?* I struggle to get my mind around the notion that he assaulted an Amish woman. I've known Dane Fletcher for years. He's been with the sheriff's office as long as I can remember. He's a solid guy. A husband and father. A volunteer. Little League coach. Why in the name of God would he accost an Amish woman in her barn? It simply doesn't make sense.

"Are you telling me Dane Fletcher accosted you in the barn last night, physically assaulted you, and demanded money?"

"He didn't demand money," she tells me. "What happened last night is about . . . something else."

I stare at them, first Loretta and then her husband, and I can't imagine where this is going. Is she telling the truth? Is it possible Fletcher and this woman are involved in some sort of illicit affair?

"Loretta, you need to tell me exactly what happened," I say firmly. "All of it. Don't leave anything out this time."

She looks away, fingers a frayed thread at the hem of her *halsduch*.

"*Fazayla see,*" Ben snaps. *Tell her.*

I lean back in my chair, irritated that I've been misled, more than a little skeptical that I'm going to get the whole truth now.

"This deputy," Loretta begins. "He thinks I know something about him. Something he doesn't want me to talk about."

"It has to do with Rachael Schwartz," Ben cuts in, glaring at his wife. "Talk."

Loretta takes a deep breath, like a child who doesn't know how to swim contemplating a dive into a deep pool. "Fletcher did something bad to Rachael. A long time ago. When she was a teenager. She told me not to tell. Now . . ." She shrugs. "I think I need to tell you."

I nod for her to continue.

"When Rachael was seventeen years old, right before she was baptized, she got a job as a stocker at Fox Pharmacy and bought a car with the money she earned. It was an old piece of junk that didn't start half the time. But Rachael loved that car." She catches herself smiling at the memory, ducks her head, embarrassed. "Leave it to Rachael to do something like that, right?"

The Amish woman sighs. "She never 'officially' got to have her *rumspringa*. Sometimes the girls don't, you know. They sure didn't want Rachael having that kind of freedom. That didn't stop her. After she'd gone through *die gemee nooch geh* in preparation for her baptism, she was sneaking out almost every night. Drinking. Listening to music. Getting into trouble. My parents didn't like me spending too much time with her." Another smile, regretful and melancholy this time. "Maybe if I had . . ."

Her mouth tightens. "Toward the end of that summer, I didn't see her for a while, which was odd. She was always coming over in that old car. To visit with me, you know. Then she stopped coming. A couple of weeks passed. When she finally came by . . ."

"She took me out to the barn." Loretta closes her eyes tightly, scrubs her hand over her face. "And she told me the most horrible story I ever heard."

CHAPTER 25

Summer 2008

Rachael Schwartz was seventeen years old the night she learned how the world worked. When she understood that getting what you wanted boiled down to how much of yourself you were willing to betray.

She'd spent the day at the county fair with Loretta and what a blast it had been. At dusk, she'd ridden the Ferris wheel with the English boy she'd met last weekend. Later, she and Loretta had bought a six-pack of beer and she'd driven out to the Tuscarawas Bridge to hang out with the usual crew, a group of both English and Amish kids, and they spent the evening swimming and drinking beer.

It had been the most wonderful day of her life. No work. No worries. No one looking over her shoulder and telling her she was going to go to hell if she didn't change her ways. She'd dropped Loretta off at ten and now Rachael was on her way home. She'd never felt so free. So *alive.* It was as if her heart couldn't contain another ounce of happiness or else it would simply burst from her chest. How could God frown upon all the things that made life so wonderful?

Most Amish girls didn't do much during their *rumspringa.* Not like the boys, anyway. Rachael had no intention of wasting what little time she had. The adults were pushing hard to get her baptized. Once that happened, she was sunk. Her parents didn't approve of her running around. They didn't approve of her friends or the choices she made. They didn't approve of the job she'd taken at the drugstore in town. But it was the car that they simply couldn't abide. Datt wouldn't even let her drive it onto the property, forcing her to park it at the end of the lane. Rachael didn't care. She wasn't going to let that keep her from doing what she wanted to do. She was finally having fun. Why did they have to go and ruin it?

No one understood. Loretta tried, but she was a good girl through and through. Unlike Rachael, who'd never quite been able to follow the rules. Just yesterday Mrs. Yoder had called her *hochmut.* Who cared if she was prideful? When you were Amish, it seemed, no one approved of anything. Did God approve? She'd been wondering about that, too. Wondering if maybe the Amish had it all wrong. Maybe she'd just find her own way. If she had to leave the fold to do so, then so be it.

Tom Petty was belting out "Breakdown," the music turned up loud enough to rattle the speakers. Rachael sang along, the windows down, the night air cool on her skin, her hair flying. How was it that she'd lived her entire life without rock and roll? And boys? And beer? Thinking about how that must seem to her Amish brethren, Rachael threw her head back and laughed out loud. She turned up the radio another notch, until the knob wouldn't go any further, and she sang along with Petty, slapping her palms on the steering wheel. She was so embroiled in the music that she didn't notice the headlights behind her until they

were right on her tail. She was just a few miles from home when the red
and blue lights flashed in her rearview mirror.

"Shit!"

She was still wearing her English clothes. A can of Budweiser sweating in the console. The empty one she'd finished before dropping off
Loretta lay on the floor on the passenger side. She didn't think she was
drunk, but she'd heard about the local cops. If they caught a whiff of
alcohol on your breath, they'd make you take the sobriety test. Even if
you weren't drunk, they'd haul you to jail.

Trying to remember if she had any gum, she slowed the car and
pulled onto the shoulder. Quickly, she picked up the can of beer, looked
around wildly, and shoved it into the opening between the console and
seat, out of sight. A glance in the side-view mirror told her the cop
had gotten out and was coming her way. Unfastening her seat belt, she
lunged at the empty can on the floor and pushed it beneath the seat.

"Good evening."

Gasping, Rachael turned in the seat to see a young Holmes County
deputy standing outside her car, bent at the hip, looking in at her.
"Oh," she said. "Hi."

"Can I see your driver's license and proof of insurance please?" he
asked.

He was young for a cop. Just a few years older than she was. Professional and clean shaven with buzz cut hair and the prettiest brown eyes
she'd ever seen.

She dug into her bag for her driver's license, then checked the glove
compartment for her insurance card and handed both to him. "Was I
speeding?"

He took her license and insurance card and studied both, taking
his time answering. She'd turned down the radio and with half an

ear listened to the Petty song end and Nirvana start in. Hopefully, he wouldn't keep her too long.

"I clocked you going sixty-seven miles an hour," he said. "Do you know what the speed limit is?"

She searched her mind for the right answer. Tell him the truth? That she knew the speed limit, but hadn't been paying attention? Tell him she thought the speed limit was sixty-five? Maybe she could tell him she was late and rushing home so her parents wouldn't be angry with her. Or that she badly had to use the restroom.

She looked up at him, saw that he was looking back at her, waiting for an answer, and she smiled. "I guess I didn't realize I was going so fast."

"Well, you were." He smiled back and cocked his head. "Are you Dan and Rhoda's girl?"

"They're my parents."

His eyes landed on her English clothes. "If you don't mind my saying, you don't look very Amish tonight."

She laughed. She almost told him she was on *rumspringa*, which wasn't quite true, but thought it might lead to a question about her drinking. Better to play it safe. "I had to work today," she said. "Then I went to the movies with my girlfriend."

"Yeah? What did you see?"

"*Twilight*."

"I hear that's a good one," he said.

She began to relax. For a police, he seemed like a nice guy. Laid-back. Reasonable. Hopefully, he wouldn't give her a speeding ticket.

He stepped back and looked at her car. "Never seen an Amish girl driving a car alone on a back road at one o'clock in the morning."

"I'm on my way home."

"Parents let you stay out this late?"

She laughed. "I'm kind of late."

"They wait up for you?"

"I hope not!" She laughed again and she thought maybe he liked her and had decided not to write her a ticket. All she had to do was be nice and polite. Charm him a little, the way she saw the English girls do. She was home free.

He laughed, too, then came closer and leaned in. "You been drinking tonight?"

"I don't drink." She punctuated the statement with a laugh, but she didn't miss the nervous tick at the back of her throat. "It's against the rules, you know."

"Huh." He scratched his head, looked around. "That's what I thought." Grimacing, he turned back to her and sighed. "I still have to check. You know, do my job. Would you get out of the vehicle? This won't take too long."

Rachael didn't move. She didn't want to get out. Didn't want this to go any further. But what could she do?

"But I haven't been drinking," she said. "I just . . . want to go home."

"It'll be all right." He reached for the door handle and opened it for her. "Come on, now. A quick sobriety test and then you'll be on your way. I'm sure you'll do fine."

"Oh. Well." Not knowing what else to do, Rachael got out of the vehicle. Feeling self-conscious now. Nervous because she thought he probably knew she'd lied to him. That she'd been drinking and maybe he wasn't her new best friend after all. What was she going to do if he wrote her a ticket? Or worse, took her to jail? What would she tell her parents? What if they had to bail her out of jail? How much would it cost them?

"Here's what you need to do," he said, indicating the painted line on the shoulder of the road. "Put your arms out like this." He demonstrated. "Take nine steps, one foot in front of the other, heel to toe.

When you reach nine steps, put your head back like this." He tilted his head back so that he was looking up at the night sky. "And touch your nose with your index finger."

Rachael took in every word, a little relieved because she thought she could do it. If she could remember all those instructions. The truth of the matter was she *had* been drinking and she wasn't exactly at the top of her game. Surely she could manage something so simple. Then she would drive straight home. Even if she got a ticket, she could pay for it herself. Her parents didn't have to know. No one had to know.

He leaned against her car and crossed his arms at his chest. It was as if he was settling in to watch a movie or something. When she hesitated, he raised his brows. "Go on," he said.

Feeling self-conscious, she walked to the painted line. She took a deep breath, stretched out her arms, and began to walk, heel to toe. Two steps in and she lost her balance, missed the line by a few inches. It was the heels, she realized. She looked back at him. "It's the shoes. May I take them off?"

He was already coming toward her, reaching for something in his belt. Alarm swirled in her gut when he pulled out what looked like handcuffs. She raised her hands, felt the tears spring in her eyes. "I can do it. It's just that these heels are—"

He reached her, set his hand on her arm, slid it down to her wrist. "I'm placing you under arrest for drunk driving."

Alarm spiraled inside her when the cuff encircled her wrist. He snugged it tight. The metal hard and cold against her wrist when it clicked into place.

"Please don't arrest me." She tried to sound calm, but panic rang in her voice.

He took her other hand, pulled it behind her, and cuffed her. "Do you have any weapons on you? Anything sharp that I should be concerned about?"

"No. Please. I didn't do anything wrong. I just want to go home."

Placing one hand at her upper arm, his other on the chain connecting the cuffs, he guided her to his car. Upon reaching the trunk, he turned her toward him, and backed her up so that her backside was against the trunk.

"I'm going to do a quick pat-down to make sure you don't have any weapons on you," he said. "Just stay calm for me, okay?"

"But I'm not drunk," she said.

"We'll get it all straightened out."

She stood stone-still while he ran his hands over her hips, squeezing the pockets, turning then inside out. He removed her pack of cigarettes, lighter, cell phone, and the twenty-dollar bill she had in her back pocket.

"Please don't arrest me," she said. "I just made a mistake. Please. I'll be in such trouble."

When he was finished searching her, he stepped back. She was leaning against the car, her hands clamped together at the small of her back. He stared at her. She stared back, aware that she was shaking, and she struggled to keep it in check.

"Looks like we got us a situation," he said.

For the first time she noticed his breathing was elevated, even though he hadn't exerted himself. Sweat beaded on his forehead and upper lip. The underarm area of his uniform shirt was wet. And for the first time, she sensed something was amiss.

"Can't you just let me go?" she whispered.

Something in his expression changed. A strange light entered his eyes. His jaw flexed, as if he were biting down on something hard. "Do you think maybe we can work something out?"

She blinked, not understanding the question, but the sense that something wasn't quite right burgeoned into a different kind of alarm. And for the first time it occurred to her that she was alone with a man she didn't know or trust. They were in the boondocks in the middle of the night. . . .

"Them jeans you're wearing are sure nice and tight," he whispered.

The alarm grew into something closer to panic. The urge to run swept through her. She looked around, wondering if she could make it to the field before he caught her.

"You got nice big titties for a seventeen-year-old, you know that?"

No one had ever talked to her like that. Certainly not a grown man. An adult. The terrible understanding that followed brought with it a gasp of shock that stuck in her throat like a chicken bone.

"Hold still now. You hear?" He reached for the hem of her T-shirt and pulled it up.

Instinctively, she leaned forward, hunched her shoulders forward, tried to cover herself. But he pressed her back against the vehicle, forced her to straighten so that her breasts were visible.

"Man." He didn't even look at her. Just stared at her breasts, a starving animal watching prey in the seconds before it attacked. "Man."

"You can't do that," she cried. "It's not right. You can't."

His eyes slid to hers. "Let me tell you something, Amish girl. If I take you to jail, you'll be there for at least three or four days. A DUI will cost your parents thousands of dollars. Plus a lawyer and they ain't cheap. You'll lose your driver's license. Your car. Everyone will know. All those self-righteous Bible-thumping Amish going to shun you. Is that what you want?"

"Please don't," she cried. "I promise not to do it again. Please."

"Well, listen up. If you let me put my hands on you, I'll let you go home. No ticket. No jail. We won't tell a soul. And no one will ever know." His voice had gone hoarse, his breaths coming faster.

Rachael didn't know what to think. Didn't know what to say. Did he just want to touch her? Did he want to do something else?

"I don't want to do anything," she choked.

"Then you're going to jail. You want to know what's going to happen when you get there? They're going to take your clothes. Strip-search you and they ain't very nice about it. Keep you locked up for days. Is that what you want?"

"No." Feeling trapped, she began to cry. "What do I have to do?"

"You don't have to do anything." Slowly, he turned her around so that she was facing his car. "I'll do everything."

Clamping his hand around the back of her neck, he forced her face against the trunk lid.

CHAPTER 26

Outrage boils in my gut by the time Loretta finishes her story. I tamp it down, grapple for distance. I don't trust my voice, so I say nothing. The only sound comes from the buzz of the overhead lights, the beelike hum of my computer.

Tears stream down Loretta's cheeks. She doesn't acknowledge them. Her gaze fastens to the surface of my desk, and the silence that follows is excruciating.

"Rachael told you that?" I ask.

She nods. "A couple weeks after it happened. She didn't know what to do. I think she needed someone to talk to."

Next to her, Ben sets his elbows on his knees and looks down at the floor.

"She named Dane Fletcher?" I ask.

"Yes."

I think about that a moment. "Did she tell her parents?"

"I don't think she told anyone. I mean, she was Amish. And she was

190

out doing things she shouldn't have been doing. How could she tell anyone?"

I don't respond. Maybe because I don't want to contemplate my answer. Would Rachael's family have supported her? Would they have believed her? Or blamed her? Would her parents have gone to the police? Or would they sweep the whole, ugly incident under the rug in the hope it would go away?

"Did she seek medical help?" I ask. "Go to the doctor?"

"No." The Amish woman tightens her mouth. "She was never the same after that."

I look at her. "How so?"

"Rachael was always bold, you know." A sad smile pulls at her mouth. "The stories her *mamm* told about her when she was a little one." She turns thoughtful. "In the weeks and months after that happened to her, Rachael became even bolder. Worse, she became unkind."

I think about Dane Fletcher. The unexplained deposits into Rachael's bank account. In my mind's eye, I see the CCTV video from the gas station next to the bar in Wooster, and I realize the silhouette of the man who met with Rachael that day could very well be Fletcher's. A theory begins to take shape.

Tears shimmer in Loretta's eyes when she raises her gaze to mine. "Chief Burkholder, Rachael was barely seventeen years old. Little more than a child. Going on twenty-five, you know? She thought she could handle what happened to her. But it changed her. Changed her view of the world and not in a good way."

"Why did Fletcher show up at your place last night?" I ask.

"He knew Rachael and I grew up together. That we were friends. He must have known she told me what he did to her that night because he told me to keep my mouth shut." Her face screws up, but she fends off tears. "He threatened my family."

Ben raises his head. I catch a glimpse of anger in his eyes before he can tuck it away, out of sight. "In light of . . . what happened to Rachael," he says, "we thought you should know."

Loretta's eyes widen on mine. She blinks. And I realize she's arrived at the same conclusion as me. That Dane Fletcher and Rachael Schwartz met at the Willowdell Motel and something unspeakable ensued.

"*Mein Gott.*" Choking out a sound of dismay, she lowers her face into her hands.

In the backwaters of my mind, I see Rachael lying on the floor in that motel room. Her broken body and destroyed face. A beautiful young woman with her entire life ahead. A woman who was difficult and flawed and didn't always conduct herself in a way becoming to her Amish roots. But she damn well didn't deserve what happened to her.

"Do you think that policeman did this terrible thing?"

The question comes from Ben. He sits stiffly next to his wife, his expression a mosaic of horror and disbelief and a possibility he can't accept.

I don't answer. I can't for too many reasons to say, let alone the fact that a law enforcement officer has suddenly become my number-one suspect.

I divide my attention between the couple. "Do you know if Rachael has been in touch with Dane Fletcher?" I ask. "By phone or text? Do you know if they've met at any time over the years?"

They exchange a look and then Loretta shakes her head. "I've not heard of such a thing, Chief Burkholder. If they did, Rachael never mentioned it."

CHAPTER 27

I was eighteen years old the last time I saw Rachael Schwartz. The Fall Harvest Festival was a huge flea-market-type event for which the Amish traveled miles to set up booths or wagons, and sell their wares, everything from produce to livestock, from baked goods to quilts. For me, it was a day away from the farm and chores, a time to see my friends, and, of course, sample all that delicious Amish food. Every September, my *datt* loaded our old hay wagon and dragged me and my siblings, Jacob and Sarah, to the festival, where we spent the day selling pumpkins of every shape and size.

By the time I was eighteen, the festival had lost some of its luster. On that particular day, I escaped the watchful eye of my *datt* under the guise of a restroom break and I made my way to a not-so-bustling area on the periphery of the festival, far enough away from my Amish brethren to sneak a smoke. I was about to light up when a cacophony of raised voices interrupted my plans.

I should have known Rachael Schwartz would be involved. The

majority of festivalgoers were Amish, after all, and they simply did not partake in noisy public discourse.

At the edge of the gravel parking lot, next to a row of Port-a-Potties, Loretta Weaver pulled a wood crate filled with what looked like baked goods from the back of a wagon and carried it to her booth, where she'd set up a nice display. A homemade easel was bedecked with a big handwritten sign that proclaimed:

HINKELBOTTBOI (CHICKEN POTPIE)—$6.99

LATTWARRICK (APPLE BUTTER)—$4.99

FRISCHI WASCHT (FRESH SAUSAGE)—$3.69

KARSCHE BOI (CHERRY PIE)—$1.99 PER PIECE/$6.99 WHOLE PIE

A few yards away, two English girls had been working on their own booth, where they were selling cakes. A printed sign pinned to the front of their table read:

PERSONALIZED CAKES FOR BIRTHDAYS,

ANNIVERSARIES, AND OTHER SPECIAL

OCCASIONS. TAKE ONE HOME TODAY!

Evidently, a territory dispute had broken out between two groups of sellers.

"Hey you! Pilgrim girl! This is our spot."

An English girl of about fifteen wearing cut-off denim shorts and a Backstreet Boys T-shirt stood in front of her booth, hands on her hips, glaring at Loretta. Behind her, two gangly teenage boys stood next to the booth, watching, their expressions expectant and amused.

Loretta Weaver went to the English girl and offered a faltering smile.

"We're just selling for the day," she said reasonably. "Pies and such, you know. We can't leave until everything is sold."

A second English girl rounded the table to join them. This one wore a white blouse and pink shorts, a nifty summer hat cocked to one side. "Yeah, well, you're putting a crimp in our style with those pies. You're going to have to take it elsewhere."

Loretta shifted her weight from one foot to the other. "But this is my booth. I'm all set up. I think we'll be fine just where we are, don't you?"

Hat Girl rolled her eyes. "We paid a week's salary for this spot, and we were told no one next to us would be competing with our shit." She pointed toward the ocean of tables and sellers set up closer to the buildings. "You're going to have to move."

Loretta looked around as if expecting someone to come to her aid and help her defend her position. But no one was paying attention. She stood there, looking from one girl to the other, saying nothing.

"I don't think she heard you!" one of the boys called out.

"Send her a frickin' text!" the other boy added, and both of them broke into raucous laughter. "All those Amish hypocrites got phones!"

Loretta looked at the boys and swallowed. "We paid, too. We can't just move. This is our table. There's no place else to go."

The Backstreet Boys T-shirt girl pointed to the more crowded area at the front of the market. "I bet there's a table over there. Just go. You'll find something."

"But this is our assigned booth," Loretta said reasonably. "They told us to use this one. We can't just take someone else's spot."

"Oh my God, she's dense." Shaking her head, Hat Girl moved closer and got in her face. "Look, be a good little pilgrim, load up that buggy, and move your shit."

Loretta opened her mouth as if to say something, but closed it as if not certain how to respond. Instead, she looked down at the ground and shook her head. "I don't want any problems."

"Well, you got one," said the girl in the Backstreet Boys T-shirt.

Hat Girl looked at her friend and shook her head. "I've heard they were dense, but this is ridiculous."

"Maybe she needs some convincing!" one of the boys called out.

The other boy started to chant. "Catfight! Catfight!"

Even then, I was aware that people were occasionally hostile toward the Amish. It didn't happen often, but I'd seen it once or twice. I wasn't exactly a quintessential example of Amish values, but I knew right from wrong. I couldn't abide a bully. Loretta Weaver was a quiet, shy, and hardworking girl who'd been raised to be submissive and nonviolent. She hadn't been exposed to prejudice or cruelty. She was light-years out of her depth and probably didn't even realize it.

"Oh, for God's sake, are you fucking deaf!" Hat Girl strode to the Amish girl's booth. There, she paused, perused the items set on the table, and snatched up a jar of apple butter.

Loretta trailed her, fingering the hem of her apron, trying to stay calm, not quite succeeding.

Mean glinted in the girl's eyes. Holding up the jar, she unscrewed the lid, stuck her finger into the goo, and brought it to her mouth. "Oh my God. This is some good shit."

Loretta stiffened her spine, met the girl's gaze. "You have to pay for it now."

The two English girls exchanged looks and burst out laughing.

A cruel expression overtook Hat Girl's face. Her eyes slanted to the boys snickering from their place at her booth, then slid back to Loretta. "How much do I owe you?"

Loretta held out her hand. "Four dollars and ninety-nine cents."

Upending the jar, Hat Girl poured the apple butter onto Loretta's upturned palm.

"Oh my God, Britany!" The Backstreet Boys T-shirt girl gasped, then slapped her hand over her mouth to hide the bark of laughter that followed.

Loretta lowered her hand, the apple butter dripping unceremoniously to the ground at her feet. Saying nothing, not meeting the other girl's gaze, she pulled a wadded-up tissue from her dress pocket and tried to clean away the sticky apple butter.

I don't remember moving. Just the buzz of fury in my head. Tunnel vision on the girl with the hat. The mean in her eyes. In the back of my mind, I was visualizing myself punching that painted pink mouth.

I never got the chance.

I was still a few steps away when movement out of the corner of my eye snapped me from my fugue. I glanced over to see Rachael Schwartz charge Hat Girl. I barely recognized her. Her face was pulled into a mask of rage. She held a pitchfork in her hand.

I was closest to Loretta, so I grabbed her arm and pulled her out of the way. Rachael swung the pitchfork, slinging horse manure all over Hat Girl with such force that I heard each individual chunk slap against her face and clothes.

For the span of several seconds no one spoke. Hat Girl looked down at her clothes, at the green-brown smears and stains on her white blouse, her bare legs. "Ewww. *Ewww!*" A shudder moved through her. "Oh my God. *Ewww!* You *bitch!*"

Rachael had already darted back to where the horse stood for a second load of manure. Breathing hard, she held it at the ready. "Get lost or you're going to get it again," she said.

That was the day young Rachael Schwartz won my respect—and pilfered a little piece of my heart. Despite our age difference, I realized we were kindred spirits. She couldn't abide by the rules, didn't fit in. She was misunderstood. She broke molds. Worst of all, she was a fighter—a fatal flaw when you live among pacifists. As much as I didn't want to admit it, when I looked at Rachael, I saw myself. Hopelessly awkward, fatally flawed, incapable of pretense. Up until the day I left, I secretly cheered her on.

I lost track of her as she entered her teens, but I heard the stories upon my return. She liked boys a little too much. At seventeen, she got a job and bought that old junker she could never quite live down. It wasn't a first because she was Amish—it was a first because she was *female.* She drank more than her share of alcohol. Smoked cigarettes. Stayed out too late. Sometimes she didn't come home at all.

As an adult looking back, her fall from Amish grace makes me incredibly sad, and I realize something important. While my parents weren't perfect, they instilled in me a foundation that gave me the tools I needed to overcome the bad decisions I made early in my life. I didn't know Rhoda and Dan well, but I don't believe they did the same for their daughter. Because they viewed her as fallen, perhaps beyond redemption, they cut her off. That intolerance—that lack of guidance and support—set her on a path to self-destruction.

A truth that breaks my heart.

CHAPTER 28

One of the lessons life has taught me is that not everyone tells the truth. People lie for all sorts of reasons. To deflect blame. To protect themselves or others. To advance an agenda. To hurt someone or exact revenge. Or any combination of the above. Sometimes, those lies are told by omission. Sometimes with reluctance and guilt. Some people lie with unabashed glee. I've seen it all, but I'm not yet so hardened that I don't feel the occasional punch of shock.

No cop ever wants to believe one of his own is morally corrupt. That he's sullied the oath he took to protect and serve. I've known Dane Fletcher since shortly after I became chief. I always considered him a solid cop and a good person. He's a father of four with a longtime marriage to a Painters Mill elementary school teacher. We've worked several assignments together. Volunteered together. Once, he helped me nab a wayward herd of goats and we ended up laughing our asses off. I liked Fletch. I enjoyed working with him. Respected him. I've trusted him with my life. As I head north toward Millersburg, I'm having one hell of a time getting my head around the possibility that he used his position as a law enforcement officer to rape a seventeen-year-old girl. I can barely entertain the notion that he beat a young woman to death with a baseball bat.

The possibilities turn my stomach. The cop inside me wants to disprove it. But outrage and disappointments aside, I know from experience that sometimes outwardly decent people harbor a shadow side. They keep the darkness of their nature—weaknesses, perversions, addictions, immoralities—hidden from the rest of the world.

Is Dane Fletcher one of them?

Because of the sensitive nature of the accusations and the fact that he's an LEO with another agency, I can't move forward until I involve the Holmes County sheriff. I call Mike Rasmussen as I head north toward Millersburg and tell him I'm on my way to meet him. He agrees—reluctantly. He's got a golf outing with the mayor later in the day and he doesn't want to miss it. I assure him I won't take up too much of his time; I don't let on that I'm about to blow his day to smithereens.

I call Tomasetti as I reach the outskirts of Millersburg. "Where are you?" I ask.

"Where would you like me to be?" he returns evenly.

"How about the Holmes County Sheriff's Office?" I give him the highlights of my meeting with the Bontragers.

When I'm finished, he makes a sound of disgust and asks, "How well do you know Fletcher?"

I tell him. "It would be an understatement to say I'm shocked."

"Any strikes against him?"

I search my memory, realize there were a few minor incidents that never went anywhere, and I feel a churning of uneasiness in my gut.

"I think a woman filed a complaint about him several years back. If I recall there was some question about her credibility and nothing came of it."

The silence that ensues brings with it a creeping dread that climbs up the back of my neck like some slimy worm.

After a moment, he sighs. "I'll be there in ten minutes."

The Holmes County Sheriff's Office is located north of Millersburg, a few miles past Pomerene Hospital. I'm in the process of signing in with the duty deputy when Mike Rasmussen opens the door and leans out.

"Hi, Kate."

I look up from the clipboard to see the sheriff standing outside the door, grinning at me. He's out of uniform, wearing a pink polo shirt, khaki slacks, and golf shoes. "Hey, Mike."

"You want to play golf with us?" he asks. "Proceeds go to the animal shelter. Save a lot of puppies."

I can tell by the way he's looking at me that he's noticed something in my expression and it's given him pause.

"Last time I played golf with you I embarrassed myself." I cross to him and we shake hands. He opens the door wider and ushers me into the hall. Side by side, we make our way to his office.

There, he motions to the visitor chair adjacent to his desk, and he slides into the chair at his desk. Grimacing, I go to the door and close it.

"Must be bad," he says.

"And then some." I take the chair. "I think Dane Fletcher may be involved with the murder of Rachael Schwartz."

"*What?* Fletch?" He starts to laugh, realizes belatedly that I'm not kidding, and blinks hard at me. "Are you serious?"

Over the next minutes, I relay my conversation with the Bontragers.

When I'm finished, Rasmussen leans back in his chair, his arms folded at his chest, staring at me as if he'd like nothing more than to pull out his sidearm and shut me the hell up.

"If I didn't know you so well, Kate, I'd throw you out of my office."

"Yep." I sigh. "Me, too."

"Do you believe this Amish couple?" he asks.

"I believe them enough so that we need to look at it. Get to the bottom of it."

A knock sounds on the door. Cursing beneath his breath, Rasmussen gets to his feet and yanks it open. He doesn't bother greeting Tomasetti and goes back to his desk, falls into the chair.

Taking his time, Tomasetti nods at me and then takes the visitor chair next to mine. "I take it you told him."

I nod, look at Mike. "I need to talk to Fletcher." I glance at Tomasetti. "We need a warrant. I want his phone records and his banking records."

Rasmussen makes a sound of annoyance. "Based on hearsay? Based on secondhand information of something that allegedly happened almost thirteen years ago? By a woman who may or may not be telling the truth? You want to ruin a man's reputation based on that?"

"I have no intention of ruining anyone's reputation," I snap. "But I have a murder to solve."

Ignoring me, he looks at Tomasetti. "Dane Fletcher is a good cop, goddamn it. He's married with a family. Been with the department for seventeen years." He turns his rankled expression on me. "You'd better be damn sure about this before you pull him into this."

"I'm as sure as I need to be." Even as I say the words, I feel the doubt crowding that certainty.

Cursing, Rasmussen slaps his hand down on the desk.

"I don't like it either, Mike," I say. "But we have to talk to him. There's no way around it."

"I don't believe he had anything to do with that girl's murder," Rasmussen says between gritted teeth.

"At the very least, we need to talk to him about the allegation of what happened between him and Rachael Schwartz."

Rasmussen says nothing.

Tomasetti cuts in. "We looked at Rachael Schwartz's banking records. She was living above her means. Way above her means. There were several substantial cash deposits made in the last year. We're trying to find the source, but as you know it's nearly impossible to trace cash."

"So you think she was blackmailing him?" Incredulity rings hard in Rasmussen's voice. "And he murdered her?"

"That's motive. A powerful one if you consider the amount of those deposits, not to mention what word of this would do to him. We're talking professional ruination. Loss of his family. If not jail time."

"We gotta look at him," Tomasetti says.

Rasmussen receives all of it with stony silence.

I look from man to man. "I need to talk to him."

"Why don't we take a look at Fletcher's file and then see if we can ascertain where he was on the night of the murder?" Grimacing, Tomasetti looks from me to the sheriff. "I'll get things rolling on a warrant."

Rasmussen scowls at me. "I'm assuming you already know he's had a couple of complaints filed against him over the years." He looks at Tomasetti. "Nothing came of either complaint due to lack of proof. Sort of a he-said, she-said thing."

"Duly noted," Tomasetti says.

With a curse, the sheriff gets to his feet. "I'll pull his file."

Access to confidential personnel records is an extremely sensitive issue and involves many potential legal concerns. For some municipalities, it requires the involvement of a police union representative.

But due to the seriousness of the situation—in this case a homicide investigation—we've no choice but to proceed. Because both Tomasetti and I are from outside law enforcement agencies—not coworkers in the same department as Fletcher—and a warrant is in the works, we are deemed fair to look at records that we would otherwise be prohibited from viewing.

Half an hour later the three of us are sitting in a small, stuffy interview room, Dane Fletcher's personnel file open on the table in front of us. Rasmussen goes through the file page by page, passing the occasional document to Tomasetti and me.

"Fletch was off duty the night of the murder," Rasmussen tells us. "He worked first shift that day. Got off at four P.M." He flips through several pages, skimming and reading, and passes another sheet to Tomasetti. "Here's the first citizen complaint form."

Tomasetti hits the highlights aloud. "Three years ago. Female complainant. Twenty-two-year-old Lily Fredricks of Portsmouth, Ohio. Pulled her over at two A.M. for a possible OVI," he says, using the acronym for "operating a vehicle impaired." "Vehicle smelled of marijuana. Fredricks claimed Fletcher offered to let her walk if she had sex with him. She refused. Became combative. He made the arrest. Her blood alcohol was point-one-nine. She was charged with OVI and possession of marijuana." He flips the page. "She filed the complaint a few days later. The department opened an investigation, sent it to the Holmes County prosecutor's office, who declined to prosecute."

I look at Tomasetti. "We need to contact her."

He writes down the information. "Yep."

Rasmussen hands him another sheet of paper. "Second citizen complaint form."

Tomasetti reads. "Six years ago. Female complainant. Nineteen-year-old Diana Lundgren. Pulled over for speeding and possession of a controlled substance. She claims Fletcher asked her for sex in exchange for letting her walk. He detained her, kept her handcuffed. She claims he raped her outside his cruiser. Investigation ensued and she was deemed unreliable. Evidently, she's got a lengthy criminal record and a history of drug use."

I look at Mike Rasmussen. He's a good sheriff and a good cop. Like most men and women in law enforcement, he's protective of his subordinates. But he also possesses the strength of character to do the right thing even when that means taking down one of his own.

"Damn, this is a mess," he mutters.

"I want to talk to Fletcher," I say.

"The instant he asks for a union rep or a lawyer, we shut it down," Rasmussen tells me. "You got that, Kate?"

"We got it," Tomasetti puts in.

We get to our feet and head toward the door.

CHAPTER 29

Dane Fletcher owns a pretty little place just south of Millersburg. The house is a newish brick ranch that sits on a three-acre lot dotted with maples and oaks. Tomasetti and I take separate vehicles, follow Rasmussen into the gravel driveway, and park adjacent to the garage.

I meet the two men next to a lamppost where a pavestone walkway leads to the front door of the house. A tricycle lies on its side in the yard. Yellow tulips in the flower beds on either side of the door are starting to bloom. Someone in the Fletcher household has a green thumb.

Rasmussen had wanted to call Fletcher and ask him to meet us at the sheriff's office, probably to save him from any questions he'll likely get from his wife. But due to the seriousness of the allegations, Tomasetti and I thought it would be better to catch him unaware. The plan is to pick him up here and transport him to the sheriff's office so he can answer our questions in the privacy of an interview room. The only thing I know for certain at this moment is that the hours ahead are going to be difficult for everyone involved.

"I'll get him." Rasmussen has just started down the sidewalk when the door opens.

Dane Fletcher steps onto the porch. His smile falls when he sees the expression on Rasmussen's face. He looks past the sheriff, his eyes holding mine for an instant, and I see a skitter of fear whisper across his features. *He knows,* I think, and a hard pang of disappointment joins the chorus of emotions banging around inside me.

"Mike?" he says. "What is this? What's going on?"

"We need to talk to you, Dane." The sheriff reaches him and the two men shake hands.

"About what?" the deputy asks.

"Dane?"

At the sound of the female voice, I look toward the back door to see a pretty woman of about forty standing in the doorway, holding open the storm door. Her expression is more curious than worried as she presses her hand against her very pregnant belly.

"Hey, Mike," she says to the sheriff, oblivious to the undertones zinging among the rest of us.

"Hi, Jen." Rasmussen raises a hand to her. "Tulips looking good," he says conversationally. "I need to borrow the old man for a few hours. Can you spare him?"

She grins. "As long as he comes home with ice cream, we're good."

"I'll get it." Fletcher doesn't look at his wife as he says the words.

"Barbecue this weekend!" she calls out.

Rasmussen has already turned away and started toward his cruiser. No one else responds.

At the sheriff's office, I sit in the Explorer, my hands on the steering wheel, and I watch Fletcher and Sheriff Rasmussen cross the parking lot and enter the building. The sense of betrayal is a knot in my gut. At the moment, that knot is so tangled and tight that I can barely draw a breath. In my mind's eye, I see the way Fletch looked at me when he came out of the house. I'd had misgivings about the allegations against him. I thought maybe the four of us would walk into the interview room and somehow Fletch would convince us he had nothing to do with what happened to Rachael when she was seventeen—or her murder. But I saw the flash of fear and guilt etched into a face well trained to remain neutral, and the truth of that moment is so powerful I'm queasy.

I think about what he did and the anger inside me roils. Not only did he betray the badge, but he betrayed himself and everyone who loves him. His family. His friends. And every single cop who's ever considered him a brother.

A knock on the window startles me from my reverie. I glance over, see Tomasetti standing outside the Explorer. Quickly, I settle my emotions and get out, aware that his eyes are on me.

"I'd ask what you're thinking," he says, "but I'm not sure I want to know."

"You don't."

"I wouldn't want to be in Fletcher's shoes."

"You could never be in his shoes." The statement comes out harshly, but I let it stand.

Thoughtful, troubled, we start toward the building. "Those women who filed complaints against him?" I don't look at Tomasetti as I speak. "He sexually assaulted them. He abused his position. I think he sexually assaulted Rachael Schwartz. Tomasetti, for God's sake, I think he murdered her."

"She was blackmailing him," he says. "He got tired of paying."

I nod, trying to get myself into a better frame of mind for the impending interview. I don't quite manage.

"That's a powerful motive." Tomasetti shrugs.

"He had a lot to lose," I add.

There's more to say, but we've reached the building. Through the door window, I see Rasmussen and Fletcher talking to the duty deputy. Tomasetti pushes open the door and we walk inside.

Twenty minutes later, the four of us are sitting in an interview room with a beat-up table and four plastic chairs. Rasmussen and Fletcher are on one side of the table, Tomasetti and I on the other. Life and experience have given me the tools I need to keep my emotions in check. Even so, I'm barely able to look at Fletcher. I'm too angry to be sitting here, partaking in a potentially life-altering interview of a peer. But this is my case. I don't have a choice.

When the small talk ends, Fletcher sits back and makes eye contact with each of us, his final gaze landing on Rasmussen. "So are you going to tell me why I'm here or are you going to make me guess?"

Rasmussen tosses me an it's-your-show scowl and spits out my name. "Kate."

I focus on the turn of events alleged by Loretta Bontrager, and I don't pull any punches. I withhold mention of Rachael Schwartz, instead focusing on what was alleged to have happened in the barn. All the while, I watch Fletcher for a reaction.

He stares back at me, stone-faced. But he can't hide the color that climbs up his throat and creeps into his cheeks. The muscles in his jaws clamping tight and working in tandem.

When I've finished speaking, he takes a moment to make eye contact with each of us. "That did not happen," he says in a low voice. "I did not threaten her. I did not assault her. I didn't so much as *talk* to her. I don't know those people. I did not drive out to their place last night." His eyes land on mine. "And I'd like to know why the holy fuck you dragged me in here for this rash of bullshit."

"She filed a complaint against you," Rasmussen tells him.

"That's crazy." Fletcher belts out a bitter laugh. "Why the hell would I go to their farm and assault an Amish woman?"

He knows instantly the question is a mistake. I see the regret flash in his eyes. He starts to speak, but I cut in.

"Bontrager claims that Rachael Schwartz told her you pulled her over for an OVI thirteen years ago," I tell him. "She alleges Schwartz told her that you let her walk in exchange for sex. She alleges in the complaint that you knew they were friends and you assumed Rachael had told her what happened. Bontrager claims you accosted her in the barn and threatened her if she didn't keep her mouth shut."

"That's not true," he says. "She's lying."

I lean back in my chair. "Where were you last night between the hours of midnight and four A.M.?"

Fletcher chokes out a sound of exasperation. "I was home. With my wife and kids."

"All night?" Tomasetti asks.

"All night," Fletcher echoes.

"You know we're going to check," Tomasetti says.

"Stay the hell away from my wife." Fletcher's eyes flick to Rasmussen. "Are you going to let them run with this? Ruin me? My marriage? My reputation?" He shakes his head. "Mike, you're going to let them move forward with this bullshit based on accusations made by someone I don't even know? Someone I've never met? I'm telling you right now, Bontrager made the whole thing up. I wasn't anywhere near their place."

Rasmussen shrugs. "You know we've got to look at it."

Fletcher smacks his hand against the tabletop. "This is bullshit."

"Did you ever initiate a stop on Rachael Schwartz?" Tomasetti steps easily into the bad-cop role.

"You mean thirteen years ago?" Fletcher shakes his head, angry. "I don't remember. How could I?" Mouth pulled into a snarl, he looks at me. "The one thing I do know for certain is that I sure as hell didn't demand sex!"

Tomasetti doesn't give him a respite. "You have two similar citizen complaints on your record."

"So do a lot of cops," Fletcher snaps. "Those two women lied. It's on record. Nothing came of either incident. I resent it being brought up now."

For the span of a full minute no one speaks. So far, we've danced around the subject of Rachael Schwartz's murder. I can tell by the way he's looking at me that he knows there's more coming.

"So if we take a look at the tread marks we picked up at the Willowdell Motel," Tomasetti says slowly, "and footage from the game cam in the field across the road, we're not going to see you or your vehicle, right?"

He glares at Tomasetti, nostrils flaring with every elevated breath. Fury in his eyes. But I catch a glimpse of a chink in the veneer. Beneath all that anger is uncertainty—and fear. Of course, there were no viable tire-tread marks picked up at the scene. Nor is there a game cam in the field across the road. Fletcher doesn't know either of those things.

"You're not going to find shit because I've done nothing wrong." He looks at Rasmussen. "This is bullshit, Mike. I can't believe you've let this charade go this far. For God's sake I've been with the department for seventeen years and this is the thanks I get?"

"Did you ever meet Rachael Schwartz?" I ask.

"I don't think so," he says. "I don't recall."

Another silence, this one filled with unbearable tension, like a razor slicing skin.

After a moment, Tomasetti sighs. "Dane, we're looking at her banking records," he says quietly. "Yours, too."

Fletcher's Adam's apple bobs. "This is a fucking hack job."

Tomasetti stares at him, saying nothing.

"Fletch." I utter the nickname even before I realize I'm going to address him.

His eyes shift to mine.

"If you want to help yourself," I say, "tell us the truth now. You're a good enough cop to know we're going to figure it out."

"Don't patronize me, Burkholder," he snarls.

It's so quiet I can hear the whistle of quickened breaths through nose hair. The creak of a chair as someone shifts.

I look at Fletcher. He's slouched now. Head down. Elbows on the table. Hands laced at his nape, staring at the tabletop. A beaten man who knows the worst is yet to come.

Up until now, this has been an information-seeking mission. The longer we talk to Fletcher, the more apparent it becomes that this undertaking now has three levels. What happened between him and Loretta Bontrager last night. What occurred between him and Rachael Schwartz thirteen years ago. And what may or may not have happened between them the night she was murdered.

For the first time I notice the sheen of sweat on his forehead. The damp rings beneath his arms. He looks at Rasmussen. "If that's the way you're going to play this, Mike, I guess I need a lawyer."

Dane Fletcher is not under arrest. We don't have enough evidence to hold him. I have no idea how any of this is going to end. The one thing I do know is that when he walks out of this room, he will not have a badge. Whether he is put on administrative leave, suspended, or fired is up to Rasmussen and policy.

"That's your right," the sheriff tells him.

"Union rep, too."

"You got it," the sheriff tells him.

Fletcher rises, takes a moment to pull himself together, gather his composure. Eyes on his boss, he removes the Glock from his holster and lays his badge on the table.

"There you go, you sons of bitches," he says.

He turns and walks from the room.

CHAPTER 30

Day 4

Early in my career, the resolution of a case—the bringing of a bad actor to justice, the closure for the victim's family, the satisfaction that comes with the knowledge of a job well done—was one of the simple and straightforward highlights of being a cop. Now that I'm older, with a few years of experience under my belt, none of those things are quite as cut-and-dried. Rachael Schwartz is still dead, her life cut short years before her time. A colleague, a man I'd worked with for years and trusted with my life—a husband and father of four young children—will likely be spending the rest of his life in prison. And for what? Money? Lust?

It's been twenty-four hours since Tomasetti, Mike Rasmussen, and I questioned Fletcher. We let him walk because we don't have enough hard evidence to arrest him. But it's coming. We procured a search warrant and confiscated his cell phone and laptop. Banking records are in the works. I spent most of the last day combing through everything I've got so far. I'm not sure if I'm looking for something that will exonerate him—or put that last nail in his coffin so I can drive it in my-self. Do I believe he forced a seventeen-year-old Rachael Schwartz into having sex with him in exchange for letting her go? Considering the two complaints on file—and later dismissed—and the detailed state-ment from Loretta Bontrager, I do, indeed, believe he's guilty. If it's true, Fletcher is a sexual predator, a disgusting excuse for a man, and a dishonor to everyone in law enforcement. As unscrupulous as that is, I simply can't get my head around the notion of him beating Rachael Schwartz to death in that motel room.

"You look like you could use some good news."

I glance up to see Tomasetti standing at the doorway to my office, his head tilted, looking at me intently.

Despite my somber mood, I smile, liking the way he's standing there with his arms crossed, his leg cocked. "A little good news would go a long way right now."

He crosses to my desk and lowers himself into the visitor chair adja-cent to me. "The IT techs hit the jackpot on Schwartz's laptop."

I sit up straighter. "Fletcher?"

"We got him." He produces his cell and taps the screen a few times. "They found texts and emails. Deleted, but easy enough to recover."

Rising, he comes around my desk to stand beside me, sets his hand on the back of my chair. I look at the screen, find myself staring at what appears to be copied texts. The first three transmissions are from Rachael Schwartz, sent on the same day, just a few minutes apart.

What is the age of consent in the state of Ohio?

Wifey has a nice Facebook page. I didn't know she was preggers! Congrats!

Bet she'd be pissed if she found out you'd pulled over and raped a 17 year old Amish girl.

No reply.

The next day, from Schwartz:

She posted pics of you and the kids. Didn't know you guys had a pool.
Nice!
Like her accent. Where is she from? Australia? London?

I look at Tomasetti. "Fletcher's wife is from New Zealand," I tell him.
He scrolls down to the next exchange.
From Fletcher:

You call my house again and I will fucking bury you. You got that?

From Schwartz:

Don't be such a pussy. Just messing with you.

"She's taunting him," Tomasetti murmurs.
"Doing a pretty good job of it," I say, but I can't take my eyes off the screen as he scrolls to the next exchange.
This one is from Schwartz and comes the next day at two A.M.

I see yur still a deputy with Holmes County. I wonder how Sheriff Rasmussen would feel if he nu U sodomized me in the back seat of yur cruiser?

No reply.

Bet yur sweating right now.
I'm going to call him.
330-884-5667

Recognizing the number, I look at Tomasetti. "That's Rasmussen's home number."

Fletcher doesn't reply.

Rachael Schwartz doesn't stop.

Maybe I'll just show up and tell him everything. Maybe I'll show up at your house and tell your pretty little wife what you do to little girls when you pull them over.

Finally, Fletcher responds.

You show up here and I'll put a fucking bullet in your head. You got that?

From Schwartz:

Don't be so sensitive! I'm jus kidding.
In case you're thinking about going all batshit . . . don't forget I got that insurance policy. Anything unsavory happens and presto! Out comes the proof.

"So they talked at some point," Tomasetti says.

"What proof is she referring to?" I ask.

"Be nice to know, wouldn't it?" he mutters. "I've no doubt we'll figure it out." He sighs. "There's more."

So if you can afford that pool you can afford to pay me a little some-thing for keeping my piehole shut all these years.
How much you got saved?
How much is your marriage worth?
How much is your job worth?

No reply from Fletcher.

Tomasetti backs out of the file and goes to the next. It looks like a listing of phone numbers. "I pulled these numbers from their devices. I compared time of day with the numbers. Fletcher called her the day after those texts were sent. They talked for six minutes."

He angles the phone so I can see the next item. I find myself looking at what appears to be some kind of financial statement.

Tomasetti continues, "Two days later, Fletcher withdrew three thousand dollars from his savings account. He withdrew another two thousand from an investment account."

He thumbs through a few more screens. "The following day, Rachael Schwartz deposited five thousand bucks into her checking account."

He flicks off the phone and returns to the chair. When he looks at me his expression is sober. "There's more, Kate. Over the last six months, she's called his house a dozen times. Calls last only a minute, so they're probably hang-ups. She hounded him, posted things on Jennifer Fletcher's social media pages. I spent half the night reading some really raw and disturbing text and email exchanges. She threatened him dozens of times. She wanted money for her silence. He'd paid her up to about twelve thousand. He threatened to kill her twice."

The information settles into my gut with the power of a stomach virus. "We have motive," I say.

"The CCTV footage at the bar in Wooster?" he says. "Expert says the car that pulled in belongs to Fletcher's wife. We enlarged it, got the plate number as it was pulling into the lot. We had an expert look at the video. He says the silhouette of the male is likely Fletcher."

"They met at the bar the day she was murdered," I say.

He nods. "A few hours later, she was dead."

We stare at each other for the span of a few heartbeats and then I reach for the phone on my desk. "Let's get the arrest warrant."

CHAPTER 31

As police chief of a small town, I deal with the occasional sticky situation that requires some degree of discretion. My department is good at maintaining confidentiality when necessary, especially when it comes to protecting someone's safety. But secrets are tough to keep in a small town. When a neighbor sees a police car pull up to someone's house—even with the overhead lights off—they want to know what's going on.

I don't expect any trouble from Fletcher. He's a stable guy with four kids at home and a wife who's expecting their fifth. Still, I've dealt with enough high-stress situations to know that when Mr. Even Keel realizes his life is about to unravel, he can come unhinged.

In my rearview mirror, I see Tomasetti pull up behind me, a Holmes County deputy behind him. I get out and we meet on our way to the front door.

"You talk to Rasmussen?" he asks.

I nod. "He's on his way."

We reach the front porch. I've just pressed the doorbell when the door opens. Jennifer Fletcher appears. She's wearing a yellow and white maternity dress. Huge belly. House shoes. Hair pinned atop her head. Her smile falters at the sight of us.

"What's going on?" Her voice rises a pitch with each word. "Is it Dane? What's—"

It takes me a second to realize she thinks we're here to inform her that her husband has been hurt on the job. It's a normal reaction. It's sad because he didn't fill her in on what's going on or warn her that he's in serious trouble.

"He's not hurt," I say quickly. "We need to talk to him. Is he home?"

"Oh." She sags, presses a hand against her chest. "Whew! You guys scared me for a second." Still, she knows there's something wrong. She pauses, cocks her head. "Is everything all right?"

I hear kids playing in the background. Splashing in the pool out back. A dog yapping. Laughter. The smell of popcorn wafting out. And I feel a wave of anger toward Fletcher because he had it all—and squandered it.

"We need to talk to Dane," I tell her. "Is he here?"

She blinks, worried now. Confused because she's realized this isn't a friendly visit and we're not going to go away until we get what we want. "He took Scotty to the Little League game, down at the elementary school." She glances at her watch. "They should be back any minute. Want to come in and wait?" She laughs. "Fill me in?"

Neither of us responds as we follow her into the house. Glossy wood floors. Open concept. Crisp gray paint on the walls. The kitchen is large and well used, with newish appliances. A plastic truck tossed haphazardly on the dining room floor.

Jennifer pauses at the island that separates the kitchen from the living room and turns to us. "I wish you'd tell me what's going on. You guys are starting to worry me."

I look through the window, see three kids splashing in the pool outside, oblivious to what's about to unfold, and I silently curse Dane Fletcher. How could a man who has so much—a family—children who need him—destroy it? And for what?

"Dane's in trouble," I tell her. "It's serious. We have a warrant for his arrest. That's all I can say at this point."

"What?" She pales, an odd shade of pink rising to her cheeks. "I'm going to call him." Spinning away from us, she rushes to the island, picks up her cell.

I look at Tomasetti. "I'm going to go get him." I lower my voice. "Keep an eye on them, will you?"

Argument flares in his eyes. The scowl that follows tells me he doesn't like the idea of me picking up Fletcher alone. "Take the deputy," he says.

"Okay."

"Who's on duty?" he asks.

"T.J."

"Call him, will you?"

"Yep." Taking a final look at Jennifer, I head toward the door.

I hail T.J. en route to the school and fill him in on the situation, ask him to meet me there.

The Painters Mill elementary school was built back in the 1960s at the height of the mid-century-modern phase of architecture. It's a two-story building fabricated of mud-yellow brick and mullioned windows set back from the street in a treed lot the size of a football field. A big sign stands guard in front, next to the flagpole, and proclaims: PANTHER COUNTRY!

I pull around to the rear of the building. Ahead is the baseball diamond, replete with freshly painted bleachers, overhead lights for night games. There's a small clapboard concession stand that sells soft drinks and hot dogs during games. Closer to the school is the public

221

pool—not yet open for the season, but there's a good-size pool house and a cinder-block public restroom. A dozen or so cars are parked in the gravel lot on the south side. I idle through and spot Fletcher's Focus at the end of the row. No one inside. I park next to it and get out.

The deputy parks next to me and we meet at the rear of his cruiser. "See him?" he asks.

I shake my head, motion toward the restroom and pool house. "Want to check in there?"

"Yeah," he says, and heads that way.

It's nearly dusk now. Golden light slants down through the treetops as I make my way toward the diamond. The quiet is punctuated by the shouts and squeals of children playing baseball and the occasional bark of an overzealous mom or dad. It's an innocent scene, but when a young batter smacks out a single, I find myself thinking of the bat used to murder Rachael Schwartz.

I speak into my shoulder mike. "Ten-twenty-three," I say, letting Dispatch know I've arrived on scene. "I got eyes on our ten-fifty. T.J expedite."

"Roger that," comes T.J.'s voice, telling me he's on his way. "Ten-seven-seven ten minutes." He's ten minutes away.

My uniform draws a few stares as I approach the bleachers. I answer those stares with a wave. A dozen or so moms and dads watch their kids play. A couple of Labrador puppies wrestle in the grass behind the bleachers. No sign of Fletcher. I look toward the field, try to ascertain if his son is one of the players, catch sight of him at the shortstop position, his eyes on the batter who's just stepped up to the mound.

I stroll between the chain-link fence and the bleachers, trying to look nonchalant. One of the coaches glances my way and waves, but I can tell he's wondering why I'm here. I'm relieved he's too busy to talk.

Where the hell is Fletcher?

I reach the end of the bleachers and head toward the concession stand. A girl with a nose piercing, the tattoo of a rose on her throat, lowers a strainer of fries into a vat of boiling oil. I go to the window. "Any fries left?" I ask.

"Going to be four minutes," she says without looking at me.

"Have you seen Dane Fletcher?" I ask. "The deputy?"

The girl straightens. She looks bored. Put out by her job. Annoyed that I'm requiring her attention. "The cop?"

I nod. "You seen him?"

She raises a ring-clad hand and points toward the park across the street. "I think he went over to the park a few minutes ago."

"Thanks." I head that way.

Creekside Park has been around as long as I can remember. There's a playground replete with monkey bars and a slide. In summertime, a fountain featuring a giant catfish spurts water and beckons kids to wade or toss pennies for good luck. There's a hiking path with a footbridge that crosses a small, trickling stream that eventually feeds into Painters Creek. All six acres of it is crowded with old-growth trees that were likely here before Painters Mill became a village back in 1815.

I make my way to the trailhead, where a sign reminds me to bring water and mosquito repellent if I plan to hike. I look down at the damp earth at my feet and see the footprints. Male boots with a waffle sole. Cop's boots, I think, and I start down the path.

I've gone just a few yards when I find him. He's standing on the footbridge, leaning, his hands on the rail, looking into the forest. I stop twenty feet away. "Nice night for a softball game," I say.

He looks at me. Something not right about his eyes. "Scotty's going to be a good hitter."

"Like his dad, I guess."

He nods, keeps his hands on the rail. He's wearing khaki pants. A short-sleeved shirt, untucked. The sheriff took his service revolver, but I know he owns a pistol. I wonder if said pistol is tucked into the waistband of his slacks. I wonder how close he is to the end of his rope.

He lowers his eyes to the trickling water. Not looking at anything in particular. His body language is off. He knows why I'm here.

"I saw a fox a few minutes ago," he tells me.

"They're out here." I pretend to look around. Hold my ground. Wait.

"I figured you'd show up sooner or later," he tells me.

"You know I don't have a choice," I tell him. "I'll make this as easy as possible for you, if that's any consolation."

"It's not." The laugh that follows is the harsh sound of ripping fabric. "Does Jen know?" he asks, referring to his wife.

"Not yet."

Silence descends. As thick and uncomfortable as a wet blanket on a freezing night. We listen to the spring peepers for a moment and he seems to relax, as if he's made some decision.

He steps back from the rail, reaches beneath his shirt. My heart rate jacks at the sight of the pistol. It's a semiauto H & K .45. Quickly, I slide out my sidearm, level on him, center mass.

"Dane." I say his name firmly. "Your son is playing baseball fifty yards away. You don't want to do this to him. Put down the gun."

He doesn't raise the pistol, but holds it at his side. At first, I think he's going to obey my command and toss it. But his finger is inside the guard.

"Come on," I say. "You know I'll do right by you."

He doesn't seem to hear me. Doesn't seem to care that I've got a bead on him and he has zero in the way of cover.

He turns to me, looks at me as if seeing me for the first time. "I didn't kill her," he tells me.

"No one said you did."

"Don't patronize me," he snaps. "I know how this works."

"I don't know what you want me to say to that. All I can tell you is that it isn't too late to end this. Put down the gun. Talk to me. We'll figure this out. Okay?"

He cocks his head, trying to decide if I'm bullshitting him. "It's over for me. This isn't going to go away."

"You made a mistake," I tell him.

"It's all going to come out. For God's sake, it'll destroy Jen and the kids."

"We'll deal with it. They'll get through. Come on. Toss the gun."

Every muscle in my body goes taut when he raises the pistol. But he only taps the muzzle of it against his forehead. "I pulled her over. I had sex with her. I did it. I fucked up. I . . . I don't know what happened to me that night. She was . . . just . . . there. For God's sake, it was like she *wanted* it. I'm telling you she . . . *knew* things. She was . . . and I . . . fucking lost it."

He doesn't have to say her name. I see it on his face. I bank the rise of disgust, bite back the denunciation dangling on my tongue. I'm keenly aware of the pistol in my hand, the pulse of anger in my veins. How easy it would be to put him out of his misery . . .

"Was she blackmailing you?" I ask.

He looks up at me, jerks his head. "For years."

"How much?" I ask.

"Twenty grand." He shrugs. "Maybe more. I lost track."

"Does Jen know?"

"She doesn't know anything." He shakes his head. "Schwartz was . . . crazy and . . . relentless. Said all sorts of crazy shit. Claimed she got pregnant that night. Had a kid. Said she had proof it was mine. Called it her 'insurance policy,' and she was going to wreck my life."

"She said the kid was yours?"

"There was no kid," he snaps. "She was a pathological liar. A fucking sadist. All she wanted was money. Ruining me was the icing on the cake." His smile sends a chill down my spine. "Looks like she got her way, didn't she?"

He looks down at the .45, makes a sound that's part sob, part laugh.

For an instant, I think he's going to use the gun on himself, so I try to engage him, keep him talking. "You met her at the bar in Wooster? The night she was killed?"

"I tried to reason with her. Told her I had a kid on the way. That I was out of money." He taps the muzzle of the H & K against his forehead again, so hard I hear the steel tap against his skull. "She didn't want to hear it."

I nod. "Okay."

He lowers the gun to his side. His eyes latch on to mine. "I've done some shitty things, Kate. I've raped. Lied. Cheated on my wife. But if you believe one word of what I say tonight, believe this: I did not kill Rachael Schwartz."

In the gauzy light I see the shimmer of tears in his eyes. The tremble of his mouth. The run of snot he doesn't seem to notice. A mask of hopelessness. The soul of a broken man.

"Then all you have to deal with is the assault," I tell him. "Fletch, you can do that. It's not too late." The statements aren't exactly true, but I'm free to tell him whatever I think he needs to hear in order to bring this to an end.

"Come on," I coo. "We'll figure it out. Just put down the gun."

He shakes his head. "You're a straight shooter, Kate. I always liked that about you."

"Dane—"

He cuts me off. "I'm fucking done. I used my badge to prey on that girl. She wasn't the only one. But I swear to God I didn't kill her. You want the truth? You'd better keep looking." A sob escapes him. "When you find it . . . make sure my wife knows."

Finality rings in his voice, as if he's going on a trip with no plans to come back. I get a sick feeling in my gut. In the back of my mind I'm wondering where the deputy is. T.J. "Dane, your kids need you. Jen needs you."

He shakes his head. "We both know I'm going to fry for this. Everything I've ever worked for. It's gone. I got nothing left." He begins to cry. "For God's sake, I can't spend the rest of my life in prison for something I didn't do. You know what they do to cops."

Taking his time, he starts toward me. Gun at his side. Finger outside the guard.

I step back. My finger on the trigger. Pulse in the red zone. "Keep your distance," I tell him.

He keeps coming. Not in a hurry. Looking down at the pistol in his right hand.

My heart stumbles in my chest and begins to pound. "Don't do this, Dane. *Don't.*"

"I didn't kill her." His tread is steady. Gun at his side. Nearly to the edge of the footbridge. Just ten feet away from me now.

I walk backward, my pistol at the ready. Cold sweat breaks out on the back of my neck. "You need to stop right there," I tell him. "Drop the gun."

He stops, tilts his head as if I'm some puzzle he's encountered and he's not sure how to solve it.

"I'm glad it was you, Burkholder."

He looks down at the H & K in his hand, fiddles with the clip, thinking about something I can't fathom. It's like watching a wreck in slow motion. Knowing it's going to be horrific, that someone is going to die. That there isn't a damn thing you can do about it. A sense of helplessness assails me.

"Dane! No! Stop!"

Quickly and without hesitation, he raises the gun, shoves the barrel into his mouth, and pulls the trigger.

CHAPTER 32

Day 5

It's been nearly eight hours since Dane Fletcher committed suicide. The scene at the park has replayed a thousand times in my head. I've critiqued my every move, my every word, everything I did and didn't do—and yet the end result is always the same. Intellectually, I know there was nothing I could have done to stop him. I should be thankful he didn't rely on me to do his dirty work for him.

By all accounts, Dane Fletcher was a duplicitous son of a bitch, a rapist, a disgrace to the badge—to all men—and likely a murderer. Despite all of those things, there is no satisfaction that comes with the end of his life.

I spent several hours in an interview room with Sheriff Rasmussen and Tomasetti. I gave my official statement to the best of my ability, but I was exhausted and shaken. I answered dozens of questions, drank too much coffee, snapped at both men a few too many times. Because I was at the scene when Fletcher committed suicide, the Holmes County

Sheriff's Office will oversee the investigation. Normally, I'd put up some token argument. This time, I'm relieved to step aside. I'm pissed at Fletcher for using his badge to prey on women, and when he got caught, for taking the cowardly way out. What kind of man does that to his wife and children? What kind of man pulls over a seventeen-year-old Amish girl and demands sex in exchange for letting her walk away from a DUI?

It was after two A.M. when I left the sheriff's office. Tomasetti followed me home. I tossed my blood-specked uniform into the hamper and went directly to the shower and stood under the spray for ten minutes. I didn't cry or curse. I didn't close my eyes, because I knew if I did, I'd see Fletcher drop, his face destroyed, the back of his head a gaping wound.

By the time I meet Tomasetti in the kitchen, I've pulled myself together. He's already poured two fingers of scotch into a couple of tumblers. The window above the sink is open and I can hear the chorus of spring peepers from the marsh down by the pond, singing their hearts out. The simple beauty of the sound makes me feel like crying. Of course, I don't. Instead, I pick up the tumbler of whiskey and take a long drink.

Tomasetti goes to the radio on the counter and fiddles with the knob. An old Led Zeppelin tune about rambling on fills the silence around us. It's a pretty song full of memories and its own unique beauty, and suddenly I'm absurdly thankful to be here in the kitchen of our modest little farm with the man I love.

"Any word on how Fletcher's wife is doing?" I ask, already knowing the answer, hating it because it hurts.

"The chaplain stayed with her until her parents got there," he tells me. "That's all I know."

I nod, take another sip. "I didn't know him that well."

"The people who did are about to realize they really didn't."

"What kind of man does that to his wife and kids? What kind of man uses his position to rape a seventeen-year-old girl?"

"A predator. A dirty cop. A sick bastard." He shrugs. "All of the above."

Leaving his place at the counter, he crosses to the table, takes the chair across from me. He's looking at me as if he's searching for something I'm not quite ready to reveal. Or maybe I'm just tired and looking for things that aren't really there.

"So what else is bothering you?" he asks.

Over the last hours, my brain has been preoccupied with witnessing the death of a man I'd once respected. On doing my job and figuring out how it fits into the investigation at hand—the homicide of Rachael Schwartz. Now that I'm settled and thinking more clearly, I'm starting to analyze more closely the exchange between Fletch and me during those final moments.

"Fletcher admitted to pulling her over and sexually assaulting her," I say. "He admitted to preying on other women. He acknowledged that Schwartz was blackmailing him. To having paid her somewhere around twenty thousand dollars over the years. He admitted to meeting with her at the bar."

Having been present for my interview and having read my official statement, he already knows all of those things. "He knew we had him."

I nod, but I'm still mulling the conversation, the words running through my head like a script. I can't get the sound of Dane Fletcher's voice out of my head. The look in his eyes.

. . . if you believe one word of what I've said tonight, believe this: I did not kill Rachael Schwartz.

I've heard too many lies over the years to believe anything an admitted rapist would say. Fletcher lied and cheated and hurt people for years. He doesn't deserve the benefit of a doubt.

So why the hell can't I set aside his sham denial and close my damn case?

I lift the tumbler, set it down without drinking.

Tomasetti sips, looks at me over the rim of his glass. "A moment ago, you reiterated all the things Fletcher had done. The one thing you didn't mention was the murder of Rachael Schwartz."

"You're pretty astute for a BCI agent, aren't you?"

"Every now and then I get something right."

You want the truth? . . . keep looking.

I meet his gaze, hold it. "I know he was a liar. Desperate and willing to say anything. But, Tomasetti, he walked onto that trail to take his life. He had nothing to prove. Nothing to lose. Why deny the murder? Why not try to rationalize or explain why he did it?"

Tomasetti looks at me over the rim of his glass and scowls. "Fletcher had motive. He had means. And he had opportunity. Rachael Schwartz was bleeding him dry and enjoying putting him through the wringer."

I hate it that I've put myself in the position of defending an admitted dirty cop. Even so, I can't shake the sense that not all of the pieces are settling into the proper circles and squares the way they should.

"Why tell me to keep looking?" I say.

"Because he didn't give a damn about anyone, including himself," he tells me.

I know this is one of those times that no matter what I say, I'll not convince Tomasetti that the situation warrants a more thorough looking-into. To be honest, I'm not certain of it myself. But if I've learned anything over the years, it is to listen to my gut. Right now, my cop's instinct is telling me to, at the very least, keep my options open.

I swear to God I didn't kill her. You want the truth? . . . keep looking . . . make sure my wife knows.

It's as if Dane Fletcher is standing outside the window, whispering the words. The thought sends a shiver through me.

"I'm going to dig around a little," I say. "A couple days. See if there's anything else there, that we haven't looked at."

Tomasetti finishes his whiskey and sets down the glass, gives me a dubious look. "Do you need anything from me?"

"Fletcher's son plays Little League. Take the bat we found to Jennifer Fletcher," I tell him, referring to the murder weapon. "If she recognizes it, I'll close the case."

He nods, but I can tell by his expression he doesn't agree with my theory and he doesn't think my request is a very good idea. "I'll pay her a visit tomorrow."

CHAPTER 33

The final vestiges of an afternoon storm simmer in a sky the color of a bruise as I turn in to the lane of the Schwartz farm. The place looks exactly the same as the last time I was here. The same Jersey cows graze in the pasture to my right. The field across the road is still in the process of being plowed and readied for seed. Same team of horses. Same young boy behind the lines. Life goes on, as it should. As it always does.

I find the couple on the front porch. Dan is sitting in a rocking chair, legs crossed, a pipe in his mouth, a glass of iced tea sweating on the table next to him. Rhoda sits in the rocking chair next to him, the parcel of a recently started afghan in her lap. They're not happy to see me. They don't rise or greet me as I climb the steps, and they watch me as if I'm some vermin that's wandered up from the field.

"*Guder nochmiddawks*," I say. Good afternoon.

"You come bearing bad news again, Kate Burkholder?" Dan's voice is amicable, but there's a hardness in his eyes that wasn't there before.

I take the jab in stride.

Rhoda pats her husband's hand to quiet him. "Would you like cold tea, Katie? I made a pot and if Dan drinks any more, he'll be up half the night."

"I can't stay." I take the final step onto the porch, go to the Adirondack chair across from them and I sit. "I wanted to give you an update on the investigation."

Dan picks up his tea and sips. The needles in Rhoda's hands still. With the music of birdsong all around, I tell them about Dane Fletcher and the turn of events leading up to his death.

"We heard about that policeman," Rhoda says.

"Everyone's talking about it," Dan adds.

"Such a horrible thing." She shakes her head. "We knew there was some connection to Rachael. We sure didn't know the rest of it. *Mein Gott.*" My God.

I'm loath to tell them the rest, but I know it's better for them to hear it from me rather than through the grapevine, where facts are scarce and the story grows with every telling.

Leaving out as many of the sordid details as possible, I tell them about what happened on that back road when Rachael was seventeen. Because the investigation is ongoing, I forgo speculation and anything not yet confirmed. It's not easy. But they deserve the truth even when I know it will break their hearts all over again.

"I'm sorry," I say when I've finished. "I know that was difficult to hear. But I thought you'd want to know."

Rhoda looks down at the knitting in her lap as if she doesn't quite remember why it's there. "She never told us," she whispers.

"She was baptized that summer," Ben says quietly.

"Left us in the spring," Rhoda adds. "April, I think."

I don't know what to say to any of that. I'm not big on the whole closure thing. When you lose a loved one to violence, the closing of the case does little in terms of easing the pain. As I stare into the Amish woman's eyes and see the silent scroll of agony, I curse Dane Fletcher.

"The investigation is still open, and the sheriff's office has stepped in to help, but we'll likely close it soon."

"Rachael is with God now." Dan's eyes remain glued to the floor. "At peace with the Lord."

"We've made all the notifications already," Rhoda tells me, referring to the Amish tradition of personally notifying those who will be invited to the funeral.

She raises shimmering eyes to mine. "We didn't see her much anymore. But we're going to miss her. And of course we take comfort in knowing that she's in good hands, and that one day we will join her."

"A man should not grieve overmuch," Dan says, "for that is a complaint against God."

Rhoda swipes at the tears on her cheeks. "Last time we talked, Katie, you asked me when we saw Rachael last. I realized this morning that I told you wrong. She came to see us *after* Christmas, not before, and we had such a nice visit." The chuckle that follows rings false. "I remembered because she'd been over to Loretta's that morning and mentioned the cast on little Fannie's arm."

I nod, listening more out of politeness than interest.

Rhoda uses her fingers to squeegee tears from her cheeks. "That girl. Christmas day. Broke her arm in two places. Fell off that old windmill over to the Cooper farm next door. Had to get some kind of pin put in to fix it."

Forcing a smile, she looks down at the knitting in her lap. "She's not the first girl we've known who's in love with adventure, now, is she? Should have been born a boy, that one."

The image of Fannie astride the horse and loping across the pasture plays in my mind's eye. "She must keep Loretta and Ben on their toes."

"She's a handful, with all the climbing and horses and such." She shrugs. "Poor Loretta was just beside herself. Dotes on that girl like she's newborn." Rhoda sighs, her face softening. "Anyway, that was the last time I saw my Rachael. *After* Christmas, not before. I don't know if that's even important now, but I wanted you to know."

She picks up the needles and resumes her knitting.

Something I can't put my finger on nags at me as I head toward the Bontrager farm. A kink in my gut that wasn't there before my conversation with Rhoda and Dan. I try to work it out, but nothing comes to me. I set it aside as I make the turn into the lane.

I'm on my way to the front door when voices from the side yard draw my attention. I head that way to find Loretta and Fannie painting a picnic table.

"You two look busy," I say by way of greeting.

Loretta, paintbrush in hand, looks at me over her shoulder and grins. "That's one way to put it."

"I like the teal," I tell her.

Stepping back, she puts her hands on her hips and studies the table. "I wasn't too sure at first, but I think I like it, too."

Fannie, a smaller brush in hand, peeks out at me from around the side of the table. "I picked out the color."

Despite the purpose of my visit, the sight of the girl makes me smile. She's got a smudge of paint on her chin. A perfect drop of it on her *kapp.* Someone will likely be scrubbing it with a toothbrush tonight.

I cross to her, offer her a high five. "Nice job."

A grin overtakes the girl's face. There's a space between her front teeth. A nose tinged pink from the sun. That odd sensation waggles at the back of my brain again, but I shove it aside to deal with later.

"We've got an extra paintbrush if you want to help."

I glance over to see Ben approach from the direction of the barn. He's wearing a blue work shirt with suspenders, trousers, and a straw flat-brimmed hat.

"I'll leave it to you professionals." I sober, let my gaze fall to Fannie, and then I focus on the couple. "I'm sorry to interrupt your afternoon, but I need to talk to you about Rachael Schwartz."

"Oh." Loretta tosses a look at her husband, then rounds the table and goes to her daughter. "Just look at that spot of paint on your *kapp*," she says. "Why don't you go in and take that old toothbrush to it before it dries? I'll be in to help in a few minutes."

The girl cocks her head, knowing the reason she's being sent inside has nothing to do with the paint and everything to do with our pending conversation. But she's too well behaved to balk.

"Use the laundry soap on the porch." The Amish woman takes the girl's brush and points her in the direction of the back door. "Go on now before it leaves a stain we won't be able to get out."

We watch the girl depart. When I hear the back door slam, I turn to the couple. "There's been a development in the case. I thought you'd want to know."

Ben nods. "We heard about the deputy," he says.

Since Ben and Loretta aren't family members, I give them a condensed version of the same set of facts I laid out for Dan and Rhoda Schwartz.

When I'm finished, tears shimmer in Loretta's eyes. "My *mamm* always said, good deeds have echoes. Now I know that bad deeds do, too."

I heard the adage a hundred times growing up and it's one of the few I believe in with my whole heart. "We'll probably close the case in the next few days."

"So it's over?" Ben asks.

"I think so," I tell him.

"It will be a good thing to put this behind us." The Amish man shoves his hands into his pockets. "Thank you for finding the truth, Kate Burkholder. I know the job put before you is a hard one and the Amish don't always approve. That makes it no less worthy."

I nod, a little more moved than I should be. Probably because it still matters to me what the Amish think.

Loretta and I watch him walk away. For the span of a full minute, the only sound comes from the *kuk-kuk-kuk* of a woodpecker followed by the rapid drum of its beak against a tree.

I watch as Loretta walks to the gallon pail of paint and replaces the lid. I think about my conversation with Rhoda and Dan Schwartz. The final moments I spent with Dane Fletcher. The kink in my gut that won't go away.

Claimed she got pregnant that night. Had a kid.

I pick up the hammer from the stepladder she's using as a table and hand it to her. "You spent a lot of time with Rachael that last summer she was here in Painters Mill," I say.

"I did." She taps down the lid to seal it. "It was one of the best summers of my life."

"You mentioned before that she changed. In what way?"

She sets down the hammer and straightens. "As strange as it sounds, she became even more forward. It's like she was in a rush to squeeze in every single experience she could before she became baptized." She pauses, thoughtful. "Sometimes she was mad at the world. Not too much, but more than . . . before. Rachael was strong. She didn't let what happened crush her."

"Loretta, when exactly did it happen?" I ask. "I mean, with Dane Fletcher?"

"Late summer," she tells me. "August, I think."

239

She was baptized that summer.

Left us in the spring. April, I think.

"Do you know if Rachael was ever *ime familye weg*?" I ask.

Loretta blinks, her brows knitting as if the question has caught her off-guard. "I don't think so," she says slowly. "Rachael would have told me."

"Would she have told you even if she terminated the pregnancy?"

The Amish woman looks down at the brush in her hand. "I wish I could tell you Rachael would never take the life of an unborn child." The sigh that follows is saturated with grief. "But she had a way of rationalizing things. If she did something like that, she didn't tell me. I think she'd have known I would disapprove."

Typically, at this point in an investigation, once an arrest has been made, the pressure is off and life returns to normal. I spend a few days catching up on the things I neglected over the course of the case, including sleep.

The Schwartz case has been anything but typical.

I'm in my office at the police station; it's long past time to go home and I've done little with regard to putting the case to rest. Instead, I've spent the last three hours grinding through the file, reading the dozens of reports and statements, and the like. I've been staring at paper for so long I'm no longer even sure what I'm looking for. I've scrutinized every crime scene photo and sketch. Viewed the videos. I've reread every statement, dismantled every word. Gone over the forensic reports with a fine-tooth comb. I've picked through the autopsy report so many times I'm seeing double. My neck hurts. My eyes feel like someone has tossed a handful of ground glass into them. All the while the little voice of reason sits on my shoulder, telling me I'm chasing ghosts.

Indeed.

The wall clock glares at me, reminding me that it's nine P.M. and I should have been home hours ago. Tomasetti is probably wondering where I am.

"What the hell are you doing, Burkholder?" I mutter.

I look down at my handwritten notes spread out on my desk and I frown.

. . . likely knew her killer . . .

. . . a fair amount of conflict in her life . . .

Setting my chin in my hand, I flip the page and come to my statement on the death of Dane Fletcher. Doc Coblentz ruled on the cause and manner of death. Suicide caused by a single gunshot wound to the head. According to Sheriff Rasmussen, Fletcher's wife and kids left Painters Mill to stay with her parents in Pittsburgh. Last I heard, they won't be coming back.

I skim my incident report, not wanting to revisit the moment he pulled the trigger. Instead, I focus on the section that recounts my final conversation with Fletcher.

Claimed she got pregnant that night. Had a kid.

Of all the things he told me the night he died, that's the one that stops me cold. Was Rachael Schwartz provoking him? Trying to inflame him? To what end? Make him suffer? Pay him back for what he did to her? Did Fletcher reach his limit? Follow her to that motel and proceed to bludgeon her to death?

In all likelihood, that's exactly what happened.

Even if Rachael *did* become pregnant, does it change the dynamics of the case? The answer is a resounding no.

The last thing I'll ever do is defend the likes of Dane Fletcher. What he did to a young Amish girl—and possibly others—is indefensible. He was a dirty cop. A liar. A phony. A danger to the community he'd sworn to serve and protect.

But was he a killer?

You want the truth? . . . keep looking.

Gathering the contents of the file, I stuff everything into the folder, drop it into my laptop case, and head for the door.

CHAPTER 34

I call Tomasetti from the Explorer as I back out of my parking spot in front of the station. He picks up on the first ring. "I was about to send out a search party," he says. "But I don't think anyone would have a difficult time finding you these days."

"I guess I'm officially busted," I say, keeping my voice light despite my mood. "If it's any consolation, I'm on my way home."

"The day is looking up."

In that moment, I'm unduly happy that I have him in my life, to keep me grounded. Remind me of what's important. "I was wondering if you had a chance to talk with Jennifer Fletcher," I say. "About the bat."

"I did," he tells me. "Two of their boys are in Little League. She bought two Rawlings aluminum-alloy bats in the last couple of years. They still have those bats; they still use them, and they have never owned a wood Louisville Slugger."

"Would have been nice to tie that up." I reach the edge of town and head north on US 62, toward home.

"Sometimes even the most open-and-closed cases don't tidy up the way we'd like them to." He pauses. "Wood bat like that one is common. Fletcher could have picked it up at a thrift store. Something like that."

I'm northbound on US 62, running a few miles per hour over the speed limit, headlights illuminating the blur of asphalt. Tall trees rise from a berm on my right. Left, through a veil of new-growth trees, I see the black expanse of a field.

"Not like you to get sidetracked by something like that," he says, fishing.

"This is one of those times when I don't want to be right."

"So you're still having doubts about Fletcher?"

"Yeah."

I'm just past Township Road 92 and closing in on Millersburg, fifteen minutes from home and concentrating on the call, when the steering wheel yanks hard to the right. The Explorer shudders. Something thumps hard against the undercarriage. Out of the corner of my eye I see a dark chunk fly past the passenger window. *Tire,* I think, and I stomp the brake.

"*Shit.*"

The Explorer veers left. My police training kicks in; I turn in to the skid. No room for error. An instant to react. The guardrail slams into my left front quarter panel. A tremendous *crash!* sounds as I plow through. I'm flung against my safety harness. Jerked left and right. A dozen trees thrash the windshield and hood as I careen down the hill. The windshield shatters. Dirt and glass pelt my face and chest. The Explorer nosedives. Straight down. Too fast. Too steep. I'm slung violently against my shoulder harness.

The Explorer hits a trunk the size of a telephone pole. The airbag explodes as the vehicle jumps right, then rolls to a stop. The windshield has been punched in, draped over the dash like a crystal blanket. I hear spring peepers. Cool night air pouring in. In the periphery of my disjointed thoughts, I hear Tomasetti calling my name.

"Kate! What the hell . . ."

The engine is running. Bluetooth still working. I don't know where my cell phone landed. "I'm okay," I hear myself say.

"What the hell is going on?" he shouts. "What happened?"

"Tire blew. I . . . ran off the road. I'm okay."

The Explorer sits at a steep angle, nose down, surrounded by trees. A branch the size of a fence post juts through the passenger window, two feet from my face. I'm covered with glass and dirt and mud. I'm shaking. Blood on the seat. I don't know where it came from.

In the periphery of my vision I see movement ahead and to my right. Someone in the trees. A motorist coming to help . . .

"I'm a police officer!" I unfasten my seat belt, reach for the door handle. "I'm not hurt!"

Pop! Pop! Pop! Pop!

The unmistakable sound of gunfire. Adrenaline kicks, followed by an electric zing of fear. I duck, shove open the door. It creaks, hits a tree. Simultaneously, I reach for my .38, yank it out. The door won't open enough for me to squeeze through. I'm in an awkward position. Leaning right, I look around wildly. Too dark to see. Too many trees. No sign of the gunman. In the back of my mind I wonder why a motorist would brave the incline only to take a shot . . . The answer hovers. No time to ponder.

Another *pop! Ping!*

A bullet ricochets. So close I feel the concussion on the seatback.

I raise the .38 and fire blindly. "I'm a police officer!" I scream. "Put down the weapon! Put it down!"

Two more shots ring out.

I fall against the seat, hunker down as low as I can, gripping the .38. I'm blind here. A sitting duck. I hit my radio. "Shots fired! Shots fired!" I shout out my location. "Ten-thirty-one-E! Ten-thirty-three!" Shooting in progress. Officer in trouble. Emergency.

Pop! Pop!

"Police officer!" I scream. "Drop your weapon! Drop it now! Get on the fucking ground!"

Pop! Pop! Pop!

A slug tings against steel. Another slams into the shattered slab of windshield, sending a spray of glass onto me. Vaguely, I'm aware of Tomasetti shouting through my Bluetooth. Too scared to understand the words. My police radio crackling to life as my call for help goes out.

I'm on my side. Jammed between the steering wheel and the seat. Not enough room to maneuver. I have no idea where the shooter is. I can't get to my Maglite. I raise my head. A single headlight illuminates an ocean of young trees. Ahead, a plowed field. No movement or sound.

Where the hell is the shooter?

If he were to approach from the side, I wouldn't see him until he was right on top of me. . . .

"Shit. Shit." Breaths coming like a piston in my lungs.

I swivel, reach for the passenger door handle, shove it open with my shoulder. The tree branch keeps it from opening all the way. Enough of a gap for me to slide through. Holding my weapon at the ready, I slither out. Shoulder sinking into mud. Cold penetrating my shirt.

Then I'm on my knees, exposed, heart raging, looking around. No sign of the shooter.

Relief rushes through me when I hear the distant song of a siren. I hold my position, trying not to notice that my gun is shaking, that the butt is slick against my wet palms. I can't quite catch my breath. I'm on my knees, using the passenger-side door for cover, when I see the red and blue lights flicker off the treetops.

"Sheriff's Office! Drop the weapon! Show me your hands!"

I call out and identify myself. "I don't know where the shooter is!"

I hear the crack of a police radio. The sound of breaking brush as the deputy makes his way down to me.

"Do not move!" he screams.

I see the flicker of a flashlight. My legs are shaking so violently, it takes me two tries to get to my feet. When I finally make it, I'm nauseous, so I lean against the door, shove my .38 back into my holster, and concentrate on not throwing up.

The approaching deputy blinds me with his flashlight beam as he skids down the incline.

"Painters Mill PD." I put up my hand to shield my eyes. "I haven't seen the shooter for a minute or two," I say.

"You know where he went? You get a look at him?"

"No," I say. "Male. Armed. He fired multiple times at me."

"Vehicle?"

I shake my head. "No idea."

He speaks into his shoulder mike. "Ten-thirty-five-E." Major crime alert—shooting. "Suspect at large."

He runs his flashlight over me. I see recognition in his eyes as he takes in my uniform. "You got a bloody nose." He reaches into his pocket, passes me a kerchief. "You need an ambulance, Chief?"

I take the kerchief. "No." Shaking my head in disgust, I look at the wrecked Explorer. "Might need a new car, though."

He grins. "Roger that."

It takes fifteen minutes for the wrecker to arrive. The driver is a Volkswagen-size man whose company contracts for the county. He's confident he'll be able to pull the Explorer from its muddy nest without the use of a chain saw.

"Went in through all those trees just fine so I ought to be able to pull her out the same way," he tells me as he hoists his large frame down the incline to attach the winch to the undercarriage.

I'm leaning against the hood of the deputy's cruiser when Tomasetti pulls up. Driving too fast. Braking a little too abruptly. He's out of the Tahoe in seconds and striding toward us.

"Kate." Worry resonates in his voice when he calls out. "Are you hurt?"

Tomasetti is known by most everyone at the sheriff's office. Even though we've been discreet about our relationship, my department is a small one and most of my officers have figured out we're involved. Most of them know we're living together. Even so, we do our best to maintain a certain level of professionality. Tonight, it's not easy.

I don't remember crossing to him. His body bumps against me with a little too much force. The next thing I know his arms are around me, his frame solid against me. Out of the corner of my eye I see the deputy I'd been talking to turn away, and I sink into the man I love.

"I'm betting that's the fastest trip you've ever made from the farm," I tell him.

"Record," he murmurs. "You like to keep a guy on his toes, don't you?"

I'm shaking, embarrassed because I feel as if I shouldn't be. Before I can think of an appropriate rejoinder, he pushes me to arm's length, his eyes running over me; then his gaze latches on to mine. "My radio lit up on the drive down. A *shooter*?" he says. "What happened?"

I tell him all of it, abbreviating when I can. "Initially, I thought it was a blowout. Bad tire. Whatever. The next thing I know the son of a bitch is coming down the hill and taking potshots at me."

Tomasetti is a stoic man. He can be a hard man. He's good at keeping his emotions at bay, especially when it comes to his job. I can tell by the flash of fury that this has hit too close to home. His eyes drift to the opening in the trees where the Explorer sits nose-down at the base of the incline.

"You recognize him?" he asks.

I shake my head. "Too dark."

He thinks about that a moment. "He say anything?"

"Not a word."

He nods. "I'll have the Explorer towed to impound. I'll get with the CSU and have them process it. See if our shooter left anything behind."

The next thought that occurs to me sends a shudder through me. "Tomasetti, those tires aren't very old."

His eyes narrow on mine. A dozen unspoken theories zing between us.

"This was no road-hazard situation," I tell him.

"What are you implying exactly?"

I look at him, trying not to appear paranoid or overreactive. "I think he knew I'd be coming this way. He shot out my tire. And then he came down that hill to kill me."

Tomasetti looks in the direction of the Explorer, where the wrecker is in the process of hauling it from its resting place. "You got a motive in mind?"

I look away, not wanting to say it, knowing I don't have a choice. "Maybe it has something to do with the Rachael Schwartz case."

He stares at me, searching my face. I see the wheels turning in his mind. After a moment, he nods. "I'll get another CSU out here and have them process this entire area."

CHAPTER 35

It's after midnight by the time Tomasetti and I arrive at the farm. He did his utmost to talk me into making a trip to Pomerene Hospital. Only after a paramedic with the fire department gave me a thorough field assessment did he concede. The BCI crime scene unit truck arrived on scene an hour before we left. The Ohio State Highway Patrol. It's a big deal when someone takes a shot at a cop. Every law enforcement agency in the area is on alert.

Because the scene is large and out of doors—with the complication of rough terrain—the odds of picking up some piece of evidence that will identify the shooter or his vehicle is doubtful. Our best hope lies with the discovery of forensic evidence from the firearm used. A spent cartridge from which we could conceivably pick up a fingerprint. Or a bullet or fragment from which we could recover striations. Both are possibilities, but no one is holding their breath.

I sustained a few bruises in the course of the wreck, so I took a hot shower upon arriving home. Tomasetti heated soup, and I downed a

251

couple of preemptive ibuprofen. I planned on a good night's sleep, getting a fresh start in the morning, and hopefully finding the son of a bitch who tried to kill me. I should have known my overactive mind would throw a monkey wrench into the mix.

It's after one A.M. now. I'm at the kitchen table, my laptop open and humming. The Rachael Schwartz homicide file is spread out in untidy piles, the logic to which only I am aware. I've filled two pages of my trusty yellow legal pad with theories and conjecture, and a fair amount of chicken scratch. Whatever pinpoint of information I'm looking for continues to elude me.

The truth of the matter is that with the suicide of Dane Fletcher, the case is tied up as tidily as a case can be. Fletcher had motive, means, and opportunity. In spades. When he got caught, he took the easy way out and killed himself. Maybe Tomasetti is right. I'm wasting my time. My gut steered me wrong. It wouldn't be the first time. . . .

So who saw fit to take a shot at me earlier? And why does the thought of closing the case feel so damn wrong?

"Because I don't think he did it," I whisper. It's the first time I've said the words aloud and they sound profane in the silence of the kitchen. But as averse I am to admit it, I've drawn the conclusion that Fletcher didn't murder Rachael Schwartz. There's something else there. Something I missed.

Something.

Sighing in frustration, I page through several reports and set them aside. I come to the copies of the texts between Rachael and Fletcher, read them again.

In case you're thinking about going all batshit . . . don't forget I got that insurance policy.

That one stops me.

Fletcher's words replay in my head. *Claimed she got pregnant that night. Had a kid. Said she had proof it was mine. Called it her "insurance policy," and she was going to wreck my life.*

Then, he'd told me there was no kid. *She was a pathological liar. A fucking sadist. All she wanted was money. Ruining me was the icing on the cake.*

"So why the hell did you keep paying?" I mutter.

Did Rachael Schwartz have something else on him? Some hidden guarantee that would pay off if something happened to her?

In case you're thinking about going all batshit . . . don't forget I got that insurance policy.

"What else did you have on him?" I whisper.

A sealed envelope tucked away in some lockbox that would explain everything when found? A lawyer poised to step forward upon word of her death?

Frustrated, I set the text messages aside and continue on. My handwritten notes on my conversations with Dan and Rhoda Schwartz are paper-clipped together. I pull them apart and read, hit the passages I highlighted in yellow.

. . . she came to see us after Christmas, not before . . .

There's nothing sinister or mysterious about Rhoda changing her story simply because she remembered a detail she'd overlooked that changed the timeline of when she'd last seen her daughter.

I come to the brown envelope where I'd tucked away the old photo of Rachael Schwartz and Loretta Bontrager. They were barely into their teens. Loretta looking awkward and shy and plain. Rachael too pretty for her own good. Even at that tender age, her smile was knowing, her eyes challenging and bold.

I get that antsy sensation at the back of my neck, a sort of pseudo déjà vu that's prickly and uncomfortable. I snatch up my reading glasses, look at the photo a little more closely.

A strange sense of . . . familiarity whispers at the back of my brain. Of course, I've seen the photo before. Plus, I knew Rachael when she was that age. Neither of those things explains the quick snap of recognition.

I set down the photo. I pick it back up.

A young Rachael Schwartz stares back at me. A pretty strawberry blonde with a nose for trouble and a complete inability to follow the rules.

I straighten so abruptly I hit my knee on the underside of my desk.

The image of Fannie astride the horse and loping across the pasture plays out in my mind's eye. I don't have a photo of the girl; most Amish don't take photographs of their children—unless they're breaking the rules. But I recall the way Fannie had looked at me. The punch of shock that follows leaves me breathless.

The two look nothing alike. Rachael had light hair with blue-green eyes. Fannie is dark haired with brown eyes—like Loretta. While their physical attributes are as different as night and day, in that instant I recognize the one trait they seem to share.

Attitude.

I knew Rachael Schwartz when she was a kid. I'd secretly admired her pluck. Though she was younger than me, I'd looked at her as a kindred soul. How many times did she get herself into some situation that required help while on my watch? When she was six, I rescued her when she climbed a tree and couldn't get down. Then there was the day she rolled down the hill in that steel drum and ended up in the creek. Later,

I saw her get into a couple of fights, which goes against every Amish tenet I can think of.

Rachael was a purveyor of chaos, invariably in pursuit of some grand adventure. When she went down the slide, she didn't go feetfirst. She went headfirst, the faster the better, with no regard for safety. She pushed the envelope. Partook in activities that weren't quite safe. She wasn't a *bad* child, but she was different from the other Amish kids.

Fannie is twelve years old. Rachael left Painters Mill about twelve years ago. The timing is spot-on. I think of the parallels between Fannie Bontrager and Rachael Schwartz, and the possibilities chill me despite the sweat that's broken out on the back of my neck.

She's not the first girl we've known who's in love with adventure, now, is she? Should have been born a boy, that one.

Rhoda Schwartz's words reverberate in my head.

Sick with something akin to dread, I dig through the papers in front of me, pull my incident report from the night Dane Fletcher took his life, and read.

Claimed she got pregnant that night. Had a kid.

What if Rachael Schwartz *hadn't* been lying—at least about that part of it? What if she *had* gotten pregnant the night Fletcher assaulted her? I'd assumed he paid the blackmail money because she threatened to go public with the assault. What if the blackmail was about something else? A child born out of an act of violence?

The questions don't stop there. In fact, the most excruciating questions have yet to be posed. Is it possible Fannie Bontrager is Rachael's child?

In case you're thinking about going all batshit . . . don't forget I got that insurance policy. Anything unsavory happens and presto! Out comes the proof.

I think about Fannie, riding the horse as well or better than any boy, breaking her arm in a fall off a windmill. A pattern of similar behaviors.

She's not the first girl we've known who's in love with adventure . . .

It's not a cohesive theory. Far from it. There's too much conjecture. Too many loose ends, none of which ever quite meet. Most importantly, and never far from mind, is the fact that an innocent child lies at the heart of it. Parents and grandparents are involved, their lives and reputations hang in the balance.

"What did you do?" I whisper, not quite sure who I'm addressing.

How does all of this affect my case? If my suspicions are correct, how much does Ben Bontrager know? And how is it that Loretta and Ben Bontrager raised the girl as their own with no questions asked? I don't dare put into words the thoughts crowding into my brain.

Movement at the door yanks a gasp from my throat. Tomasetti stands in the kitchen doorway, arms crossed at his chest, hair mussed, frowning.

"You've been busy," he says.

I look down at the papers and reports and notes strewn about the table and floor. I'm aware of how I must look. Exhausted. Fixated. "Dane Fletcher didn't kill Rachael Schwartz."

"Why am I not surprised to hear you say that?" Despite the frustration evident on his face, his voice is kind.

"I could use a sounding board," I tell him.

"I'll make coffee."

A few minutes later, he's sitting across from me, nursing a cup of dark roast, looking at me over the rim. "All right, Chief," he says. "Hit me with your best shot."

I lay out my theory, holes and all, struggling with every word because I'm not sure of any of it.

"Rachael Schwartz and Fannie Bontrager don't share any physical characteristics," I say. "They do, however, share a psychological trait that could be even more important."

"Like what?" he asks.

"A predilection for reckless behavior. For breaking the rules, the norms set forth by the adults in their lives."

"I think the official term for that is 'being a kid,' " he says.

I'm talking too fast, stumbling over the words because I'm attempting to explain something I'm not well versed on. "There's a difference." I take a breath, slow down, and tell him about some of the behaviors I witnessed in Rachael Schwartz when she was a kid.

"You're asserting that behavior carried over to adulthood." He's listening now, but skepticism rings hard in his voice.

"What if this . . . propensity for thrill seeking is hereditary?" I ask. "Fannie Bontrager displays some of the same tendencies." I tell him about her riding the horse with such utter confidence. The broken arm.

"You believe Fannie Bontrager is Rachael Schwartz's daughter?" he asks.

"I think Rachael Schwartz got pregnant the night Fletcher assaulted her. She wasn't prepared to raise a child. Didn't want a baby. Especially *that* baby. Loretta on the other hand had just gotten married. I remember hearing the birth of her first child was a little too close to her wedding day."

"How old is the girl?"

"Twelve."

The silence that follows breaks beneath its own weight. "So if Fletcher didn't murder Rachael Schwartz, who did?" he asks after a moment.

He knows where I'm going with this. He wants me to say it. I hate it that it's so damn difficult. Doubt sits on my shoulder, stabbing me with its steely little knife. "What if Rachael Schwartz had a change of heart?" I say. "What if she came back to Painters Mill, not only to extort money from Fletcher, but to see her daughter? What if she wanted more? More than Loretta and Ben were willing to grant?"

Tomasetti holds his silence for a full minute. I see the wheels of thought spinning in his eyes. He doesn't like this any more than I do, but he knows it's something we cannot ignore.

"Even if the girl is the biological child of Rachael Schwartz, it doesn't prove Loretta Bontrager committed murder. We can't place her in that room. We can't tie her to the bat."

"It gives her motive," I say.

"Maybe." But he frowns. "What about Ben Bontrager? Do you think he's involved?"

"I don't know. He has to know that Fannie isn't their biological child. Whether he knows Fannie is Rachael Schwartz's child . . ." I let the words trail when the image of Rachael Schwartz's broken body flashes in my mind's eye. "That said, the level of violence . . . the strength required to do that kind of damage . . . maybe."

"It's flimsy."

"I know."

"Any human being capable of doing what was done to Rachael Schwartz needs to be taken off the street," he says.

I nod. "DNA would be a good place to start."

"No judge in his right mind is going to sign off on a warrant."

"I can get something."

He scoffs at the notion. "You know surreptitious sampling isn't admissible."

"It doesn't need to be. But at least we would know. It would change the way we look at the case." I think about that a moment. "Who we look at."

"If you're wrong?"

"I drop everything, leave it as it is, and close the case," I tell him.

He scowls at me. "If you're right, you're going to have to prove your case."

"I'm aware."

"At the moment, you've got nothing."

Except that kernel of suspicion that's been nibbling away at my gut from the start. "For now, I'm going to do some research, see what I can find." I shrug. "The rest . . . I'll cross that bridge when I come to it."

CHAPTER 36

Day 6

It's just after eight A.M. when I walk out of the Butterhorn Bakery in downtown Painters Mill, a baker's dozen of still-warm doughnuts tucked into a paper bag. I didn't sleep last night after my conversation with Tomasetti and the ensuing research marathon. I couldn't turn off my brain. Couldn't stop thinking about Rachael Schwartz and Fannie Bontrager and all the ugly implications of a theory I'm still not sure of.

I wasn't surprised to discover several academic studies on "sensation seeking in children." One of the articles I read used phrases like "novelty seeking" and "desire to engage in activities involving speed or risk" and "behavioral difficulties." A second study used the term "heritable trait," and I had my answer.

I don't like the idea of obtaining a DNA sample without a warrant. It's not illegal in the state of Ohio, but as Tomasetti pointed out, even if I'm able to prove that Fannie Bontrager is Rachael Schwartz's daughter,

I can't use the information as evidence. The one thing it will do is establish a motive for Ben and Loretta Bontrager, and set me on track to take a hard look at them.

The warm cinnamon aroma of the doughnuts fills the interior of my rental car as I make the turn onto the township road and idle past the Bontrager farm. I look for garbage cans at the end of the lane, but like most Amish, the Bontragers burn their trash. No help whatsoever in terms of my gaining a DNA sample.

Half a mile down the road, I make a U-turn and pull onto the shoulder. I don't expect any problems with Ben or Loretta, but it's always prudent to let a fellow officer know where you are no matter how benign the assignment.

I call my on-duty officer, Skid. "Where are you?" I ask.

"I just stopped Ron Zelinski's kid," he tells me. "Caught him doing ninety out on Township Road 89. Claims he was late for school."

That particular stretch is smooth, flat, and wide, which makes it a favorite spot for all sorts of illicit driving activities, everything from street racing to car surfing. Two years ago, a sixteen-year-old was thrown from a pickup truck and sustained a serious head injury.

"Now he really *is* going to be late," I say. "Don't cut him any slack."

"Wouldn't dream of it. Kid's a shit."

Like his dad, I think, but I don't say it. "Look, I'm about to swing by the Bontrager place. I shouldn't be there more than twenty minutes or so. I'll call you when I finish up."

A beat of silence and then, "Something going on, Chief?"

"Fishing expedition, mostly." Because I'm not sure of any of my suspicions—because I'm dealing with the welfare of a minor child and the reputation of a well-thought-of family—I keep it vague. "I need to talk to them about the Schwartz case. There are a couple of things that don't add up. I'm not sure I got the whole story from them."

"You want me to meet you out there?" he asks. "I can tie this up in two minutes."

"With their being Amish, I think they'll be more apt to speak openly if I'm alone. I don't expect things to go south—I just want you to know where I am."

"If I don't hear from you in twenty, I'll call out the posse."

"Roger that."

I pull onto the road and make the turn into the Bontrager lane. The horse I'd seen Fannie riding a few days ago grazes in the field to my right. I continue on past the house and park in the gravel area between the house and barn. The reek of manure drifts on the breeze as I take the sidewalk to the front porch. I've barely knocked when the door swings open.

"Katie! Hello!" Loretta motions me in. "*Kumma inseid.*" Come inside.

"I won't take up too much of your time." I hold up the bag of doughnuts. "I come bearing gifts."

"Oh, how nice." She smiles. "The Butterhorn Bakery. Fannie's favorite." She laughs and touches her backside with her hand. "Mine, too, as if you can't tell. What brings you to our neck of the woods this morning?"

"I'm about to close the case and I wanted to tie up a couple of loose ends."

Her expression turns thoughtful. "This has been a dark time for all of us. I'm glad it's over. I reckon you are, too." She glances over her shoulder toward the kitchen. "I've got bone broth on the stove. We can sit in the kitchen if you'd like."

I follow her through the living room, to a big typically Amish kitchen. Cabinets painted robin's-egg blue. Formica countertops. The cast-iron woodstove throws off a little too much heat. A kerosene-powered refrigerator vibrates in the corner. Ahead, a doorway leads to the mudroom. There, I see the coat tree, laden with *kapp*s and a man's flat-brimmed hat.

"Bone broth smells good." I set the bag of doughnuts on the table and pull out the three paper plates and napkins I brought with me.

"It's my *mamm*'s recipe. An old one." At the stove, she stirs the broth and replaces the lid. Mild surprise registers in her eyes when she sees that I've set out plates and napkins. "Well then, while Ben's in the barn, maybe the three of us will just sneak a few of these doughnuts.

"Fannie!" she calls out, and then to me, "*Kaffi?*"

"*Dank.*" Using a napkin, I set doughnuts on the plates.

Fannie appears in the doorway. She's wearing a green dress. White *kapp*. Gray sneakers. I'm surprised to see the pediatric sling that secures her left arm in place across her chest.

"Hi, Chief Burkholder," she says with a smile.

"That's a nice-looking sling you're wearing," I say to the girl. "What happened?"

Loretta pours coffee from a percolator, looks at us over her shoulder. "Snuck out of the house to ride that horse last night is what happened." She clucks her mouth. "Going too fast, I imagine. Fell off down by the creek. Broke her clavicle." She carries two cups to the table, sets one in front of me. "We knew she was going to get hurt sooner or later."

I look at Fannie. "You weren't speeding, were you?"

A not-so-guilty grin. "The rein broke and I couldn't stop him."

"*Sitz dich anne un havva faasnachtkuche.*" Sit yourself down and have a doughnut.

The girl pulls out a chair next to me and sits. Despite her injury, she goes directly for the doughnut and bites into it with relish.

At the counter, Loretta pours milk into her coffee. "You'll be lucky if your *datt* doesn't sell that horse."

"He's a good horse," Fannie defends.

Knowing I don't have much time, I smile at Fannie and touch the side of my mouth with my finger, indicating to her she's got a speck of doughnut on her lip.

"Oh." She scrubs the napkin across her mouth and raises her brows.

"Let me." I take her napkin, blot in a place where I'll likely get spit. "There you go."

The girl grins, takes the napkin, and for an instant I can't look away. Rachael Schwartz had strawberry-blond hair, eyes the color of a tropical sea, and a face so pretty it hurt to look at her because the world somehow never seemed to measure up. Fannie is brown haired and brown eyed. She's plain, her face unremarkable. Except for that dazzle of light in her eyes . . .

"Katie?"

Loretta hands me a cup of coffee. She's looking at me oddly. Fannie, too, and I realize one of them said something I didn't hear.

"*Dank.*"

"Are you feeling all right?" Loretta asks.

"Just a little sleep deprived," I tell her.

"Well, now that this horrible mess is over, maybe you can get some rest," the Amish woman tells me.

I glance toward the doorway to the mudroom, where the coat tree holding the *kapp*s stares back at me. Most Amish women have at least two. One for every day and one for worship. From where I'm sitting, I can see that one of the *kapp*s has a tiny bow at the back. A shadowy spot of teal paint on top. Fannie's *kapp*. The one she wears every day that's waiting to be washed—and likely laden with DNA. If I can't get Fannie's napkin into a baggie without being seen, I might be able to pocket the *kapp*.

"All right, my girl." Loretta brings her hands together. "Why don't you run next door and see if Mrs. Yoder wants some of this nice broth, so Katie and I can talk."

"Can I have another doughnut?" The girl rises, scoots her chair back to the table.

I look at the napkin on her plate. The one I used to blot her mouth. I'm aware of the baggie in my jacket pocket.

"She eats like her *datt*." Loretta shakes her head. "Go on now. Tell Mrs. Yoder I got plenty."

I rise to gather the paper plates.

At the doorway, Fannie looks at me and smiles. "Bye, Katie."

I grin, look at her over my shoulder. "Stay out of trouble."

Aware that Loretta is at the stove, replacing the lid on the Dutch oven, I snatch up the girl's napkin. Keeping my back to Loretta, I flick out the baggie, tuck the napkin into it.

"Oh, I can take care of the throwaways, Katie. You just sit and enjoy your *kaffi*."

"No problem," I say easily. "I've got it."

I'm sealing the baggie when I hear the creak of a floorboard. I look up to see Ben Bontrager standing in the doorway of the mudroom, looking at me.

"What was it you wanted to talk about?"

I hear Loretta's voice behind me. The tap of her spoon against the Dutch oven where the bone brother simmers. I can't stop looking at Ben. I don't know how long he's been there. If he saw what I did. If he understands what he saw.

"I mainly just wanted to bring the doughnuts." As nonchalantly as I can manage, I shove the baggie into my jacket pocket.

I meet Ben's stare, force a smile. "If you like doughnuts, you're in luck."

"I like them just fine."

He steps into the kitchen. He's been working. Leather gloves in his left hand. A shovel in his right hand. Mud on his boots. Bits of hay stuck to his trousers.

"Now just look at all that mud you've tracked in," Loretta says.

Ben says nothing. Continues to stare at me. The hairs prickle at my nape. I'm aware of my police radio clipped to my shirt. My .38 pressing against my hip. "I've got to get back to work," I say.

The blow comes from behind. A *clang!* of steel above my ear. The force snaps my head sideways. A lightning strike of pain as my scalp splits open. Before I even realize I'm going to fall, my knees hit the floor.

I shake myself, glance right, see Loretta swing the cast-iron lid lifter. I block the blow with my forearm. The steel zings against bone. Another explosion of pain. The length of cast iron clatters to the floor between us.

I yank out the .38, bring it up. "Do not move! Get your hands up!"

I get one foot under me, lurch to my feet when another blow smashes against the back of my head. My vision narrows and dims. I swivel, catch a glimpse of Ben. Shovel at the ready. Lips peeled back. Teeth clenched.

I fire twice, the sound deafening in the confines of the kitchen. My timing is off, my balance skewed. I sway right. The shovel goes up again.

"Drop it!" I shout.

The steel spade crashes against my crown with the force of a freight train. Consciousness spirals down, water being sucked into a drain. The lights flicker. Then my cheek slams against the floor and the darkness welcomes me in.

CHAPTER 37

Spring 2009

For the first time in her life, Rachael Schwartz mourned the loss of her faith. Tonight, the darkest of nights, she needed the comfort of knowing she wasn't going to die alone and in agony, and that she wasn't the last person left on earth.

She should have been prepared. She'd known this moment would come. She and Loretta had discussed it. For months now, they'd planned everything down to the last detail. But Rachael had been in denial. She'd spent weeks ignoring the changes, hiding the weight gain and the swelling of her breasts. Not only from her parents, but from herself. She'd denied the cold, hard truth of what had happened.

Of course, Fate didn't give a good damn if she was ready or not.

Pain screamed through her body. The power of it took her breath, frightened her. It shook her physically, emotionally. Rachael was no stranger to pain. She'd broken her arm when she was nine. Last year, she'd had her wisdom teeth pulled by the English dentist. This was like nothing she'd ever experienced.

Rachael hadn't told anyone. Not even her *mamm*. No one in the Amish community knew she was *ime familye weg*. She'd known they would judge her harshly. And so she'd weathered this storm alone.

The pains had started after supper. At first, Rachael thought it was indigestion. By midnight she was pacing and upset and she knew it wasn't going to go away. If she didn't leave soon, everyone would know; her life would be over. And so after her parents went to bed, she'd sneaked from the house. She cut through the cornfield, fighting her way through mud, panting like an animal, bending and clutching her belly with every wave of pain. She called Loretta from the phone shack and asked her to meet her at the bridge, like they'd planned. By the time Rachael got there, she was hysterical and crying and certain this would be her last night on earth.

Relief swamped her at the sight of her friend's buggy.

"Rachael!" Loretta rushed toward her. "What's wrong?"

"It's time," she cried.

Loretta reached her, set her hand on her back. "You're going to be all right. Come on. Let's go."

She choked out a sob as another cramp ripped through her middle. She staggered right, leaned against the beam. A warm flood gushed between her legs, soaking her underthings and shoes. Horrified, Rachael looked down, watched it run down her legs, and splash onto the ground at her feet.

She knew what it was; she'd read about all the things that would happen. But to see it was an out-of-body experience.

"I don't want to do this!" she cried.

"It's okay," Loretta said. "It's normal. But we don't have much time."

Loretta put her arm around her. Rachael closed her eyes and let her friend guide her to the buggy. For the first time in hours, she didn't feel alone. Still, she sobbed while her friend climbed onto the driver's bench. She lost herself to the pain as they drove, the horse's shod hooves clanking against the asphalt.

The Willowdell Motel was a trashy old place that had been sitting on an unsightly slice of land for as long as Rachael could remember. For weeks now, she'd debated where she would go. She'd thought about the abandoned Hemmelgarn place down by Dogleg Road. The old barn out on Township Road 1442. At one point, she'd even considered going to the midwife in Coshocton. In the end, she'd decided on the motel, where there was a bed and towels and a shower.

Lying in the back seat of the buggy, Rachael rode out another cramp while Loretta went inside and paid for a room. Rachael had given the money to her a week ago, after she'd made the decision to do it here.

"Room 9."

Rachael looked up from her misery and watched her friend climb into the buggy. "Park in the back," she said. "Where no one can see the buggy. Hurry."

The room was furnished with a single bed draped with a blue coverlet. A window covered with ill-fitting curtains squatted over a metal air conditioner that blew air reeking of mildew and rattled like a train. While Loretta tethered the horse, Rachael went inside, dropped her overnight bag on the chair next to the bed, and went to the bathroom.

Fear and a terrible sense of disbelief roiled inside her as she stripped off her clothes. Bare feet on a broken tile floor. A smear of blood on her leg. A bright red drop of it on the tile next to her toes. Fear pulsing in a body that was no longer hers. A body she didn't recognize or understand. Pain so frightening she could do nothing but sob as she stepped into the tub. She soaped up, not caring that her hair got wet. Twice she went to her knees. Not to pray, but to ease the pain.

Still damp, she crawled into the bed, pulled the sheet and coverlet over her. She barely noticed when Loretta came in. But she saw the uncertainty on her friend's face as she took the chair next to the bed. "I brought Tylenol."

Rachael knew it wouldn't help. Nothing would help. She didn't even care at this point. "Give them to me. Hurry."

Quickly, Loretta went to the bathroom and filled a plastic glass with tap water. Next to the bed, she tapped out four acetaminophen tablets and handed them to her.

Rachael snatched them up, tossed all four into her mouth, and swallowed them with a gulp of water. She'd never been prone to tears; not like some girls. She was tougher than that. But at some point, she'd begun to cry again. The helpless, whimpering sobs of a dying animal.

"I don't think I can do this," she cried.

"Yes, you can. Women do it all the time."

Agony ripped at her insides, turning her inside out. Nausea seesawed in her gut and for a moment she thought she might throw up. "I have to . . ." Rachael bit down on the word, grinding her teeth. "Use the bathroom."

"No, you don't," Loretta said. "It's just the baby telling you he's ready to come into the world."

Rachael fisted the sheets, turning left and right, trying to find a position that would ease the pain. Angry now because nothing helped. "I don't know how to do this! I don't—" A wail squeezed from her throat. "I have to . . ."

"Shhh! Quiet!"

Rachael squeezed her eyes closed, brought the pillow to her face and screamed. "It hurts!"

Straightening, Loretta rushed to the bathroom and returned with two face cloths. A damp one, which she placed on Rachael's forehead.

A dry one, which she rolled up and handed it to her. "Bite down on this when the pain is too much," she whispered.

Rachael grabbed her friend's hand, squeezed it hard. Before she could say anything, the pain gripped her. Writhing, she fumbled with the cloth, jammed it into her mouth, and bit down as hard as she could. She rode the wave that way, biting down so hard she thought she might shatter her teeth.

The urge to push overrode her fear that she would mess the bed. She bore down hard, felt her insides cramp and tear. She screamed into the towel, pulled it hard against her lower molars. Body wet with sweat. Hair still damp from her shower.

This time, the cramp didn't subside. It came and came and came until she couldn't breathe. Thought she would pass out. Or die. She bore down again, grunting, the ugly sounds of a mindless beast. She opened her legs, spread them wide, not caring about modesty or the sheets or anything else. All she knew was that she wanted this thing out of her. She wanted the pain to stop. She wanted to be done with it.

She pushed against the pressure with all of her might. At some point, she looked at her friend, saw her pale face suffused with horror and fascination. Before she could speak or think, another riot of pain ripped through her.

She grabbed her knees, pulled them to her shoulders. She wanted to sit up, but couldn't. Another cramp rolled through her, movement in her abdomen. Pressure low and building. An elongated scream tore from her throat as she pushed. She bore down hard, unable to catch her breath, and the room spun. She closed her eyes, sucked in a breath, held it as she tried desperately to force it from her body.

A tearing sensation between her legs. Lessening pressure, like bowels breaking free.

"I see the top of his head!" Squealing, Loretta took her hand. "It's coming out! Go ahead and push!"

Lying on her back, she gripped both knees, curling upward with the effort. Sounds she didn't recognize tearing from her throat. Everything else falling away.

Loretta moved to the foot of the bed. Bent over her, looking at her. "Keep going!" she said. "Push. You can do it. Push!"

Rachael closed her eyes and bore down. The sensation of tearing. The knowledge that her body would never be the same.

"Oh! Oh! It's a girl!"

Rachael caught a glimpse of her friend's face. Eyes wide and excited and filled with awe.

"She's out," Loretta said. "I've got her."

Rachael fell back into the pillows. Breaths rushing. Body slicked with perspiration. The sheets around her damp with it.

"There's a cord."

Loretta set the baby in a ratty towel. A tiny body slicked with fluids. An instant later, Rachael heard a cry, like a kitten's mewl. The sensation of the cord still within her.

She looked away. "Cut it," she said, and for the first time since the first pang of labor, she thought about what came next.

"I brought Mamm's shears." Loretta cut the cord, capturing the blood with a face cloth. "There."

She then swaddled the baby tightly in the towel, rolling her from side to side and tucking in the edges. "That's how the midwife does it," she said. "Tight, like this, so she doesn't scratch herself with those little fingernails."

Loretta got to her feet and looked at Rachael, her expression uncertain, questioning. "Do you want to hold her?"

Rachael didn't look at her friend; she didn't look at the baby. She shook her head.

"Oh, but she's so cute. Just look at her." Smiling, Loretta looked down at the baby, running her finger over the little cheek. "Such a precious thing. Her lips are like a satin bow."

When Rachael said nothing, she added, "This child is a gift from God. No matter how she came to be, this little angel is—"

Rachael cut her off. "You're not having second thoughts, are you?"

A moment of hesitation and then, "Of course not. It's just that . . . you're exhausted and overwhelmed. Maybe *you're* the one having second thoughts. I wouldn't blame you, especially after what you've been through."

"I don't want her," Rachael said. "I don't want to be a mother. You know that."

Loretta looked down at the baby, tears glittering. "Are you sure?"

Rachael studied her friend, wondering how she could be so happy— so *good*—when life dished out such terrible things. Having children and a family are a key part of being Amish. Children are welcomed with joy and considered "a heritage of the Lord." She wondered what was wrong with her. Why didn't she want her own baby?

"You and Ben have been married for what? Seven months now?" Rachael asked. "And yet God hasn't seen fit to bless you with a child."

"These things take time," Loretta said. "God will not be rushed."

"It's a sign, Loretta. It means everything we talked about is the right thing to do."

Loretta looked up, met her gaze, her expression serene. "But how . . ."

"Ben still thinks you're *ime familye weg*?" Rachael asked.

Loretta nodded. "Mamm, too. Everyone does. I made that pillow, you know. I've been wearing it under my dress for weeks now." She looked down at the baby, but not before Rachael discerned the hint of shame in her eyes.

"So we go through with our plan," Rachael said. "Just like we talked about."

"What if it doesn't work?" Loretta whispered. "What if someone finds out?"

"No one is going to find out," Rachael assured her. "All we have to do is stay calm and stick to our plan."

Looking down at the newborn in her arms, Loretta blinked back tears. "I love her already."

"See? You're a natural," Rachael said, watching, relieved. "You'll see. Everything will work out. Ben is going to be so happy. Your *mamm* and *datt*. You, too."

Loretta's brows knit. "It sounded so . . . easy when we talked about it. I mean, before. Now that the baby is here, how do I explain—"

"I got it all worked out." Rachael tapped her temple with her index finger. "I thought of every last detail. Every question. Here's what we're going to do."

And she began to talk.

CHAPTER 38

"Hello? Anyone home?" Skid knocked on the door hard enough to rattle the glass.

No one came.

He'd tried the front door, the back door, and the side door off the porch by the garden, all to no avail.

Puzzled, he hit his shoulder mike and hailed the chief. "I'm ten-twenty-three," he said. "What's your twenty?"

Radio silence hissed, same as it had the first time he'd tried to reach her, ten minutes ago.

He took the steps to the sidewalk and started toward his cruiser, which was parked in the gravel area between the house and barn. He'd been looking forward to a quiet shift. A breakfast burrito from LaDonna's Diner. Coffee from that new café on Main. He'd especially been looking forward to using the men's room somewhere.

Where the hell was Burkholder?

Cursing beneath his breath, he hailed Dispatch. "Mona?"

"What up?"

He grinned at the sound of her voice—which he liked a little too much these days—and he was glad there was no one around to see him. She was filling in for Lois today, which meant she'd be there when he ended his shift. "Any idea where the chief is?"

"Last I heard she was headed out to the Bontrager place."

"That's what I thought." He looked around. "She's not here."

"That's weird." A beat of silence. "Did you try her cell?"

"I'll try again. Over and out." Skid pulled his cell from his pocket, hit the speed dial for Kate. Four rings and then voicemail. "Well, shit."

Puzzled, he walked to his cruiser, opened the door to get in, and then closed it. Fingers of something that felt vaguely like concern pressed into the back of his neck. One of the things he liked most about the chief was that she was reliable and always available. Day or night.

"So unless you're in the damn shower," he muttered, "you ought to be picking up the phone."

Had she run into some problem on her way here? Or was there something else going on?

Leaning against the hood of his cruiser, he checked his phone again and looked around, wrinkled his nose at the waft of manure coming from the barn. Damn, he hated dairy operations. They were all mud and stink and he'd had enough of both to last him a lifetime. He was reaching for the car door handle when he noticed the barn's sliding door standing open about a foot. Wondering if there was someone inside who hadn't seen or heard him, he started that way.

He reached the barn, pushed the door open another foot, and peeked inside. "Hello?" he called out. "Police department! Anyone here?"

The interior smelled of cattle and sour milk, the stink made worse by the manure pit out back. He entered, his eyes adjusting to the murky light. A dozen or so stanchions ahead. Milking apparatus that didn't look too clean. A big generator that smelled of kerosene and sludge. To his right were the stairs to the hayloft above. Skid glanced left. Everything inside him ground to a halt at the sight of the vehicle parked halfway down the aisle. It was a newish Toyota Camry. Red. If he wasn't mistaken, that was the rental car the chief was driving.

Senses on alert, he strode to the vehicle, set his hand against the hood, found it warm to the touch. Did she have some mechanical problem after she'd arrived? Dead battery and no jump? If that was the case, why was the vehicle parked in the barn?

He spoke into his radio. "I'm ten-twenty-three out at the Bontrager place. Mona, I got a vehicle out here. I'm pretty sure it's the chief's. Can you ten-twenty-eight?" He read the license plate number to her. "She been in contact?"

"Negative."

Skid looked around. No one in sight. Not even a damn cow. He was reaching for the Camry's door handle when he spotted a smear on the window. Not dirt or mud. Pulling out his mini Maglite, he leaned close for a better look. Blood.

"Shit."

"What's going on?"

"I got blood." He yanked open the door. His heart did a slow roll at the sight of the .38 revolver on the seat. Her clip-on mike. "Get County out here. Ten-thirty-nine." Lights and siren. "I'm going to take a look around."

CHAPTER 39

Consciousness returns with the ebb and flow of a gentle tide. Warm water lapping against sand and then rushing back out to sea. I'm aware of movement and light and the vicious pound of pain in my head. Something coarse scraping my cheek. The smells of old wood and dust and moldy feed. Nausea bubbles like hot grease in my stomach. Bile in my mouth.

I spit, realize I've been slobbering. I try to lift my hand to wipe my mouth, but I can't move my arms. I have no idea where I am. All I know is that I'm in a bad way. Confusion is a bottomless pit. But the muscle memory of fear hovers just out of reach, coiled tight and ready to spring.

Get up, a little voice whispers. *Get up.*

I open my eyes. I see a mound of loose hay a foot from my face. I'm lying on my side, my face against weathered wood. I'm being jostled, bumped and rocked back and forth. I hear the jingle of a harness. The clip-clop of shod hooves.

I raise my head, look around. My vision blurs, so I blink it away, try to focus. Pain roils in my head. The jostling triggers another rise of nausea. I spit, set my head back down, close my eyes.

Get up, Kate. Get up! Hurry!

The memory of the events that brought me to this moment rushes back. Adrenaline jets into my muscles, making them twitch. The fear that follows sends me bolt upright. I'm in the back bed of a hay wagon. Two horses pulling it along a dirt road. There's an open field to my left. Thick woods on the right. I see blood on the wood where I'd been lying. My hands are bound behind my back. Ben Bontrager sits in the driver seat, leather lines in his hands, looking at me over his shoulder. Blank expression. Mouth set. Loretta sits next to him, staring straight ahead.

"Ben, what the hell are you doing?" I grind out the words as I test the binding at my wrists. Wire, I realize, tight enough to cut off my circulation.

"Stay where you are." He turns back to his driving. "We're almost there."

"Ben, you can't do this." I work at the wire, twisting and tugging as I speak. "I'm a cop. There's an officer on the way."

The Amish man ignores me, jiggles the lines, continues on.

I take in my surroundings, try to get my bearings. Nothing is familiar. I have no idea how far we've traveled or how long I was unconscious. We're not on a public road. No sign of the farmhouse. My best guess is that we're somewhere in the back of his property.

I glance down at my right hip. My .38 is gone. My radio and shoulder mike are gone. Shit. *Shit.*

"Ben." I say his name firmly, as if I still have any say in a matter that has spiraled out of control. "Stop the horses. Untie me. Right now. Before this goes too far."

No response. No indication that he even heard me.

"Where's my gun?" I ask. "My radio. For God's sake, people are looking for me. Cops."

Nothing.

"Turn around and look at me," I snap, adding authority to my voice that's ridiculous at this point.

Loretta looks over her shoulder at me. Her face impassive.

"Take me back to the house," I tell her. "So we can talk about this. Get things worked out."

No one responds.

I try another tack. "Where are you taking me?"

The couple exchanges a look, but they don't answer, they don't look at me.

I shift, try to get my legs under me. I'm unsteady, but manage to get to one knee. I'm about to rise when, without warning, Ben swings around. He lifts the buggy whip and brings the thick handle end of it down on my shoulder. "Stay there," he warns.

I duck and turn away. The second blow strikes my back. The lash of pain roils my temper. "Cut it out," I hiss.

He offers up a third blow. A glance off my right cheekbone. I grit my teeth, take it. Nothing else I can do.

"*Mer sott em sei eegne net verlosse,*" the Amish man snaps. One should not abandon one's own. "You did, Kate Burkholder. You left the Amish way. You abandoned God. He no longer sees you as one of us."

I stare at him, wondering if he's got my .38 on him. "God loves all of His children," I hear myself say. "Amish. English. It doesn't matter to Him."

"*Huahrah.*" Whoremonger. Making a sound of disgust, he turns away and goes back to his driving.

I lean against the side of the wagon, the wood rasping my back. Desperation presses down. I'm unarmed and incapacitated, in the middle of nowhere, with a man who will likely do me harm. I remind myself that Skid is probably wondering where I am. It's only a matter of time before he comes looking. My feet aren't bound, which means I can run if I get the chance. If I can reach the woods, I might be able to elude them until backup arrives.

I stare at their backs a moment before speaking. "What about Fannie?" I ask. "Have you thought about what this will do to her?"

Loretta turns to me. No longer is she the mouselike woman with the dish towel tossed over her shoulder and her eyes cast down. Now, she is a mother whose child is under threat, willing to do whatever it takes to protect what is hers.

"You are *veesht*," she hisses. Wicked. "Your heart is filled with *lushtahrei*." Immorality. "You are not *Amisch*. You were never Amish." She raps the heel of her hand against her chest. "Not inside. Not here, where it counts."

"This isn't about me," I tell her. "It's about Fannie."

"Leave her out of this," Loretta spits.

My mind races for some way to reach her, land upon some point that will help me negotiate my way out of this or at least defuse the situation until help arrives.

"I know what happened," I tell her. "I know it wasn't your fault."

Neither of them engage, so I keep going. "I think Rachael became *ime familye weg* the night Dane Fletcher assaulted her. I think she hid it from her family. From everyone. She had the baby. An innocent little girl. Only she didn't want it, did she?"

The Amish woman stares straight ahead. "Be quiet, Katie."

I keep pushing. "I know what she did. I know what you did. I'm not blaming either of you."

"*Leeyah.*" Liar. She turns to me, eyes flaring. "You know nothing. Backslider. Who are you to judge? We will not let you take her."

In the minutes I've been talking, I've worked at the wires wrapped around my wrists, bending and flexing, but the steel holds fast. At some point, I've cut my skin. I feel a dribble of blood making its way across my knuckles.

"No one's going to take her from you." I say the words with a gentleness that belies the situation. "There may be some legal issues, but there's no reason why you can't legally adopt Fannie and continue to raise her as your own."

It's not true, of course. This couple has committed multiple felonies. They will be prosecuted and, if convicted, probably spend time behind bars.

"All you have to do," I say, "is untie me. We go back to the house and come up with a plan. I know we can work it out."

The Amish woman slants a questioning look at her husband. For the first time, she appears uncertain. She wants the words to be true. She wants the problem of me to go away. Most of all, she wants Fannie.

"I think it's too late," she whispers.

"Do the right thing," I coax. "The police will be here any moment. Whatever you have planned isn't going to work."

Ben casts a warning look at his wife. "*Sell is nix as baeffzes.*" That is nothing but trifling talk. "No one is coming. Don't listen to her."

I look around. The woods are about fifty yards away. The field to my left looks fallow. There's no cover, not a single tree or fence. I have no idea what they have planned or where they're taking me. They're not going to let me go. If I'm going to get away, now is the time.

Never taking my eyes from the couple, I set my heels against the wood bed. The jingle of the harnesses, the wagon bumping and rocking over the rough road, cover the noise I make as I scooch my feet closer to the side of the wagon. Using the side for balance, I get to my knees. The horses are trotting, but the pace is slow enough for me to jump without getting hurt.

Eyes on the backs of my captors, I get to my feet, set my right foot atop the side. Out of the corner of my eye I see Ben's head swivel. I jump, land on my feet, and hit the ground running.

"*Ivvah-nemma!*" Take over.

Ben Bontrager's voice rings out. No time to look. I keep going, sprint toward the tree line fifty yards away. I hear Loretta shout, but I don't comprehend the words. I train my eyes on the woods ahead. Old-growth forest, thick with bramble.

"*Shtobba!*" Stop!

Ben's voice, scant yards behind me. I pour on the speed, too fast. Praying I don't trip. My balance off because I can't use my hands.

There's a ditch at the edge of the woods. Too wide to hurdle. I plunge into a foot of muddy water, muscle through, charge up the other side. Then I'm in the trees, zigzagging between trunks as wide as a man's shoulders. I hear the sound of breaking brush behind me. Another jet of adrenaline hits my muscles. A branch comes out of nowhere, punches my cheek, opens the skin. I duck, ignoring the pain, keep running.

"Skid! *Skid!*" I know there's no one around. I call out anyway. "Police Department! Help! *Help me!*"

I know Bontrager is going to catch me. It's inevitable. He's faster, not hampered by bound hands. Still, it's a shock when his fingers clamp around my arm. One moment I'm running full out, the next I'm being yanked backward with so much force that my feet leave the ground. I land on my backside and roll. I'm scrambling to my feet when Bontrager puts his boot on my back.

"Get off me," I snarl.

He looks down at me, breaths labored. Sweat beaded on his forehead.

I see stress etched into his every feature, and I know the fear of losing the child he's raised from birth has sent him over the edge. Looking into his eyes, I see something else, even more unexpected. The regret of a man who knows he's about to make a mistake that cannot be undone.

"Please don't do this," I say.

"*Greeyah ruff.*" Get up. There's no rage or high passion in his voice— just the steel resolve of a man who expects complete submission.

"I'm not going anywhere with you," I say.

Bending, he hauls me to my feet and shoves me toward the wagon. "*Gay.*" Go.

When I don't move fast enough, he shoves me in the direction of the wagon. "Keep walking."

We leave the cover of trees. I listen for a distant siren. The rumble of an engine. Where the hell is Skid?

Ahead, I see Loretta standing near the wagon, looking around, her hands on her hips. "*Dumla,*" she says. Hurry.

I slow, stalling, but Ben shoves me again.

Only then do I recognize where we are. We've left the Bontrager property and entered adjacent land upon which a two-room Amish school once stood. I attended school here. A few years ago, a tornado leveled the structure. The only thing left is the decrepit foundation and stone chimney. Beyond, there's a gravel two-track that continues on for another half mile or so, eventually opening onto County Road 60.

Why the hell have they brought me here?

"Bring her." The Amish woman strides past the foundation to an area overrun with high grass and the spindly stalks of last year's weeds.

"Walk." Ben shoves my shoulder again.

I have no idea what they have planned or hope to accomplish. What are my options? Appeal to reason? Their Amish mores? Threaten them with the consequences of their actions? Losing custody of their daughter?

Loretta stops next to the stump of a long-dead tree. I've been here before, I realize. The school outhouse once stood on this very spot. The only thing left is the pit, where the refuse was stored and removed.

Uneasiness quivers in my gut at the sight of the pit. It's about five feet deep with crumbling cinder-block walls choked with roots and tangled with weeds. A huge pile of freshly excavated dirt is next to the pit. Someone has recently taken a shovel to it, cleared out most of the debris and earth.

"This is not the way we wanted to do this," Loretta whispers.

"Don't do anything stupid," I say. "It'll only make things worse for you. For Fannie."

"You should have let things lie." Ben says the words as if he didn't hear me. "You've left us no choice. Whatever happens here today is between you and God."

I'd been working under the assumption that I'd be able to talk them out of whatever crazy scheme they'd hatched. For the first time it occurs to me they didn't bring me here to convince me of their cause. I'm in danger. The ripple of fear that follows is so powerful that the ground trembles beneath my feet.

"I know what we are about to do is a sin against God," Ben says. "That we will go to hell for it. But I will not let them take Fannie."

My heart begins to pound. If I were to be pushed into the pit, I'm pretty sure I could eventually climb out, even with my wrists bound. In the back of my mind, I wonder if he's going to pull out the .38 and kill me and then push all that dirt into the pit. . . .

"You have brought the wrath of the Lord down upon yourself," Loretta says. "You are *eevil*." Evil. "You are a threat. Not only to us and our daughter's life. But everything that is decent and good—"

I launch myself toward the trees. Ben lunges so quickly, I don't have time to brace. He shoves me with so much force that I fly sideways and plummet into the pit. I hit the ground so hard that the breath is knocked from my lungs.

I roll, spit dirt, try to suck in a breath of air. I struggle to my knees, look up in time to see the shovel. I duck, avoid the blow, but it's so close I feel the puff of air against my face.

Holding the shovel like a bat, Ben swings again. Purpose etched into his features. Lips drawn back. I lunge sideways, but I'm not fast enough. The blade grazes the top of my head with enough force to open the skin. I feel the warm trickle of blood.

"Don't do this!" I shout. "Think of Fannie! She needs you!"

Staying low, watching for the shovel, I look around for a way out. A place where the wall isn't vertical. A foothold, a broken cinder block or root or jut of rebar. The pit is about five feet square, the muddy floor littered with dead vegetation and loose dirt.

Ben jabs the shovel at me again. I'm far enough below him that I'm able to get out of the way and he misses again. I stumble to the opposite side of the pit, spot the jut of root. I rush to it, step up on it, press my shoulder against the wall to keep my balance. If I can find another foothold, I might be able to wriggle high enough to escape. . . .

The shovel strikes the side of my head with so much force that I'm knocked off my perch. I hear the *tink!* of the blade strike my skull. The zing of pain down the side of my face. Then I'm falling into space and the darkness swallows me whole.

CHAPTER 40

Skid was well versed in all the ins and outs of police procedure. He'd had it drilled into his head since his first day at the academy a lifetime ago. He figured his finding the chief's abandoned vehicle and .38 qualified as just cause to enter the premises sans a warrant. He didn't bother knocking. It took him just a few minutes to ascertain there was no one in the house. He even went into the basement and attic. All to no avail.

"House is clear," he said into his shoulder mike. "You got an ETA on County?"

"They're ten-seven-six."

"Put out a BOLO for Ben and/or Loretta Bontrager's buggy." The request didn't feel right, because he'd seen a buggy in the barn. Did Amish people have more than one?

"Roger that."

"Something's wonky here, Mona," he said. "I'm going to look around."

"Pickles is ten-seven-six."

287

"Ten-four."

Skid left the house, jogged to the gravel area between the house and barn. There was a rusted steel gate next to the barn and a muddy two-track that ran toward the back of the property. He got into the cruiser, idled to the gate, and got out. Sure enough, marks in the dirt told him someone had recently opened the gate. On the other side were fresh horse tracks and the ruts of tires. He pushed open the gate. Back in the cruiser, he drove through.

At the top of the hill, he hailed Pickles. "What's your twenty, old man?"

"I'm two minutes out."

"I'm headed to the rear of the Bontrager property. Do you know if you can get in through the back? There a gate back there?"

"I think there's an old two-track down where that old schoolhouse used to be. You want me to meet you back there?"

Skid didn't know about the old schoolhouse. In fact, he wasn't counting on much help from Pickles. The guy might've been a good cop back in the day, but he was almost eighty now and sneaking a smoke every chance he got.

"That's affirm. Keep your eyes open, old man," he said. "I'm pretty sure someone's come back this way."

I don't remember falling or striking the ground. The next thing I become aware of is the press of damp earth against my cheek. Pain above my ear. The smell of dirt and decaying organic matter. I can't move my arms. . . .

I open my eyes to find myself staring at a wall of dirt and concrete block, dangling roots, and nondescript vegetation. I'm prone, the ground cold and wet beneath me. Raising my head, I look up to see Ben Bontrager slide a shovel into a pile of loose dirt.

It's a surreal scene. So strange that for a moment, I wonder if I blink, it'll go away. A shovelful of earth clatters onto my back. I try to sit up, but I'm tied to something heavy. I twist my head, smell the creosote an instant before I recognize the railroad tie.

A hot flare of panic courses through me as the hopelessness of the situation hits home. A railroad tie weighs about two hundred pounds; there's no way I can move it. I'm lying in the base of a deep pit and from all indications Ben Bontrager is planning to bury me alive.

"Loretta!" I look around for the Amish woman. "Don't do this!"

She looks down at me, then walks away without speaking, leaving my line of vision.

"*Help me!*" I work at the wires binding my wrists, no longer noticing the pain. My feet aren't bound, so I use the strength in my legs to try and disengage myself from the railroad tie. I dig my toes into the dirt. I grunt and scramble, like an animal snared in a trap. All to no avail.

A torrent of earth rains down. It goes into my hair. Down my collar, into my eyes. I look up to see Ben upend a wheelbarrow. "Stop!" I scream.

Blinking dirt from my eyes, I see Loretta come up beside him, pushing a second wheelbarrow. Ben usurps the handles and upends it.

Dirt and small stones come down atop me. It gets into my mouth. This time, there's so much, I feel the weight of it on my back.

I struggle mindlessly against the bonds, twisting. Back and forth. Back and forth. I kick my legs, throwing off the dirt. I buck against the railroad tie, clods rolling off me. Another wheelbarrow full of dirt plummets. I suck in dust and begin to cough. Panic smolders inside me, but I tamp it down, knowing it will do nothing but hinder my efforts.

Abruptly, I go still. I take a deep breath, release it slowly. I close my eyes. Grapple for a calm that isn't there. I hear the rattle of the wheelbarrow. The hiss of the shovel penetrating earth. I focus on the wires at my wrists. Try to pinpoint the weak point. I go at it again. Ignoring the steel slicing my flesh.

I remind myself Skid is on his way. He's a good cop; he'll find me. Eyes closed, I take a deep breath and scream at the top of my lungs. "Skid! I'm here! Help me! Help!"

My cries echo against the walls of the pit. I quash another wave of panic. A payload of earth hits my back, the weight pressing me down. I kick my legs, twist to rid myself of it. But the railroad tie locks me down tight. The dirt stays, and I can't help but wonder: How long before my face is covered? How long until I can't breathe? How long until I'm completely buried and even if someone comes, they won't find me?

Another volley of dirt pours down, strikes my face. It goes into my left ear. My eyes. My nose. Grit in my mouth.

Dear God.

I lift my head. Spit mud. "Skid!"

The wire on my wrists snaps. I twist my head around, look up to see Ben Bontrager. His back is to me. Loretta is nowhere in sight. I twist my hands and the remaining wire falls away.

I lie still. Facedown. Listening. My mind racing. Even with my hands free, if I try to climb out, one of them will bludgeon me and force me back down. I don't have much time. In the periphery of my vision, I see Ben move away, leaving my line of sight. No sign of Loretta, but I hear her speaking to him.

I jump to my feet, look around wildly. For a foothold. A weapon. Anything I can use. A three-foot length of rebar lies on the ground. I snatch it up, spot the jut of a broken cinder block. Heart pounding, I set my boot on the cinder block and heave myself up.

I hear the whoosh of air before I see the shovel. I glance left, see Ben swing it like a nine iron. But his angle is bad. I flatten myself against the earthen wall, feel the gust against the back of my head. I throw my leg over the top of the pit, scramble out. I roll, get to my knees, swing the rebar with all my might. Steel clangs against his shin with such force that I nearly lose my grip.

A howl tears from his throat. He drops the shovel. Goes down on one knee. Face contorted. But his eyes are on me. Enraged and filled with intent as he rises.

I scramble to my feet, kick his shovel away. Gripping the rebar with both hands, I swing it with all my might. The steel clocks him across the chest. He dances sideways, bends, snatches up the shovel, comes at me.

"Drop it! Do it now!"

Skid.

I swivel, catch sight of my officer rushing toward us, weapon drawn, moving fast.

Ben Bontrager swings the shovel at me. I pivot, reel backward. Trip on a clod of dirt. Lose my balance. I land on my backside.

The shovel arcs 180 degrees. A heavy hitter smacking in a home run, inches above my head.

"Drop it!" Skid screams. "Get your hands up! Now!"

A dozen things happen at once. I see Loretta rush Skid from behind, shovel raised over her head. "Behind you!" I shout.

Skid spins, fires once as the shovel comes down on his shoulder. The Amish woman drops. The shovel clatters to the ground. Cursing, Skid lowers his weapon, goes to his knees, injured.

Ben Bontrager charges Skid. Shovel at the ready. Footfalls heavy and pounding. A roar pouring from his mouth.

"Get on the ground! Show me your hands!" Pickles lumbers toward us. Ten yards away. An old man's run. But his weapon is trained and steady on Bontrager. Authority rings in his voice. "Do not move or I will put you down! Do you understand me? Get the hell down!"

For a moment, I think Bontrager isn't going to comply. That he's going to force Pickles to fire his weapon. But the Amish man's stride falters. A couple of feet from his wife, he stops. He looks down at her. The shovel clatters to the ground. He goes to his knees and raises both hands.

Pickles goes to him, works the handcuffs from the compartment on his belt. "Get down. On your face." He sets his knee on the Amish man's back. "Do not move."

Bontrager doesn't resist. Doesn't seem to care as Pickles snaps the cuffs onto his wrists and pats him down. The Amish man never takes his eyes off his wife.

I get to my feet. My legs are still shaking as I cross to where Loretta lies. I'm aware of Skid standing a few feet away, speaking into his shoulder mike, requesting an ambulance. Of Pickles standing over Ben Bontrager.

I kneel next to her. She's lying on her side, one arm stretched over her head, the other bent with her hand pressed against her abdomen. I can see the rise and fall of her chest. Her eyes open and blinking.

"You're going to be all right," I tell her.

Wincing, she shifts, rolls onto her back. "He shot me."

"I know," I say. "Be still. An ambulance is on the way."

Her hand falls away from her abdomen as if she no longer has the strength to keep it there. I see a hole the size of my thumb in the fabric of her dress, just below her rib cage. Blood runs from the wound, soaking the fabric and pooling on the ground.

"Here you go, Chief."

I look up to see Skid approach, his first aid kit in hand. He sets it on the ground, then passes me a sterile pack of gauze and a pair of disposable gloves.

"You okay?" I ask him.

"Didn't need that rotator cuff anyway." But he manages a half smile.

Snapping on the gloves, I turn my attention back to the injured woman. I open the gauze and press it firmly over the wound.

Loretta squeezes her eyes closed against the pain. "It was me," she whispers.

Blood soaks quickly through the gauze. I look up at Skid. He nods, letting me know he's listening, and he hands me a fresh wad. Saying nothing, I press it to the wound.

"Rachael," the Amish woman says. "She asked me to meet her at the motel. She'd been calling. I knew what she wanted."

"Fannie?" I ask.

"She said she wanted to know her daughter. I didn't believe her. Not for a moment. Rachael might've been curious, but she had no use for a twelve-year-old girl. Not with the kind of lifestyle she led. All she cared about was the money."

"What money?" I ask.

"I paid her four thousand dollars. To stay away from us. Away from Painters Mill. It wasn't enough. I knew it would never be enough. So I stopped her. To protect Fannie."

"How did you stop her?" I ask.

Her face screws up, in pain from the gunshot wound—or anguish because of what she did. I don't know. "I remember getting Fannie's bat out of the buggy. I was just going to scare her, you know. Tell her to take the money. To go away and never come back."

Loretta begins to cry. "She was actually happy to see me. Can you imagine? And then I just . . . I don't know what happened. I was so angry. I hit her and then she was on the floor. The bat was in my hand. It was as if the devil took over my body. He made me do ungodly things."

Skid hands me another wad of gauze and I put it to use. "How much does Ben know?" I ask.

"He didn't know any of it. Just that Fannie was adopted. He never questioned me. It all came out the night that deputy attacked me in the barn. I told him everything."

I hear the wail of sirens. I'm aware of Pickles and Skid standing next to us. The bark and hiss of their radios. Most of all, I'm aware of the blood soaking the gauze, oozing between my fingers at an alarming rate, and the growing pool beneath her.

"I was always the good one," she whispers.

"Loretta, stay with me," I say. "Stay with me."

The Amish woman fades to unconsciousness.

CHAPTER 41

There is comfort in what is familiar. An inner calm that comes with ritual and routine. We find reprieve from turmoil when we partake in the things we know. The heart finds solace in the company of those we love. I'm lucky to have all of those elements in my life, especially the people I love.

I'm sitting on a gurney in the emergency room of Pomerene Hospital, wondering where the doctor has gone, debating whether I should make my getaway while the getting away is good. The side of my head is numb where two nasty lacerations were cleaned and closed. I've been X-rayed, injected, and CT-scanned. Hopefully I'll get a clean bill of health and be on my way soon. I've no intention of spending the night.

I'm wearing a hospital gown with a paper sheet covering my legs, which are bruised and smeared with mud. Someone tucked my trousers, shirt, and boots into a bag and placed them on a shelf. I can see the caked mud from where I'm sitting.

Through all the tests and good humor, I haven't been able to stop thinking about the case. About Rachael Schwartz. About Loretta and Ben Bontrager. And, of course, Fannie.

I understand why they did what they did. To protect the child they'd loved since birth and raised as their own. Rachael Schwartz threatened to destroy all of it. After she was gone, I became a threat. What I can't reconcile is that these two people were willing to commit multiple violent crimes—including murder—to protect their secrets. What they did goes against the very foundation of what it means to be Amish. How could they possibly believe that God would forgive them their sins and they would be welcomed into heaven? Were the stakes so high that they convinced themselves the risk of hell was worth the gain?

Ben Bontrager was booked into the Holmes County jail. Loretta was taken by ambulance to Pomerene Hospital. Last I heard, Fannie was picked up by Children Services shortly after. The girl faces a great deal of upheaval in the coming hours and days and weeks. Likely, she'll be placed with a foster family initially, and then probably with her biological grandparents Rhoda and Dan Schwartz. I don't know how she'll fare. The one thing I do know is that the Amish community will step in to help with the transition and support her.

"Someone said there's a dirty cop back here."

I look up to see Glock shove aside the privacy curtain and pause upon seeing me.

"Dude, we're not supposed to be back here." Behind him, Skid glances over his shoulder as if expecting some stout nurse to stop them and escort them out.

Next to him, Pickles and Mona struggle to see past the curtain.

"You decent, Chief?" Mona asks.

Despite the headache pulsing above my left ear, I find myself grinning. "Decent enough."

I'm embarrassed because I'm pretty sure my smile is lopsided. Not only did the doc numb my scalp before applying a the staples, but they gave me some pain medication that's a little stronger than I expected.

When the men hesitate, Mona pushes her way past them and thrusts out a pretty bouquet of flowers she probably bought at the hospital gift shop. "How're you feeling?" she asks.

"I'm fine." Ignoring the thickness of my tongue, I watch my other three officers crowd in behind her, the men feeling awkward, trying not to show it.

"Nice mohawk, anyway," Skid says.

Mona elbows him. "Dude."

He shoots her a what-did-I-do look.

All of it for my benefit, which I appreciate more than they can know.

"Any word on Loretta Bontrager's condition?" I ask.

"They airlifted her to Cleveland Clinic in Akron," Glock tells me. "No word on her condition, but they think she's going to pull through."

No one looks at Skid, including me. We're following that unwritten script. The one that tells us to give him some space, and a little time to shore up before you talk about it. Even if your suspect is going to be all right, having to fire your weapon at another human being is a traumatic experience that takes a toll.

Mona hefts the flowers and looks around for a place to put the vase.

Glock taps the side of his head with his index finger. "How's the head?" he asks me.

"The proud recipient of nine staples," I say, deadpan.

"That's pretty impressive." He looks at Skid. "You just got your departmental record beat."

He shakes his head, whistles. "Guess I'm going to have to up my game."

I turn my attention to Pickles. The old man is frowning at Mona, who's set the flowers atop a shelf that's too small and likely used for medical supplies.

"I owe you a big thank-you, Pickles," I tell him. "Situation would have turned out a lot differently if you hadn't gotten there when you did."

The old man raises his gaze to mine. He's a surly guy. He doesn't like the fact that he's getting old. That he can't move as fast as he once did. That he's past putting in long hours and being in the thick of things.

"Just doing my job, Chief." He can't quite meet my gaze. And in that moment, I see how much my recognizing him before his peers means to him.

Glock grins. "Don't let that go to your head, old man."

Skid follows suit. "Can't run worth a damn," he says good-naturedly.

Pickles huffs a laugh, but not before I see the flash of emotion in his eyes.

The curtain whooshes aside. All of us look that way, guilty because too many visitors have crowded into an otherwise quiet ER. Tomasetti stands there a moment, looking from person to person, and then offering me a look that's part smile, part scowl.

"Evidently, I'm late for the party," he says.

Glock clears his throat. Pickles brushes at a nonexistent speck of lint on his uniform. Skid looks down at his cell phone. Mona fiddles with the vase of flowers.

"I'll see if I can get a status on Loretta Bontrager," Glock says.

Nodding at Tomasetti, Mona makes a beeline for the still-open curtain. "Glad you're okay," she says.

"See you around, Chief." Skid offers a mock salute.

I look past Tomasetti to see Glock holding the curtain open and the rest of my team file out.

I smile at Tomasetti. "Took you long enough to get here."

He stares back. "Can't leave you alone for more than a few hours, can I?"

"Once again you underestimate my ability to get myself into trouble."

"Apparently, you are correct."

He crosses the distance between us in two strides, his eyes intense and steady on mine. Upon reaching me, he leans close and presses a kiss to my temple. "You scared the hell out of me," he whispers.

I close my eyes, overcome by his presence, his closeness, the sight and smell of him, the feel of his lips against my skin. "Not the first time," I whisper.

"Probably not the last."

His arms go around me. He pulls me tight against him. I feel the warmth of his face against mine. His hand against the back of my head. "I heard you had a close call."

"Too close," I say. "If it wasn't for Pickles and Skid . . ."

He shushes me with a kiss, then pulls away, runs his knuckles down the side of my face. "I heard about Pickles," he said. "Not bad for an old guy."

"You old guys are so underappreciated." My smile feels tremulous on my lips. "Any news on Fannie Bontrager?"

He grimaces and I'm reminded this man I love was the father of two girls who were about Fannie's age when they were killed. "Children Services picked her up. Foster parents will probably keep her for a day or two, until they can figure out the family situation."

I think about Rhoda and Dan Schwartz. Already mourning the loss of a daughter. A granddaughter they didn't know existed about to enter their lives. "The Amish believe children are a gift from God," I tell him.

"Most of us believe that," he tells me.

I nod. "If there's any good news to come out of this, it is that Fannie has family here in Painters Mill."

"Do you think they'll—"

"Yes," I say. "They will. They're Amish."

"I guess that just about says it all," he murmurs.

I motion toward my clothes on the shelf. "What do you say we get out of here before the nurse comes back and tries to cart me out in a wheelchair?"

He grins. "I think that's the best idea I've heard all week."

CHAPTER 42

Life is a river that never stops flowing. You can dam it, you can harness its power, you can poison it, but you can't stop it. A river never ends. It changes course and cuts through the land. It floods and damages and kills. It can be weakened by drought. But it never stops. It is the fundamental giver of life.

It's been two weeks since Loretta and Ben Bontrager tried to murder me in the field where the old Amish schoolhouse used to stand. My cuts and bruises are healed for the most part. The nightmares have dwindled. Tomasetti and I don't talk about it, but he always lets me know he's there for me if I need to.

This afternoon, I'm on duty and covering for Glock, who had an appointment with his wife, LaShonda. He hasn't made the announcement yet, but I'm pretty sure they're expecting their fourth child. That river of life, I think. It's a beautiful thing that fills me with hope for the future.

I'm idling down Folkerth Road, watching a team of horses pull a plow through river-bottom soil, when Lois's voice snaps over my radio.

"Chief, ten-twenty-nine."

A 10-29 is a general code my department uses for any type of juvenile situation and usually entails the Tuscarawas Bridge and a can of spray paint. "What's the twenty on that?"

"I just took a call from Rhoda Schwartz," she tells me. "Seems their granddaughter is missing."

A thread of worry whispers through me at the mention of Fannie. I'm not surprised. "Any idea how long she's been gone?"

"She thinks maybe a couple of hours. She called from the phone shack. She and her husband are out in the buggy looking."

"I'm ten-seven-six," I say, letting her know I'm on my way to the Schwartz farm.

I hang a U-turn in the middle of the road and head that way. I haven't seen or spoken to Fannie since the day Loretta and Ben Bontrager accosted me at their farm. But I've spent quite a bit of time thinking about her. Twelve is a difficult age for a girl, whether you're Amish or English. That's usually about the time you leave childhood behind and take that first tentative step—or misstep—into adulthood. There are a lot of unknowns, a lot of fears, none of which are easy to talk about. Add the kind of upheaval Fannie has been through to the mix, and it's a time that can become emotionally chaotic.

I'm passing by the Bontrager farm, which stands vacant now, and nearly to the greenbelt at the edge of the pasture when in the periphery of my vision I spot the horse and rider. I know immediately the rider is Fannie. I brake hard, hang another U-turn, and head that way.

If the girl notices me, she doesn't show it. The horse is galloping in the ditch alongside the road at a speed that would give any parent a panic attack. The girl leans forward, reins in one hand, a tuft of mane in the other, keeping perfect time with the animal's stride. I stop the Explorer a hundred or so yards ahead of her, so I'm visible to both horse and rider.

I pick up my radio. "I've got eyes on our ten-twenty-nine."

"Roger that."

I get out, walk around to the front, and lean against the hood. I watch her ride, a little awed because she's good, a little sad because at some point she probably won't be allowed to continue. A few yards away from where I stand, she straightens slightly, tugs gently on the reins.

"Whoa," she says quietly.

The animal slows to a trot and then to a walk; its steel shoes crunch against the gravel on the shoulder as it walks up to me. Ten feet away, she stops the animal. It's the same horse she was riding the day I met her. His nostrils are flared. There's a bit of lather on his flanks and where the saddle blanket rests on his shoulder.

"He's beautiful," I say.

She's not happy to see me. "You arrested my *mamm* and *datt*," she says.

"I don't blame you for being angry." I pretend to study the horse, but I'm cognizant of the girl, too. She's been crying. There's a smudge of dirt on her left cheek, and her tears left a trail.

I go to the animal, run my hand over its forehead, along its neck. She's braided the mane, securing the ends with rubber bands. I find myself thinking about Rachael Schwartz and that long-ago day when I found her sitting on that rocky shoal in Painters Creek, grinning like an imp, her face aglow with the aftereffects of adrenaline—and the eternal question of nurture versus nature stirs.

"I know professional horse trainers who can't ride like that," I tell her.

Her gaze jerks to mine, untrusting of the compliment, too angry with me to accept it. She doesn't quite know how to reject it, so I simply let the statement stand.

"I guess they sent you to pick me up," she mutters after a moment.

"They love you. They worry." I shrug. "Might've helped if you'd let them know where you were going."

"Like they'd give me permission," she huffs.

I don't know how much they've told her about Rachael Schwartz or the Bontragers. I don't know how much she's heard via the grapevine. I don't even know whether to call the Schwartzes her grandparents. Does she know that Rachael Schwartz was her mother? Does she know Loretta Bontrager took her mother's life?

"They don't like me to ride," she tells me. "They're probably going to sell him."

"Maybe you can come up with some kind of compromise."

"It's because I'm a girl." She speaks over me. I almost smile, because Rachael used to do exactly the same thing. "Amish girls don't ride."

I nod, pretend I don't notice when she swipes angrily at the tears that have begun to fall. "It's not fair," she spits.

This is where I have to bite my tongue. The truth of the matter is the Amish *are* a patriarchal society. Sometimes the boys and men are allowed to do things the women and girls are not. What some people fail to recognize is that while those roles are defined and separate, they're also equally important.

"You're right," I tell her. "Sometimes life isn't fair. It's a hard lesson, but we do the best we can. And we try not to worry the people who love us."

Fannie rolls her eyes at my philosophy, sniffs.

The clatter of shod hooves draws our attention. I look past Fannie to see a horse and buggy coming down the road at a fast clip. Dan Schwartz stands abruptly, cranes his head, and speeds toward us. A few yards away from where I'm parked, he stops the horse. I watch as Rhoda climbs down from the buggy and rushes toward us, the remnants of worry etched into her features.

"Fannie." The Amish woman reaches us, presses her hand to her chest. "Hi, Katie."

"She was exercising the horse," I say in *Deitsch*.

I feel Fannie's eyes on me, but I don't look at her. "*Sell is en goodah,*" I say, referring to the horse. That is a good one.

Neither Dan nor Rhoda was born yesterday. They know their granddaughter was out here, riding like the wind. Even so, I suspect both of them have learned something important in the wake of Rachael's death. Something that feels a little bit like . . . forbearance.

Nodding, Rhoda steps forward, runs her hand over the animal's sweaty shoulder. "He's young," she says. "Looks strong, too."

"He's too strong," Dan grumbles from his place in the buggy. "Pushes too hard. Shies in traffic."

"He's the fastest trotter in all of Painters Mill," Fannie tells him.

Dan grunts. "We've already got a buggy horse."

"Nellie's getting old, Dan." Rhoda touches the braids with her fingertips. "Got a nice mane on him and just look at that pink nose."

Knowing he's being played, but sensing this is an important moment, Dan leaves the buggy and crosses to the horse in question. He smooths his hand over the animal's rump, frowning dubiously.

"Needs work," he mutters.

"Good buggy horse costs a pretty penny," Rhoda counters.

I shrug. "If you find someone to work with him, he might just surprise you."

Fannie clears her throat and climbs down from the horse. "I can do it," she says quietly. "Train him, I mean. Turn him into a better horse."

"Riding a horse . . ." Frowning at his wife, Dan shoves his hands into the pockets of his trousers. "Is no place for a girl."

Rhoda waves off the comment. "*En bisli gevva un namma is net en shlecht ding, eh?*" A little give-and-take is not a bad thing, eh?

I look at Fannie. "I think that's called compromise," I say to her. When the girl says nothing, I add, "It takes two."

Dan looks at his granddaughter over the rim of his glasses. "You think you can do this thing?"

"*Ja.*" She says the word a little too quickly.

"You have to stop running him," the Amish man tells her. "Train him to be calm and steady so he's safe on the road."

"I can do it," she says.

Rhoda looks at me. "Thank you for finding her for us, Kate Burkholder."

I nod, then turn my attention to Fannie, and I wait until the girl meets my gaze. "*Vann du broviahra hatt genunk, du finna vassannahshtah mechta sei faloahra,*" I say. When you try hard enough, you find what otherwise might be lost.

I hope the girl understands that the phrase encompasses more than one meaning. That one is more complex than the other, and yet both are equally important.

CHAPTER 43

A spring storm hovers on the western horizon when I pull into the gravel lane of the farm I share with Tomasetti. It's dusk and I can just make out the occasional flicker of lightning within the roiling clouds. I roll down the window, breathe in the fragrant air, humid and rich with the smell of growing things and life. For the first time in days, I notice the new foliage on the trees that grow alongside the driveway. The grass in the pasture is an ocean of green, made even greener by the slant of sun beaming through the thunderheads.

I park behind Tomasetti's Tahoe, grab my laptop case, and start toward the house. I'm midway to the back door when I hear the *clang!* of a hammer against something solid. I round the corner and a few yards away, down the hill about halfway to the pond, Tomasetti stands next to a stone firepit that wasn't there when I left this morning. Yellow and orange flames dance a couple of feet into the air, illuminating the circle of meticulously placed stone and the sight of a man I suddenly can't wait to touch.

"You've been busy," I call out as I make my way down the incline.

He turns. My heart stutters in my chest when his eyes sweep over me. His expression warms as he takes my measure. "If you want someone to stay out of trouble," he says, "give them a job."

I break into a run, drop my laptop case on the bench seat, and go to him. Holding his gaze, I put my arms around his neck, and fall against him, set my face against his shoulder.

"If I'd known building a firepit would get me that kind of reaction," he says, "I'd have done it a long time ago."

Laughing, I pull back, give him a playful punch on the arm.

"What do you think?" he asks.

"I think the chief of police is incredibly glad she has a certain BCI guy to come home to."

"Well, in that case . . ." Tilting his head, he looks at me, a little puzzled but pleased nonetheless, and presses a kiss to my mouth.

I try not to be moved, but I am, on too many levels to sort through at the moment. "You smell like woodsmoke," I tell him.

Without speaking, he eases me to arm's length and looks at me closely. "Everything all right, Chief?"

I choke out a laugh, but I can't hide the note of melancholy in its depths. "Fannie Bontrager took off without telling her grandparents."

"Ah." He runs both hands down my arms. "You find her?"

"At the Bontrager place. On her horse."

He motions toward the bench seat constructed of old wood from the barn. I sit, look out across the land where the red-winged blackbirds swoop over the pond to the weeping willow at the water's edge. The last of the spring peepers sing their final song. Before long, summer will arrive. Another chapter, different, but just as beloved.

Tomasetti sits next to me. "I take it that's not a good thing?"

"Fannie's not going to stay Amish," I tell him.

"In case you need a reminder, Kate, *you* left the fold and everything turned out all right." He takes my hand, squeezes it gently.

I know what I want to say. What I *need* to say. What I feel in my heart. But to put it into words is no easy feat. "Rachael Schwartz was no-holds-barred, fearless to a fault, and traveling at a hundred miles an hour." Loretta Bontrager's description of her floats through my mind and I mumble it, realizing that of all the terms I could use to describe Rachael, that one is the one that best captures the essence of her. "*Frei geisht.*" Free spirit.

"Fannie is exactly like her," I tell him. "She's being raised by the same parents who raised Rachael. The Schwartzes didn't give Rachael the tools she needed to . . ." I almost say the one word I don't want to say: "survive."

He looks into the fire, thoughtful. "That doesn't mean Fannie is bound for the same fate as her mother."

"The kid's got a nose for trouble, just like her mom."

Thunder rumbles in the distance. The sun has sunk behind the clouds. The birds have gone silent. The tempo of the bullfrogs from the pond strikes a crescendo.

"Fannie Bontrager has a couple of things going for her that Rachael Schwartz didn't," he tells me. "The people raising her have learned a thing or two about life since they raised their daughter." He looks at me. "And Fannie has a good-hearted chief of police to keep an eye on her over the next few years."

The wind has picked up, sending the flames into a frenzy. The first fat drops of rain splat against the stone, sizzle when they hit the glowing coals.

"You know, Tomasetti, if you ever decide to leave BCI, you could probably make it as a shrink."

"Or a bartender."

"Same thing, right?"

We grin at each other and, hand in hand, hightail it through the rain toward the house.

ACKNOWLEDGMENTS

As is the case with every book, I've many talented and dedicated people to thank at Minotaur Books—for their expertise and hard work, their willingness to go above and beyond, their belief in me and the story, and, most of all, for the friendship. My editor, Charles Spicer. My agent, Nancy Yost. Jennifer Enderlin. Andrew Martin. Sally Richardson. Sarah Melnyk. Sarah Grill. Kerry Nordling. Paul Hochman. Allison Ziegler. Kelley Ragland. David Baldeosingh Rotstein. Marta Fleming. Martin Quinn. Joseph Brosnan. Lisa Davis. A heartfelt thank you to all!